Midnight Memory Lane

FULL STEAM AHEAD

By
Donna Anderson

Gotham Books

30 N Gould St.
Ste. 20820, Sheridan, WY 82801
https://gothambooksinc.com/

Phone: 1 (307) 464-7800

© 2024 *Donna Anderson*. All rights reserved.

No part of this book may be reproduced, stored in a retrieval system, or transmitted by any means without the written permission of the author.

Published by Gotham Books (August 27, 2024)

ISBN: 979-8-3303-5495-5 (H)
ISBN: 979-8-3303-5493-1 (P)
ISBN: 979-8-3303-5494-8 (E)

Because of the dynamic nature of the Internet, any web addresses or links contained in this book may have changed since publication and may no longer be valid.

The views expressed in this work are solely those of the author and do not necessarily reflect the views of the publisher, and the publisher hereby disclaims any responsibility for them.

FOREWORD

Before Jeannette was attacked, Clay asked her to write him two songs for a new album he and The Band planned to record. She was reluctant in the beginning. Jeannette had not played or written anything since Robert passed.

One evening she joined Clay and Amy for dinner at *My City Restaurant.* Little did Jeannette know the couple had a few ulterior motives? An introduction was made to her of the owner, Mark. He gave her hand a kiss and sent a spark that went through both of them.

The restaurant had a stage where live music from the Big Band era was playing. Over the microphone, Mark asked Clay and The Band to play a song for them. Clay introduced Jeannette, without warning, and asked her to join them on the stage. After the shock of the introduction, she refused at first. With Amy and the audience's encouragement, she reluctantly joined Clay and the band on stage. It was the most fun she had had in several years.

The next day Jeannette was attacked by Jim Westcock. He stabbed her in the right arm several times. A neurosurgeon performed a delicate surgery to repair all the damage Westcock had done. Mark stopped to see her Just after surgery while Jeannette was still feeling the effects of anesthesia and pain meds. Without realizing it, Jeannette told him how she felt about him. He left with a smile on his face, knowing he had made an impression on her.

It was not long after, Jeannette was in love with a special man named Mark. He told her he loved her and promised he would never hurt her, but he did. Together, they settled their issues and were more in love than before.

Now, Jeannette would have to face her attacker in court. Would Jim Westcock go to prison? Will Jeannette and Mark get married? What will happen with *Windy City* and *My City*?

It was time for **Full Steam Ahead.**

Contents

Chapter	Page
1	1
2	13
3	39
4	62
5	85
6	98
7	111
8	136
9	143
10	155
11	160
12	180
13	193
14	221
15	236
16	256
17	273
18	285
19	287
20	293
21	300

22 317
23 324

1

Monday morning arrived. The workweek began. Jeannette walked through the door at *Windy City* with a smile that covered her face. She had a glow about her.

"Good morning, Jeannette," Bridgett said, staring with surprise at how good her boss looked. "You look wonderful! Oregon did wonders for you."

"Well, I cannot give Oregon all the credit. Mark and I worked our problems out when I got back. We are a couple again," Jeannette announced.

"Oh!" Bridgett could not conceal her shock.

Jeannette giggled and said, "You are surprised. The look on your face is worth a million."

"You think I am shocked? Just wait! Greg is NOT going to approve of your choice."

"Buzz him for me, please? Ask him to come to my office. I would like him to join you and me." Jeannette said.

"Greg! Good to see you. Both of you, have a seat." Jeannette said with a smile that made Greg think she had lost her mind." Did everything go smooth while I was away?"

"Fine. Are you okay? Should I call a shrink? Ambulance? You are making me jittery," Greg said, his nerves on edge.

"Tell me your opinion of Mark," Jeannette asked.

Greg jumped to his feet and began to pace.

"I almost paid him a visit, but I changed my mind when I heard your voice in the back of my head saying, *'now what good would that do?'* I think the man is a jerk. I told him he was not to see you anymore. The man does not know how to treat a woman!"

"Before you get too carried away, why don't you sit back down? You are probably not going to like what I have to say. I agreed to meet Mark when I got back on Saturday. First let me tell you what happened to upset me," Jeannette began to explain a short version of what took place.

"Mark and I talked about what was going on in his head to flip his switch. The thought of marriage terrified him. He was engaged once. He came home early from the restaurant one day and found his girlfriend in bed with another man. Flashbacks immediately played in his head, then doubt of my faithfulness popped in to join the party. It snowballed from there," Jeannette explained.

"My brain jumped to doubts. I thought he didn't love me, and I was being played. Flashbacks of Jeff and his manipulations whirled in my head. I was sure he had been lying to me all this time, and all he wanted from me was to add another notch to his belt. Both of us went a little crazy. Mark would not talk to me about what was going on in his mind, so naturally, my brain started making up all kinds of reasons why he didn't want me. I did not talk to Mark about my feelings either. We were both at fault. In the end, he begged for my forgiveness, and I gave it. I warned him if he did anything stupid like that again, it is over." Greg and Bridgett looked skeptical. "Mark is a good man. He felt overwhelmed. I jumped to conclusions and look where it got us? Our communication skills left something to be desired."

"I am not convinced he is trustworthy," Greg said.

"I'm with Greg on this one, Jeannette. Are you sure this is not a story he has fabricated?" Bridgett asked.

"If you had seen Mark Saturday night you would know he was telling the truth. He looked horrible. He lost weight and there were dark circles under his eyes from no sleep," Jeannette informed them.

"He is going to have to prove himself to me and do a lot of sucking up! Do you honestly believe him? You think he can be trusted?" Greg asked.

"I do believe him. Yes, I believe I can trust him," Jeannette said, looking back and forth from Greg to Bridgett.

"So, are you a notch?" Greg asked with one eyebrow raised.

"Greg!" Bridgett yelled.

"Like that is any of your business!" Jeannette raised her voice at his question. "No," she answered reluctantly.

"Good. Make Mark wait. We need to check this guy out. Dinner may be in order at *My City* this evening," Greg said.

"I don't think that will happen, Greg," Jeannette said with a grin.

"Oh, yes, it will! I can eat anywhere I please!" Greg said.

"I mean, you need a reservation. It is always filled to capacity and more waiting to be seated. I always get a table because I am special," Jeannette bragged.

"Whatever," Greg said as he stood. I am still going to find time to talk with him. "Nobody treats you like that!"

Jeannette put her arms around Greg and whispered, "Thanks for watching out for me. You are a good family member." He left the room without saying a word.

"If anyone knew that I confide in my employees with personal issues, they would be appalled. That is a business no-no. But my company is different from the average. We operate as a family. If I make you uncomfortable telling you things, don't hesitate to say something. I mean it, Bridgett! From time to time, I need a sounding board. If you do not want to hear it, just say the word," Jeannette said.

"You do not have to worry about it. We are all wrapped up together. Any problem is everyone's problem. Whether it is work or personal. Sometimes it takes a clearer head to prevail. Why do you think no one quits working for you? We care. We pitch in to help each other. No matter what the problem is, if we can help, we will without hesitation. We deeply care about you and *Windy City* as well as every person here," Bridgett said.

"Thank you for saying that. It makes me feel better. Mark is going to have to figure out how to get back in Greg's good graces. I have no idea how he will pull it off, but it will be interesting to watch. Okay. Now, it is time for business. What is on my schedule?" Jeannette asked.

Bridgett went through everything that had taken place while she was in Oregon and reminded her of physical therapy and a doctor's appointment.

"One last thing. Clay will be stopping by late this afternoon to talk about his album."

"Good. I wanted to see Clay. Thank you, Bridgett. I will be working through lunch, so would you order me a sandwich around noon, please?" Bridgett put it on her list then left the room.

She had just gotten her mind focused on work when her cell phone rang. It was Mark. "Good morning, Sweetheart. Did you sleep well?" Jeannette asked.

"Yes. I finally got some peaceful sleep. I cannot tell you how good it is to have you home. Would you consider having dinner with me tonight? I believe Clay and Amy will be joining us," Mark told her.

"I do need to eat, and you serve a delicious steak, so yes. I would love to," Jeannette accepted.

"Don't do that, Jeannette! You scared me when you hesitated. It makes my heart skip a beat," Mark said slightly out of breath.

"Okay. I promise I will not do it any longer. Have you thought about how you are going to get back on Greg's good side? I told him this morning we worked out our issues, and we are back to being a couple. I also told him part of the problem was my fault. You were not completely to blame. He did not seem happy about us being back together, but I am confident he will come around. It will take some time to regain Greg's trust. Remember, this is my family here at *Windy City*, and we are a close-knit group. Greg is like my big brother," Jeannette explained.

"I figured that out when he called me a jerk. Oh! You reminded me of my family. I want you to meet them. Is Thursday a good night for you? I finally pinned them down on a day."

"Thursday will work. What time? What should I wear?" Jeannette asked.

"Eight o'clock. Wear anything that makes you comfortable. You have a great sense of style."

"Alright. I will see you about 7:30 tonight," Jeannette said.

Later in the afternoon, Bridgett announced Clay had arrived for his appointment as he burst though Jeannette's office door.

"Hello, Pretty Lady! You are looking happy today."

Behind him Bridgett was shaking her head. She was unable to stop him any time he came to see Jeannette.

"I am happy, Clay," Jeannette answered.

"I am very happy to hear it. I heard a rumor you and Mark split. It concerned me, especially from the looks of Mark. It was awful. Amy was worried he was going to have a breakdown! The poor man looked horrible while you were gone. We felt so bad for him. After all, Amy and I introduced you."

"Yes, you did. Thank you. For your information, we have worked it out, and are very happy, together. Mark told me this morning you and Amy will be joining us for dinner tonight."

"That is the plan. Let's talk about the album. How are the songs progressing?" Clay asked.

"First, I will tell you, I can play chords again! None of the fancy stuff, yet. I have one almost finished. It is a love song I wrote last week when I was so depressed. Would you like to hear what I have so far? See if it meets with your approval?"

"I am all ears!"

"Let me buzz Greg and ask if he has a client." She pushed a button on her phone labeled 'booth.' "Greg, is the room open right now?"

"Almost. We just finished recording. The musicians are packing their gear now. Give us five maybe ten minutes."

"Will do. While we wait for the sound room to empty, let's have a drink of the good stuff," Jeannette suggested.

They sipped the whiskey and made small talk while waiting. Jeannette looked at the clock and said, "Enough sipping, Clay. Down it! The room should be open."

Jeannette took her place on a stool in the middle of the room with her headset in place. She was able to hear Greg clear as a bell if he wanted to talk to her from the booth.

"Clay, grab a stool and sit in here with me. Keep me company while I play. It will not take long. My arm can only handle five minutes at a time."

He set up next to Jeannette, bringing his guitar in with him. Clay never went anywhere without bringing along his old friend, the guitar.

"I am ready whenever you are Pretty Lady."

She began to play. Greg started to record. It was a song that had a lot of emotion about heartbreak. The song touched deep down in the soul. As Jeannette played and sang, Clay joined in and occasionally sang harmony. When she finished, tears were rolling down her cheeks. Greg and Clay were silently in awe.

Clay broke the silence, "Pretty Lady I have never heard a more beautiful, gut-wrenching song. It will take the music world by storm. Do not write one more word. The song is finished. It needs to end with the listener wondering what happened. You know? Up in the air. I love it." He hugged Jeannette and gently patted her back as if he were her father.

From the booth, Greg said, "Jeannette, I recorded it. It is wonderful. It is better than wonderful, but I don't know what the word would be to describe it. You need to hear it."

All three sat and listened. When the recording stopped, Jeannette said, "I did a good job. I think it is my best work so far. How about you, Clay?"

"It is the best, and this song is mine!" Clay declared. "I will bring you a check tonight at dinner. You need to perform this on the album. Sing it just like you did a few minutes ago. On my other albums you have recorded one song. We have to keep the tradition going. Is it a deal?"

"Okay. You have a deal," Jeannette agreed. "I promise the next song will be a knee slapper, up-tempo tune. My mood is always a dead giveaway by the songs I write. I was upset. Now I am happy."

"I have to go, Pretty Lady. Greg, will you make me a copy of the recording we just did? Is it possible to send it with Jeannette this evening?" Clay asked.

"You bet! It will only take about ten minutes," Greg promised. Clay left sniffling. "Jeannette, you outdid yourself with this song. Maybe it was worth the pain?" Greg asked.

"If it helps Clay and the band with notoriety, then it was worth it. I will be leaving in about an hour. Can you bring me the disc when it's finished? Thanks, Greg."

Mark met Jeannette at the head waiters' desk at *My City*. He wanted to escort the most beautiful woman in the world to her table.

"Hello, Beautiful. You look lovely. You are right on time, but I was hoping you would be early so that I could steal a kiss. Clay and Amy just arrived. I guess it will have to wait."

"You smooth talker. I love it," Jeannette confessed.

"I think you love this, too," Mark said and brought her hand to his mouth for the gentle kiss she knew so well. She gently placed her other hand on his cheek. Her eyes rolled with enjoyment. He felt a spark deep in his stomach, stronger than ever before. Clay and Amy sat watching the two lovebirds.

"Ahem. I said, ahem! Good evening, Jeannette. You look glowingly charming. Did you bring the disc and the contract?" Clay asked anxiously.

"I did. Did you bring your checkbook?" Jeannette asked, and Clay cringed.

Mark pulled her chair out, then kissed her cheek before seating himself. He moved his chair close to Jeannette so he could hold her hand or touch her in some way.

Jeannette handed Clay the contract and disc. He signed it and gave her an envelope. Song number five now belonged to Clay.

"I would love to hear the song. Could I be in the booth when you record it?" Mark asked.

"I think I can talk the owner into allowing you to sit in. Clay? Do you mind if he sits in on one of the sessions?" Jeannette asked.

"Not at all. When will that be?" Clay wanted to know.

"How soon will the band have the song ready to record?"

"Two weeks for this one. We have a few other songs ready, so if we could have some time in the sound room, that would be great," Clay negotiated.

"I already thought of that. When you and I talked about the album, I booked one full afternoon after you left. It just so happens it is in two weeks," Jeannette informed him.

"Let's order a bottle of champagne! I have a new song that will hit number one on the charts as soon as it is released and more to come!" Clay beamed.

It was a wonderful evening. They laughed, ate, and sipped champagne. Mark was never further away from Jeannette than twelve inches. Most of the time, he held her hand. Amy observed how much in love they were from across the table. She put her arm through Clay's and hugged him.

Amy whispered in Clay's ear, "I love you. We made a good match. I hope they invite us to the wedding."

It was a week later on a beautiful starlit night; Mark took Jeannette to their special place overlooking the night lights of Chicago. They stood holding each other like they always had.

Mark spoke quietly in her ear, "Jeannette, I love you with all my heart. I have loved you from the moment I saw you. I love everything about you. You are perfect, in my eyes. I want to be by your side for the rest of my life." He let go of her. She turned around to see he was on one knee and holding a small velvet box. "Jeannette, will you marry me and be by my side for the rest of our lives. To grow old together and be grandparents together? To love one another unconditionally?"

He opened the box. The ring was glistening in the moonlight. It was made of yellow gold, with a three-carat square diamond in the center and two one carat square cut sapphires on either side. The wedding band had a row of small diamonds set in yellow gold.

"Oh, Mark, I love you. I would be proud to be your wife."

He stood to slide the ring on her finger. He kissed her with a passion neither had experienced before.

Lesson learned: Learn the facts before you ASSUME what they are. Do not go off the deep end until you understand the reasoning behind the situation. Never assume. Think. You can hurt someone with words OR your actions. How would you feel? Stop and think before you react or open your mouth.

Love is a gift.

Be careful with a heart that has been given with love. If you break that heart, it might end up hurting you more.

2

It was May 15th and the first day of the trial for Jim Westcock, Jeannette's mugger. Her physical wounds have healed, but what will happen when she faces her attacker? Would it trigger a panic attack? She will know in short order.

Mark escorted Jeannette into the courthouse. He could feel her heart rate quicken.

He tried to reassure her by squeezing her hand and saying, "I know you are nervous. Any normal person would be in your situation. Take a few deep breaths and try to calm yourself. I will be with you the entire time. He will never hurt you again. I will protect you and he will be guarded by police officers with guns."

"Thank you, honey. I know everything you just said is true. I have told myself the same thing over and over. As we traveled closer to the courthouse, I could feel emotions start to bubble to the surface. Give me a minute to get my feelings in check."

"Jeannette, it is not my intention to rush you, but you might want to speed it up a bit. I see the media headed this direction," Mark told her.

She did not bother to look. Instead, she took a step forward toward the entrance. She was determined not to be seen as a victim, but as a survivor.

The District Attorney was waiting for her outside courtroom #4.

"Jeannette, good to see you. Is David coming? Having both of you makes for a very solid case. Are you ready for this?" He asked Jeannette.

She squared her shoulders, held Mark's hand, and said, "I am. David will be along as soon as he parks the car."

"Excellent. Oh, here he comes now. Remember everything we have gone over and the questions I will ask. Answer them truthfully and to the point. Mr. Westcock's attorney will want to cross-examine. Answer truthfully, to the point and do not offer any more information. Keep your answers short. Do not look at the defendant. He will try to intimidate both of you. Focus on Mark or me if need be. We will get you through this."

"Thank you for the reassurance. I am ready. David, are you prepared for this?"

"I am very ready. I want him in jail!" David answered.

"Is it time for us to go in?" Jeannette asked.

The D.A. looked at his watch and said, "Yes. Sit behind me in the first row. If I need to ask a question or give you instruction, I can. Okay, here we go."

The D.A. led the way into the room. She saw Westcock being brought in with his wrists cuffed. The shackles attached to his ankles rendered him with having great difficulty in walking to his appointed chair. Jeannette quickly looked away. Mark squeezed her hand.

"I am fine, Mark. I am not going to let him rattle me."

"That's my girl," Mark replied.

After they were seated, Jeannette looked around the room for the other witnesses the detective said would be testifying.

She tapped on the D.A.'s shoulder and asked, "Are there more witnesses here to testify against Westcock? It was my understanding there would be several."

"They changed their mind. The other witnesses were scared. You and David are my only witnesses. With your testimonies, we will get a conviction. Don't worry," he told her.

"Please rise," the bailiff thundered. "The honorable Judge Morgan presiding. You may be seated."

The court recorder read the charges against Westcock. They were extensive — attempted murder, assault, robbery, kidnapping, and stalking, to mention a few. The attorney for Westcock, Mr. Bentley, gave opening remarks. To listen to him, you would think Jim Westcock was a model citizen! Jeannette was shocked. The D.A., Mr. Craig, gave his opening remarks and portrayed the defendant as what he is, a criminal.

"Mr. Bentley, call your first witness," the judge instructed.

"I call Madison Anderson to the stand." She was sworn in, and the questioning began.

"Will you please tell the court your name and relationship with the defendant?"

"My name is Madison Anderson. I am Jim Westcock's girlfriend. We share an apartment."

"Please tell the court how long you have shared an apartment."

"He and I have lived together for two years," she testified.

"When you say he, do you mean Mr. Westcock?"

"Yes."

"On March 11th will you tell the court about your day?" He asked.

"Jim and I spent the entire day together. It was the anniversary of our first date. After breakfast we did a little sightseeing. We had lunch, then he took me shopping for a new outfit," Madison said.

"When you say Jim, you are referring to Mr. Westcock, correct?"

"Yes."

"So, you are swearing he did not leave your side at any time during that day? Remember you are under oath," Mr. Bentley reminded Madison.

"Yes," she responded. She appeared to be nervous. More like scared to death. Madison kept looking at Westcock. He was glaring at her with the intent of scaring her and keeping her in line with the questioning.

Mr. Bentley continued, "What time did you return home?"

"It was at six o'clock in the evening. I remember looking at the clock and thinking I needed to start dinner," Madison answered.

"I have no more questions at this time, your honor," Mr. Bentley stated and took his seat.

"Mr. Craig, do you have any questions?" Judge Morgan asked.

"Yes, your Honor, I do. Ms. Anderson, Madison, you swore to tell the truth and nothing but the truth. Before you answer, keep in mind if you do not tell the truth, you are committing perjury and can go to jail. Are you sure Mr. Westcock was with you the entire day?" Mr. Craig asked.

She looked at her boyfriend, bit her lip, and answered, "Yes."

"Can you tell me where you had lunch?" Mr. Craig asked.

"I don't remember the name of the restaurant," Madison was showing more visible signs of nervousness. She was wringing her hands and could not sit still.

"You said Mr. Westcock took you shopping. Did you purchase anything?" Mr. Craig asked.

"No, I mean, yes," Madison answered nervously.

"Which is it, yes or no?"

Madison looked at her boyfriend for an answer.

"Yes. Jim bought me an outfit."

"What was the name of the store you shopped at?" Mr. Craig asked.

"I don't remember."

"Really? I know when my wife goes shopping, she knows every store she visits, how many outfits she tried on, and the name of the clerk who helped her. I find it hard to believe you do not remember," Mr. Craig argued.

"Objection!" Mr. Bentley shouted.

"Sustained," the judge responded. "Mr. Craig keep your remarks directed to the case. Ask a question."

"Sorry your Honor. To be clear, you are telling the court you were with Mr. Westcock all day? You had lunch you do not know where, went shopping with him by your side, you bought an outfit, but you don't know from what store? Are these the facts? Is this true? I remind you one more time about the oath you took."

Madison looked at Westcock. She didn't want to go to jail for lying, but she also didn't want to reap the wrath of such an evil man staring back at her. Wringing her hands and biting her lip, she began to shake.

"I really could go to jail if I lied?" She asked.

"Yes, Ms. Anderson. You could spend up to a year in jail. I will ask you again. Was Mr. Westcock by your side all day while you had lunch, shopped for a new outfit, and arrived home at six p.m. on March 11th? Is that a true statement?" Mr. Craig asked.

"Yes, I guess that's right."

"You guess? Please answer with a yes or no."

She looked one more time toward Westcock for the answer. He was glaring at her and barring his teeth. He looked completely evil.

"Yes." Madison began to quietly cry.

"I have no more questions at this time but reserve the right to question her again at a later time," Mr. Craig said.

"You may step down. Call your next witness, Mr. Bentley," the judge ordered.

Mr. Bentley stood to say, "My other witness is not in the court room at this time."

Judge Morgan asked, "You have no other witnesses?"

"No, your Honor," Mr. Bentley replied and hung his head as if defeated.

"Mr. Craig. You're up. Call your first witness," Judge Morgan ordered.

"I call David to the stand."

As David walked to the stand, he looked directly at Westcock. He was an evil sight to behold. A cold chill swept over David.

Mr. Craig began, "Please state your name and what you do for a living."

"My name is David, and I am a professional diver for *Windy City Publishing and Recording Company* here in Chicago."

"David, who, specifically, do you drive for at the Recording Company?" Mr. Craig asked while walking back and forth.

"Jeannette, the CEO."

"Were you driving her on the morning of March 11th?"

"Yes, I was."

"Tell me about the events of the morning on March 11th."

"I picked Jeannette up at 7:45 from her apartment and drove her to work at *Windy City*. I was then scheduled to pick her up from *Windy City* at 10:30 for an appointment. When I arrived, she came out of the building right on time. I held her door. She sat on the passenger side of the backseat, just like she always did. I shut her door, walked to the other side of the car and got behind the wheel. I started to put the car in gear, suddenly I heard a loud thud and a short scream from Jeannette. I turned as quick as I could while calling out Jeannette's name." David shook his head trying to get the sound out of his head. He was reliving a nightmare.

"Did you know at that time what had happened to Jeannette?" Mr. Craig asked.

"No. When I turned around that man," David pointed to Westcock, "was holding a knife I estimated to be at least ten to twelve inches long in my face."

"Let the record show David identified Jim Westcock, the defendant. This is the knife that was found in the car with Mr. Westcock's fingerprints and DNA on it." Mr. Craig gave the knife to the bailiff who handed it to the judge for evidence and then showed David.

"Do you recognize this knife?"

"Yes! It was the knife that was inches from my face!"

"Let's proceed with the events in the car. Go on David. Then what happened?"

"He told me to drive or he would cut Jeannette and then me. I called out for Jeannette again. This time she answered. Westcock yelled drive. I asked where. He said just drive and he would tell me when to stop. He still had the knife in my face until I pulled away from the curb then his attention turned back to Jeannette. He was yelling something about her owing him money. All I could think about was trying to get him away from her. So, I swerved the car to throw him off balance."

Mr. Craig asked, "Were you successful in throwing him off balance?"

"Not at that time."

"Then what happened?"

"He slashed through Jeannette's coat with the knife and cut her arm. She screamed. At that point I didn't hear what he said to her. I didn't know what to do to help her. She screamed again and I hit the brakes. Mr. Westcock hit his head on a hard piece on the back of the seat. It rattled his brain for a second. Jeannette grabbed the knife and held him down until I could get the attention of a police cruiser."

"When you stopped the car, what did you see?"

"I opened the door where Jeannette was at. She was on the driver's side of the backseat. She had hold of Westcock's arm pulling as hard as she could while her foot was buried in his shoulder so he couldn't move. There was blood everywhere. She did not let go until the police arrived and took him into custody."

"That is quite a story. David, have you ever seen the defendant before?"

"Yes. Once a week or less before March 11th. It was on a weekend. I picked Jeannette up at her apartment and drove her to the office at Windy City to work for a while. When she called to have me pick her up, I was waiting outside *Windy City*. I saw him trying to get in the building but when he discovered the doors were locked, he left."

"Did you inform Jeannette?"

"Yes, I did. We also informed security at *Windy City* thinking someone was trying to break in," David recounted.

"Is that man in the courtroom?" Mr. Craig asked.

"Yes. He is sitting at that desk."

"Let the record show he identified Mr. Westcock," Mr. Craig stated. "I have no other questions for this witness."

"Does the defense have any questions for this witness?" Judge Morgan asked.

"Yes, your Honor, I do. David, are you absolutely positive you saw my client trying to get the door open at *Windy City*?" Mr. Bentley questioned.

"I am positive."

"How can you be sure it was Mr. Westcock? Were you close enough to identify his face?"

"Yes. When he was unsuccessful at opening the door, he turned his face in my direction. He was spouting obscenities and was wearing the same clothes he had on then, as he did on March 11th."

"You were about fifteen feet away when he turned? Is that correct? And you were able to identify him without a shadow of a doubt?" Mr. Bentley questioned.

"Yes," David answered with confidence.

"Let's talk about the morning of March 11th. You said you heard a thud and quickly turned around. Did you see my client cause that sound?"

"No."

"Then how do you know he caused it?"

"Jeannette was crumpled in the seat and unconscious. There were only three of us in the car!"

David was starting to get mad. He looked at Jeannette. She smiled and shook her head no to remind him not to let Mr. Bentley upset him. That would work in Westcock's favor.

Even though David wanted to call him an idiot, he calmed down and prepared for more questioning.

"When I turned around, Mr. Westcock was hovering over Jeannette and holding that knife. Then he stuck the knife in my face."

"One more time, David. You are positive you saw Mr. Westcock try getting into *Windy City,* and then again on March 11th when he was in your car, even though you heard his girlfriend testify he was with her all day?" Mr. Bentley asked.

"Yes. I am positive."

"No more questions, your Honor." Mr. Bentley blew out his breath and took his place next to his client.

"The witness may step down. Mr. Craig, call your next witness."

"I call Jeannette to the stand," Mr. Craig said with authority. Jeannette was sworn in. She sat straight, her head up with a down to business expression.

"For the court, would you please state your name and your occupation?"

"My name is Jeannette. I am the owner and CEO of *Windy City Publishing and Recording Company,* here in Chicago."

"Jeannette, would you please tell the court what you did on the morning of March 11th?"

"My driver, David, picked me up at 7:45 a.m. at my apartment to take me to *Windy City.* When I arrived, I went into my office, discussed my schedule for the day with my assistant, and drank a cup of coffee while I worked on contracts for our clients. At 9:30, David picked me up at *Windy City* to take me to an appointment," Jeannette answered.

Mr. Craig paced as he asked, "Was this a normal morning for you?"

"Yes."

"What happened next?" Mr. Craig asked.

Jeannette looked to Mark for support. He smiled, hoping to make her feel at ease. She took a deep breath and began.

"David had just taken his place behind the wheel when suddenly my door flew open. I was struck with such force that I slammed into the door on the opposite side of the car with my shoulder. My head hit the window, breaking the glass, and knocking me out."

"How long do you think you were unconscious?"

"Not too long. Maybe thirty seconds," Jeannette answered.

"What happened then?" Mr. Craig asked.

"I was not out for too long. When I came to, David was calling out my name. That man . . ." She pointed at Jim Westcock.

"Let the record show she identified Mr. Westcock," Mr. Craig instructed the court. "Please continue."

"Mr. Westcock was hovering over me holding a huge knife in my face," Jeannette continued. "He smelled awful, and his breath stunk. I shouted at him to get out. He refused and threatened to cut me. He yelled at David to drive. He said if David didn't do as he told him, Westcock would cut me and then him."

"Mr. Westcock threatened you and David, your driver?" Mr. Craig asked.

"Yes. Then Mr. Westcock turned to me again and told me I had to pay him for the services my ex-husband had hired him to do."

"What services was Mr. Westcock talking about?" Mr. Craig asked.

"I was married to Jeff at the time and Mr. Westcock was hired by Jeff to follow me and report back to him about every move I made throughout the day, and if I had talked to anyone. My ex was a very paranoid, insecure man who controlled my every move."

"So, Mr. Westcock was hired to follow you?" Mr. Craig questioned.

"Yes."

"Was he a licensed private detective?" Mr. Craig asked.

"I do not know."

"Did he do the job Jeff hired him to do?" Mr. Craig asked.

"Yes, and very well. Jeff knew every move I made throughout my day, every day. I had a suspicion someone was watching me, but I did not know for sure."

"Did he ever make contact with you before March 11th?"

"Yes, he did. Once at a restaurant. I had a business lunch with two men, my boss at the time and a prospective client of *Windy City*. I was at that lunch to take notes for a contract. I went to the register to pay the bill. He was the cashier. He called me by name. I had never seen him before, so I asked him what his name was. He told me it wasn't important."

"Did he threaten you at that time?" Mr. Craig asked.

"No, not directly. Mr. Westcock said he would see me."

"And by saying, 'he would see you,' what did you think he meant?"

"Objection! There is no way for the witness to know what he meant," Mr. Bentley said.

"Sustained," Judge Morgan ruled.

"Let me rephrase that. Can you tell the court what you, in your mind, believe Mr. Westcock meant?" Mr. Craig questioned.

"I believed Mr. Westcock would be watching me so he could report back to Jeff."

"Thank you. Let's go back to March 11th. Okay. He is hovering over you with a knife threatening you, and telling you to pay him. Is that correct?"

"Yes. Mr. Westcock tried to collect the money Jeff owed him. But Jeff told Westcock he would have to get it from me. I was rich, and I would pay the debt. I refused. I told him he was out of his mind, that I did not owe him a penny, and to get out of the car. He was irate. David was shouting at Westcock from behind the wheel of the car to stay away from me. When Westcock started threatening me again, David made a sharp turn to the left trying to get him away from me," Jeannette recalled and took a deep breath. "The turn David maneuvered did not work as he had hoped. It only made Mr. Westcock angrier. Westcock shouted that he warned him and slashed at my arm. The knife cut through my coat and inflicted a long gash on my right arm down to the bone. I screamed with pain. He called me names and demanded the money. I refused. That is when he stabbed my arm. Once again, I screamed. David slammed on the brakes, sending Mr. Westcock into the back of the seat, hitting his head on something hard. He was stunned for a second, making him loosen his grip on the knife. I grabbed it out of his hand, kicked him in the head and I held him on the floor by pulling on his arm as hard as I could while pushing on his shoulder with my foot. He could not move. He screamed obscenities at me. I told David to drive fast or crazy to get the attention of a police officer. We were stopped by a police cruiser in short order. I did not let go until the officer said he had him. An ambulance came to take me to the hospital."

"Your honor, I would like to submit pictures of Jeannette's injuries to the jury," Mr. Craig said holding photos in his hand.

"Bailiff, give the pictures to me to examine first," Judge Morgan said. He inspected the evidence then handed the photos to the bailiff and instructed him to show them to the jury.

"Jeannette, would you please stand and show the jury your scars left by the attack?"

As instructed, she stood, removed her jacket, and pulled up her sleeve to reveal the scars. Several of the female jurors gasped. Jeannette's face turned pink. She did not like showing the scars left from her attack.

"I have no further questions at this time, your honor, but reserve the right to question the witness again."

"Granted. Mr. Bentley, do you have any questions for the witness?" Judge Morgan asked.

"Yes, I do. Jeannette, how can you be sure it was my client that hit you, to begin with?"

"He was leaning over me when I came to, holding a huge knife in my face. His face was inches from mine."

"Did you see him hit you?"

"No," Jeannette remembered what the D.A. had told her. 'Do not give any more information than asked of you. Short to the point answers.' She almost broke that rule to tell the attorney what she was thinking, "*You are an idiot! There were only three people in the car. David could not have done it. He was in the driver's seat. I certainly did not do it to myself, idiot.*"

"I see. You said the man was dirty. Could you say for sure it was my client? Take a good look at him before you answer," Mr. Bentley demanded.

Jeannette turned her attention to Jim Westcock. He was glaring at her like he did that day in the car. A shiver ran down her spine. She was determined not to let him intimidate her.

She turned to Mr. Bentley and said, "Yes. That is, without a doubt, the man that assaulted me on March 11th."

"But you said he was dirty. How can you be sure it was him? Maybe he was too dirty at the time for you to identify him now?"

"He was not dirty enough that I couldn't identify him now. He had the same sneer he has on his face he has right now. His eyes are two different colors. One is blue, the other brown and he has a scar on his right cheek. His face was inches from my face. Jim Westcock is, without a doubt, my attacker," Jeannette said with confidence.

"No further questions, your honor," Mr. Bentley stated and sat down. He had a look of total defeat on his face.

"Mr. Craig, do you have any more questions for the witness?" Judge Morgan asked.

"No, your Honor."

"Witness may step down. Mr. Craig, do you have any more witnesses?" Judge Morgan asked.

"No, your honor, not at this time."

"In that case, I will hear closing statements. Mr. Bentley, you're up."

Both attorneys gave their rendering of what took place. Jeannette sat with no expression listening to Mr. Bentley defend a guilty man. She wondered how a person could work so hard to set a man like Westcock free. Mr. Bentley knew he was guilty, and yet he argues that Westcock is innocent. It did not make sense to her.

After the attorneys finished with their closing remarks, the judge instructed the jury about their responsibility to weigh the evidence and testimony presented before making a decision. The judge excused the jury from the court to deliberate.

"Court is in recess until the jury has made their decision," Judge Morgan stated and hit his gavel.

"All rise," the bailiff commanded in a loud voice. The judge disappeared through a side door.

Mr. Craig turned to Jeannette, "You were marvelous on the stand. You were calm, cool, and collected, as the saying goes."

"Thank you. I remembered what you told me about my answers," Jeannette said. "I wanted to call him an idiot for asking me if I saw Westcock hit me."

The D.A. chuckled and said, "I wish all my witnesses were as succinct as you."

"What happens now?" Mark asked.

"Now we wait for the jury to come back with a decision. The court will notify me. I, in turn, will call you. I assume you want to be here to hear the verdict?"

"Absolutely!" Jeannette raised her voice with the answer.

"Okay, keep your phone handy," Mr. Craig said and left the courtroom.

"How are you holding up, Sweetheart?" Mark asked.

"I am a mess on the inside but holding it together on the outside. I will be glad when this is over. I noticed when we walked into the building this morning that there is a coffee shop down the hall. How does coffee and a snack sound? My treat," Jeannette asked Mark.

"I would love it."

The two were able to relax and enjoy a moment together until a journalist with a camera saw her. Jeannette heard a click. She immediately turned to see the same man that interviewed her outside *My City* after the attack. Her spirits took a downward turn.

Mark rose from the table and said, "I will take care of this."

Jeannette did not stop him this time. She wanted to be left alone until the jury had announced their decision. Mark stood beside the journalist. Holding his arm, Mark said something quietly in the man's ear. Whatever it was, the reporter, with camera in hand, left.

Jeannette's phone rang, "Hello, Jeannette speaking."

"The jury is back with a verdict," Mr. Craig said.

She looked at Mark and informed him it was time to see what the jury had to say. In the courtroom, the D.A. told her it was a good sign they were back so quickly.

"All rise. The Honorable Judge Morgan presiding," the booming voice of the bailiff was heard throughout the courtroom. "You may be seated."

The room was quiet and ready to hear every word.

"Has the jury made a decision?" The Judge asked.

The jury foreman stood with a paper in his hand and said, "We have your Honor."

The bailiff handed the paper to the judge. He then gave a nod and said, "What say you?"

The counts against Westcock were, once again, read by the jury foreman. Jeannette held her breath.

"Your Honor, we find the defendant guilty on all charges."

Relief flooded Jeannette. Mark squeezed her with the arm he had put around her shoulders.

The judge was quiet for a moment, then said, "Before I pass sentence, do the witnesses have anything to say to Mr. Westcock?"

Jeannette stood, to Mark and Mr. Craig's surprise, and answered, "Yes, your Honor, I do," she answered with confidence.

"Please come forward," Judge Morgan instructed.

"Proceed."

Jeannette glanced at the judge, then faced her attacker, and began, "Thank you, your Honor. Mr. Westcock, I do not know what drove you to commit this crime against me as well as your other victims who were not here to see you were punished. It does not matter," she said without emotion while the vile man bared his teeth and growled at her.

"You are an angry man. In my opinion, your anger has consumed your spirit, causing you to take it out on others to blame them for your unhappiness. I feel sorry for you," Jim slammed the table he sat at with his fist. A police officer and the bailiff quickly stood by the evil man with a hand on either shoulder to hold him in place. Jeannette did not move. She stood her ground, not showing any fear.

She continued, "You don't scare me anymore. I agree with the jury. You have to be stopped, take responsibility for your actions, and accept your punishment. I want to tell you. I forgive you for whatever possessed you to hurt me. I am no longer your victim."

She returned to her seat beside Mark, but not before seeing the D. A's jaw was agape from her words.

Judge Morgan watched Jeannette with amazement until she sat.

"Ahem. Will the defendant please rise for sentencing?" The judge instructed. "Jim Westcock, because of the violence of your crimes, you are at this moment sentenced to seventy-five years to life in the Illinois Maximum Security Prison with no possibility of early parole. Bailiff, take Madison Anderson into custody for perjury."

The gavel came down. It was over. Applause broke out through the courtroom. It was directed at Jeannette. Her face turned red with embarrassment. The praise didn't stop until they were out of the courtroom.

"Take me home," Jeannette said to Mark. "It is time you made love to me."

"Really?" Mark asked as they walked out of the courthouse.

"Yes. You have waited long enough. I need you, Mark. Are you ready to make love to me?" Jeannette whispered in his ear.

Mark's eyes grew wide, and his brow wrinkled. "I want you so much. I am past ready! Let's go!" Mark said, excitedly in her ear.

He started getting fidgety, like a teenager, as David drove them to Jeannette's apartment. He whisked Jeannette past, Sid, as he tipped his hat.

"Hi, Sid! Bye, Sid!" Jeannette said. There was no doubt what the lovers had in mind.

Sid thought, "It's about time. A person would have to be blind not to see the love they have for one another." He tipped his hat and only got out the word, 'Miss,' and they were gone.

Mark danced in the elevator as if he was a young child doing the pee-pee dance. "Why doesn't this elevator move faster?" He shouted.

Jeannette reached over and pressed the stop button then turned to Mark with a big smile.

"I know you have waited until I was ready. I appreciate it very much."

She stepped towards him, leaving no trace of air between them. She ran her hands up his chest and around his neck. She kissed him with such passion and love that it made Mark vibrate.

"What are you doing? We are not going to have our first time in an elevator, are we?"

"No. I wanted to show you how much I love you first." She nibbled at his lower lip while she ran her hands down the length of his body to the bulge in his pants. She felt his heat and the throbbing of his big muscle straining to get to her.

Mark's eyes rolled back in his head. He let out a groan from pure pleasure. He pushed the button on the elevator to make it move again.

"Jeannette, I don't know if I can wait one second longer!"

The elevator doors opened. Jack, her neighbor, was standing there with a big smile. "Hello, Jeannette. It looks like you are feeling better," he said.

She pulled away from Mark just before the door opened. She saw Jack and said, "Hi. Nice to see you. Sweetheart, would you carry my purse for me while I unlock my door?"

Jeannette carried a large purse that was big enough for contracts. She knew Mark needed something to hide the bulge she had helped create.

"Sure," Mark thankfully agreed. They stepped off the elevator and whispered as they walked to her apartment, "You are so lucky I have not ripped your clothes off yet! Please open the door, quickly?"

"Here we are," was all Jeannette got out of her mouth before Mark crushed his lips to hers.

"Thank God! Come on!" He grabbed her hand and spun her around. Mark had her in the bedroom in nothing flat. His breathing was heavy and labored. "I want to be inside you right now!"

Jeannette pulled back and said, "Okay, okay. Slow down a little and let me catch my breath. You've got me." She began slowly unbuttoning her blouse, revealing a see-through bra. Nothing was hidden. She was exposed.

Mark was fumbling with his belt. He had forgotten how a buckle works. He stopped when Jeannette's blouse hit the floor. He needed his hands on her breasts immediately!

"Honey? Honey? Slow down a bit. Let me take your pants off." She prolonged the release of his manhood that was rock hard. She slid the final thin piece of clothing to the floor that stood between him and Jeannette's naked form.

"Oh, God! If you touch me that will be all it will take for me to explode." He didn't take his eyes off Jeannette as he pulled her to him and gently laid her on the bed. "I have dreamt of this moment for a long time. It is nothing like I thought it would be. It is more, so much more than I dreamt. I am going to make you mine completely right now."

Jeannette and Mark were still wrapped in each other's arms an hour later. They had fallen asleep.

Jeannette stirred. She kissed him on the chest, and his arms tightened around her.

"My sweet sleepy man, you probably need to get back to the restaurant, don't you?"

Mark moved with an effort to open his eyes. "What time is it?" He asked.

"It is almost time for the dinner rush. It is a good thing I called Bridgett from the car and told her I would not be in until tomorrow," Jeannette said, all the while kissing him all over his naked body.

"Oh, Baby, you know what I like. That's the spot. Are we going for round 2? Because I am willing to go a second round, but I will need about a liter of fluids first."

"Well, before we get to the edge of no return, maybe you should call the restaurant and make sure everything is running smoothly?" Jeannette asked him and ran her tongue around his nipples. "Here's the phone, sweetheart." She had a knowing something was happening at *My City*.

"Oh, God! What was I supposed to do? Oh, yea. I forgot the number."

"Press one on the speed dial."

"Ahem. Yes, this is Mark. Any issues that need my attention? What? Keep them separated. I will be right there. I have to go. Two busboys are fighting over a tip. They have them in the alley so the entire restaurant cannot hear them. My manager called the police. I have to go fire two busboys!" Mark explained while he got dressed. "I love you. I will call you later."

Jeannette laid back on the bed, looked to the ceiling, and said, "Thank you God for the wonderful gift of Mark. Keep him safe."

"I need to call the boys and Tia and tell them about Westcock." Jeannette dialed Sean and then conferenced Tyler in on the call. "Sean have you got me on speaker so Tia can hear? Great. The trial is over. He had a lot of charges against him. The other witnesses didn't show up. David and I were the only ones. They got scared and wouldn't testify against that evil man."

"Is that jerk in jail?" Sean asked with a raised voice.

"Yes, and he will never get out. The judge really gave it to him! Seventy-five years to life at the Illinois Maximum Security Prison without the possibility of early parole. Westcock's girlfriend testified that she was with him the entire day, which was a lie. He sat there and growled and showed his teeth the whole time like some animal. She was scared to death of him.

After David and my testimonies the judge knew she was lying. He put her in jail for perjury! He didn't say for how long, but she could be in jail for up to a year for lying under oath."

"Oh Mom! Thank God you will never see him again!" Tyler exclaimed. "I am so proud of you for standing up and testifying against that rotten man. Good riddance to bad rubbish."

"After he was found guilty the judge asked if the witnesses had anything to say before he passed sentence on Westcock," Jeannette took a deep breath before going on. "I stood and walked over to Westcock's table and faced my attacker. He tried to scare me, but I didn't waver. I told him I didn't know why he attacked me, but I forgave him. Sean? Tyler? Say something."

"Mom! How could you forgive someone like him? He is evil!" Sean shouted.

"Because I did not want to carry the burden of hatred and unforgiveness. It takes too much energy. He is not worth that much attention. Now I can move on with a clean spirit. I am free of him."

"You are a better person than I am, Mom. I might have taken a swing at him in the courtroom!" Tyler told Jeannette.

"It is over, and I am fine. He is never going to hurt another woman again. Okay I have reported all the action from today. Bye for now, I love all of you."

She rolled over and went to sleep with a smile on her face.

Lessons learned: If you cannot control what is happening to you, control the way you respond in whatever situation you find yourself. That is where your power is!

FORGIVE! It will set you free! Do not let hatred take away the good things in your life.

I believe the hardest part of healing after a traumatic experience is to find, once again, the part of you that was taken.

3

College Graduation for Tia and Sean was two weeks away. Jeannette was still struggling with what to give them for a graduation gift. They both had sacrificed and worked hard for their degrees — Tia in business law and Sean in business. Jeannette was hoping to make a position available for the pair at *Windy City* if they were interested in a few years. But for now, the business at hand was graduation.

If a person did not know Jeannette and Tia, they would swear they were mother and daughter. Jeannette's first call of the day was to Tia.

"Hi, Tia. It's Jeannette. I wanted to talk to you about three things. The first is, what are you and Sean planning on doing after graduation?"

"We want to move to Clark City. We have submitted job applications around that area. No word yet."

This news made Jeannette happy her oldest son and his bride wanted to live in Clark City.

"Would you like me to put a word in for you with Mr. Baker? My late husband, Robert, worked with him. His office deals in business law. I know him very well," Jeannette informed her.

"That would be great!" Tia exclaimed.

"Does Sean have any prospects? Or ideas?" Jeannette asked.

"He has been applying for positions mainly in Carson City. It is a bigger city with more jobs that are suited to his degree," Tia answered.

"It sounds like you and Sean are on the right track with a plan in place. I will be in Eugene the day before graduation. I assume your parents will be attending? We need to get acquainted. I want to take everyone out for dinner," Jeannette offered.

"I am not sure, yet. Neither one has committed. Dad will probably show up, although he has not given me a definitive answer, and no guarantees from mom. She uses the excuse that 'something came up' a lot."

Sadness for Tia washed over Jeannette. She tried to keep the conversation light. "Oh. Well, if they decide to come, we can have a nice dinner together. If they don't come we will eat without them. The second thing I wanted to talk to you about is your wedding. Have you decided on a date?"

"We finally pinned it down last night. We are going with your suggestion for Labor Day weekend," Tia announced.

"Wonderful! Have you decided about having your wedding at the estate?" Jeannette asked.

"I have not seen it yet, but from what I hear, it would be perfect. So, yes, we would like to if it is alright?"

"It is better than alright! It is wonderful! I am thrilled! I have a million things to do to the landscaping before the nuptials. Can you and Sean make a trip to Clark City this weekend? I can show you around the estate. We can brainstorm ideas for the ceremony."

"Funny you should ask; we were just now talking about the very same idea. We were thinking about making the drive Friday evening," Tia informed her.

"Marvelous! I will call Tyler to ask him if he will come home for a family weekend. I will ask Mark if he would like to join us also. Oh, I am excited! Lots of noise and chatter! I love it when my house is full. The third and last thing is a guest list. Have you talked to your mother?"

Tia hesitated for a moment and said, "I talked to her briefly a few days ago. I told her I needed a list of people she wanted to invite. She told me the same thing she always does, 'When I get a free minute, I will do it.' So it is hard to say if she has even started a list."

"Okay, well, this is what we will do. While you are in Clark City this weekend, we will call her together. You can introduce us over the phone," Jeannette suggested.

"That is a good plan, but no guarantees if she will talk to us about it. Work always gets in her way."

"Keep a positive thought. I can be persuasive. What about your father? Has he started a list?" Jeannette asked.

"His girlfriend is working on it."

"Okay, that is all I needed. I will let you go. See you Friday night. Bye," Jeannette ended the conversation.

She called Tyler right away. He agreed to join them on Friday, of course, Zach would be coming with him. Those two had been best buddies since high school. She was sure others would be dropping by also. Jeannette thought to herself, *"This will be a good weekend."*

"Bridgette, I need you to change my flight to Friday morning. Thank you. Wait a minute before you do, I need to call Mark to see if he can get away." She was hoping he had enough faith in his manager to leave the Restaurant for the weekend. "Hello, Sweetheart. Will you be able to fly to Oregon with me on Friday? We are going to have family time. My boys and Tia will be there."

"Nothing would make me happier than to spend *special* time with you in Oregon."

"Oh, that's wonderful, Mark! I am so anxious to show Oregon to you. Well, not the entire state, but the important part, Clark City. I will have Bridgett take care of the plane tickets," Jeannette almost sang.

David drove the couple to the airport, so Mark did not have to leave his car in the parking garage at the airport. Jeannette was so giddy about going to Oregon she giggled all the way to the airport.

"You are goofy today. Did you drink some happy juice or take some leftover drugs?" Mark asked.

"No happy juice, no drugs. I am just excited!" Jeannette declared.

"David, have you ever seen her like this?" Mark asked.

"Never. This is new," David declared.

"When we get on the plane, we are going to settle you down with alcohol," Mark promised.

"I am happier than ever before! I have my love by my side, we are going to have family time, I get to show you some of Oregon, where I was born and raised, and you will get to see my beautiful home. To me, this is a perfect weekend. I could not ask for more," Jeannette explained. "David I will bring pictures of my home so you can see what I am always talking about."

"Okay, I get it," Mark replied.

Mark drove Jeannette's car from the airport to her home with Jeannette giving him driving instructions. He was astounded as he turned off the engine in front of a beautiful, huge, but welcoming house that Jeannette called home.

"This is your house? You told me it was big, but holy cow! It's gorgeous! How can you stand to be away from it?" Mark asked with surprise.

Jeannette giggled and said, "Yes, this is my humble abode. Come on. Let's go in so I can show you around." Walking through the front door, she called out, "Irma! I'm home! Where are you?"

"Right here, Miss Jeannette. Oh, you look so happy!" Irma hugged her and looked at Mark with a cautious look. "And who is this?"

"Irma, this is Mark. Mark this is my longtime friend and housekeeper, Irma," Jeannette introduced.

"It is nice to meet you. I have heard wonderful things about you," Mark said, shaking her hand.

"It is...Interesting to meet you. I have heard a lot about you, too," Irma said, raising an eyebrow.

Mark smiled at Irma and said, "I hope it was all good?"

"Why don't we put the bags away, Mark? I will show you where," Jeannette said, "Sean, Tia, Tyler, and Zach should be here in a couple of hours," Irma told them.

"What are you cooking, Irma? It smells wonderful, as always," Jeannette asked.

"It is a special weekend, so I have a prime rib in the oven. Sound good?" Irma asked.

"Like heaven. I love your prime rib. Irma could give your chef a run for his money," Jeannette told Mark with a snicker.

For the next hour, she was in tour mode, showing Mark everything inside and out until they were back where they started, the living room.

"Would you like a glass of wine, Sweetheart? We have time to relax for a bit before everyone arrives."

"I would love one. Woman, you have worn me out! Being in the restaurant business, you would think I would be in shape with all the walking I do. We just proved, I am not. Your home, the grounds, the pool, everything, I am in awe," Mark said.

Jeannette began to tell Mark about her life years ago.

"Around twenty years ago, I was struggling to make enough money from ironing so I could pay bills and keep food on the table. Once in a while, I had enough money to buy my boys an ice cream cone or a small toy as a treat. It seems like a lifetime ago. We didn't have much, in the material sense, but we three had a lot of love."

"It shows. You have taught Sean and Tyler respect, a good work ethic, excellent manners, not to be showy about what they have, and most importantly, what love is. You have grounded them."

"Thank you, Mark. I could never ask for a better compliment. As teenagers, my boys had jobs before they could drive. They have had a job while attending college and have pretty much supported themselves. I have not handed them everything. They saved to help buy their cars. When they headed off to college, I upgraded their cars to new ones. I wanted them to have something reliable. Oh! I just had a great idea about what I can get Sean and Tia for graduation! A new car for each of them!" Jeannette exclaimed.

"Whoa! Isn't that rather extravagant?" Mark asked.

"After all the work they put into college, held down a job, helped pay for their education, never complained, and still got good grades? Sean is Valedictorian! Tia has been on her own since she was eighteen. Her car barely runs most of the time. I think a car is a much-deserved gift! I can afford it, especially since I receive royalties from Clay's albums. I keep selling him songs and I earn a pay check from *Windy City*. Yep! That is what I'll do."

"Now that you have explained the reasoning behind it, I agree with you. Sean and Tia do deserve it," Mark said with a smile.

"Did I tell you they are having the wedding here? It is going to be gorgeous! A Labor Day wedding. Perfect weather," Jeannette gushed.

"Mom! We're home!" Sean yelled.

Jeannette left Mark sitting on the couch and hurried to Sean and Tia. "Oh, my kids are home!" She exclaimed. She gave them big bear hugs.

"This is the first time I have seen you without a sling!" Tia shouted. "You look great. Fit as a fiddle."

"Tia don't hog my mom. Let me get in there," Sean demanded. "You are looking delightfully happy. I like it. Did Mark come with you?"

"Mark? Are you still in the living room?" Jeannette yelled.

"I am on my way to you if I don't get lost. I am not used to all this walking. I am afraid to guess how many miles we covered on our tour of the grounds," Mark said tiredly with a smile.

Jeannette giggled, "You are going to have to get in shape to keep up around here." She turned her attention to Sean and Tia for introductions, "Have I introduced you to Mark? I do not remember if I did. Things were kind of blurry a few months ago. Before you answer, I will introduce you, just in case. Sean and Tia, this is Mark. Mark, this is my oldest son Sean and his fiancé, Tia." They shook hands.

"I am excited to be here. Oregon is a beautiful state, and your home is gorgeous! From what Jeannette has told me, there is going to be a wedding here on Labor Day weekend. Congratulations!" Mark exclaimed.

Sean gave Mark the once over to size him up before he said, "Thank you. It is nice to meet you. Welcome to our home." Sean turned to his mother, "Is Tyler here yet?"

"No. Tyler should be rolling in any time. Why don't you put your bags in your room? Irma is making a prime rib for dinner."

"Oh, yum. No wonder I like coming home," Sean said, rubbing his hands together. "Tia, follow me? My room is down the hall."

"Sean and Tia make a handsome couple," Mark commented.

"They complement each other. Oh! I think I heard a car! It is Tyler and his best friend Zach," Jeannette squealed.

"Mom! No sling! Things are back to normal," Tyler said, hugging his mother.

"Jeannette, you look good without your sling. As Tyler said, things are back to normal," Zach said hugging Jeannette.

"Tyler, Zach, I would like you to meet Mark. Mark this is Tyler, my youngest son and my adopted son, Zach," Jeannette introduced.

"Gentlemen, it is nice to meet you, again," Mark said with a wink and shook their hand.

"Smells like Irma is cooking. What's on the menu?" Tyler asked.

"Prime Rib."

"When do we eat?" Zach asked, anxiously.

"I think it is ready. I will check with Irma. You boys know which bedrooms are yours, put your bags away so we can get dinner underway," Jeannette instructed. "Mark, would you please pick out a wine for dinner? The wine keeper is to your left. While you open it, I will help Irma."

"Are you always this bossy?" Mark asked with a smile and a wink.

"Yes. Get used to it. I run a tight ship around here," Jeannette answered with a little laugh.

"Yes, captain. I have my orders!" Mark said with a salute.

Jeannette sat at the head of the table where she belonged. As silverware clinked and conversations commenced, Jeannette stopped to look at her family enjoying themselves. Her heart was full.

Mark joined in on a conversation about baseball and who will win the series this year. It was fun bantering back and forth. Of course, it was all in jest. Irma had joined them for dinner and even had her say on who would be the champions this year. Mark fit right in.

Dinner came to an end with moaning from around the table after eating their fill.

Jeannette broke through the moans and said, "Why don't all of you men, go out to the fire pit and build a fire? We girls will clean up the dishes, make coffee, and bring it out in a few minutes."

"Gentlemen, we have our instructions. I have been informed your mother runs a tight ship," Mark said.

"Does she ever! We can show you scars we got when we disobeyed," Sean said.

"You are so full of bologna! We will be out in a few minutes. Go! Tia, how do you put up with him?" Jeannette asked, shaking her head.

"It's a dirty job, but somebody's got to do it," Tia said. The girls laughed as they quickly cleared the dishes.

By the time Tia and Jeannette joined the men, the fire was roaring. After coffee was served, the couples cuddled under an almost full moon with millions of stars twinkling above.

Jeannette looked at Tyler and Zach sitting alone.

She told them, "You two need girlfriends. Don't you have anyone special?"

They looked at each other. Tyler spoke up, "Well, I have been kind of seeing someone, but Zach has a girlfriend!" Tyler pointed his finger at Zach, laughing.

"Aw, man. Why did you tell your mom that?" Zach moaned. All Jeannette had to do was look at Zach for him to confess. "Yes, I have been seeing a girl for about four months. I am not sure she is the one, or I would have asked if she could come here this weekend. I am keeping my options open."

"So, you are playing her?" Jeannette asked.

"No, no. I want to make sure this girl is the special one before I introduce her to you. She lives in Klamath Falls. Long-distance relationships do not usually last. I am being cautious."

"Okay, I will accept your answer. Tyler, you are getting a big kick out of this, aren't you? What is all the giggling about?" Jeannette asked.

"Because he knew you would question me! He is seeing someone also! He threw me under the bus, so now it's his turn!" Zach said.

"Tyler. Tell me about her. Is there something you are hiding?" Jeannette asked.

"Nothing like that, mom. Zach doesn't like her. They do not get along. That makes me question how I feel about her. If she cannot get along with my best friend, it will probably be a deal-breaker, so I didn't say anything," Tyler explained.

"Let's change the subject. How about fun in the pool tomorrow?" Jeannette suggested. "Invite some of your friends that are in town, and we can make shake chick on the outdoor stove. Or hamburgers. Your choice."

Tia and Mark both said at the same time, "Shake chick?"

"We will demonstrate tomorrow if it is what they choose for dinner," Jeannette explained.

Sean spoke up, "We can have a burger anytime. We eat those a lot. I vote for shake chick." It was unanimous.

The next morning Jeannette and Tia were up early. They wanted to get an early start touring the grounds and talking strategy for the wedding. In the kitchen, the four men stood with a coffee mug in hand watching Jeannette and Tia through the window. Both women were making arm gestures and talking a mile a minute at the same time.

"What are they doing? How can they hear what each other is saying? They are both talking at once!" Sean said.

"Sean, they are women. We don't understand how they do it, but they do. It is a talent they are born with. You should know that by now. Women are a mystery. Just agree with them, and remember these four words: *happy wife, happy life*. A wise man had to have come up with that saying. My married friends have told me those are brilliant words. Here they come. They are still talking!" Mark said, shaking his head in disbelief.

"It is going to be gorgeous, Tia! You have great taste," Jeannette complimented.

"Thank you, Jeannette! A gazebo decorated with flowers and tiny twinkling lights. I can picture it in my mind," Tia said dreamily.

"We don't have a gazebo, mom," Sean protested.

"That is easy to fix. I will get my contractor on the phone tomorrow. Tia wants a gazebo for the wedding. Then we will have a gazebo for your wedding. Besides, I think it would make a nice addition to the grounds. It would be nice to sit in, have a glass of wine, and listen to the crickets or whatever critters are lurking in the bushes," Jeannette said.

Mark looked at Jeannette and mouthed the word critters with a questioning look.

"Yes, Mark. Critters is an Oregon, country word."

"Tia, aren't you getting a little carried away?" Sean asked her.

"I don't think so. I have dreamed of this kind of wedding, but thought it was way beyond my reach," Tia said.

"Sean, you are not paying for the gazebo, I am. It enhances the estate. It will be a nice permanent fixture. Your wedding gives me an excuse to have it built," Jeannette told him. "It will be the dance floor after the ceremony, so it will serve several purposes."

"Okay. Please do not get too carried away? We have talked about a budget," Sean reminded Tia.

"Yes, I know about the budget. Remember, we do not have to rent a venue. That saves us about $2,000. We will incorporate some of the flowers around the grounds, saving more money. Jeannette knows a store that is very reasonable for the cost of my dress. There are other things that we are saving on since we are having it here," Tia retaliated.

"Okay, I trust you and mom. Do not tell anyone, Tia, but my mom is the frugal queen!" Sean declared.

"Okay, okay. What activities have you four come up with for this afternoon?" Jeannette asked.

Tyler announced, "I have four or five friends coming over to swim about 2:00."

"I have invited another couple to join us. I want to introduce Tia to them. They will be here about two also," Sean said.

"It sounds like we are having a pool party! Mark, will you go with me to pick up extra chicken and paper bags? It will allow me to show you a little bit of Clark City." Jeannette suggested.

"Of course. It sounds like we have an agenda for the day. Shall we go into town now?" Mark asked.

"Did you eat breakfast?"

"Yes, I fixed us boys toast and coffee. Very nutritious," Mark said with a serious face.

"I see. We have quite a while before everyone arrives. How about I take all of us for a light breakfast at my favorite place? The Blue Bucket. It is going to be a long time until we eat again," Jeannette offered.

"I'm in!" Zach yelled.

"You are always in when it comes to food! Count me in also." Tyler said.

It was agreed — breakfast at the Blue Bucket.

Upon arrival, Mark looked intently around the restaurant. It was his first restaurant in Oregon and wanted to compare it to *My City*.

"I like it. The atmosphere is welcoming. How is the food?" Mark asked.

"I have always liked it. We used to come here a lot. Tia, what do you think of this place?"

"I reserve my judgment until after I taste the food," Tia said.

A waitress stepped to their table and said, "Hi, my name is Cyndi. Are you ready to order?" Heads nodded around the table.

"I believe we are," Mark said, smiling.

Cyndi wrote down their order and disappeared through a doorway. Jeannette looked up to see Mr. Baker walking in the door.

"Oh! Mr. Baker is here. Would you excuse me for a moment?" Jeannette asked and greeted Mr. Baker with a hug. They shared a short conversation before he escorted Jeannette back to join her family. She made introductions and added, "This is Tia, the young woman I was telling you about."

"Very nice to meet you, Tia," Mr. Baker said. "Jeannette tells me you are looking for an entry-level position with a law firm. I have a position opening in July. Here is my card. Call me, and we can set up an interview. Please excuse me. I have a client waiting for me. Nice to meet you." Mr. Baker gave Jeannette a quick hug and a kiss on the cheek.

Tia sat very still with her eyes wide and her mouth slightly open. "I am going to have a job interview! My first job as a lawyer! Sean! Can you believe it?" Tia exclaimed, trying not to squeal in the restaurant.

"Oh, Baby, I am so happy for you! Things are looking up! Does this mean you want to move to Clark City for sure?" Sean asked.

"Yes!" Tia said excitedly. "How can I thank you, Jeannette?"

"Take good care of my firstborn, that's how," Jeannette said. "I have been thinking. My house is empty a lot of the time. How about you and Sean living there, at least until after the wedding? If you think you can get along with Tyler for the summer?"

Tia's eyes leaked tears of joy.

"I am overwhelmed. A job interview, a beautiful home to live in, what more is there? It has all happened in less than an hour!" She no sooner said that when Tyler spotted Jeff, his biological father.

He quietly got his mother's attention and tipped his head in Jeff's direction. The smile on Jeannette's face faded. She could see he was walking in her direction.

She warned Mark, "Before anything is said, I want you to know my ex-husband is walking in this direction. Don't worry. I can handle him." She looked up to see him standing beside their table. "Jeff. When did you get out of jail?"

"A month ago. Listen, I wanted to thank you for the phone call. I wanted to say I am sorry for controlling you and all the other mean things I did. Boys, I apologize to you, also, for not being the father I should have been. You can thank your mother for the way you have turned out. If I had raised you, well, who knows where you would have ended up? I have said my piece and don't want to bother you. I just wanted to say I am truly sorry." Jeff confessed then left.

"Well, that was a shock. Sorry, I didn't introduce you, Mark," Jeannette said.

"I am glad you didn't," Mark replied.

"What phone call, mom?" Sean asked, sternly. "Why in the world would you call him?"

"Settle down, Sean. Mark was with me when I called. I told him I forgave him for what he put me through."

"You what?" Tyler said, raising his voice. "Mom! He was horrible to you! Sean and I were lucky. We didn't have to deal with him very often. You were on the front-line running interference for us!"

"I know what I did. Tyler, I meant what I said. I forgave him. I didn't need to carry hatred around with me anymore. Don't you see? I went through all that hell for a reason. I learned a lot of lessons. It helped shape me into the woman you can be proud to call mom. That was my goal to make you boys proud of me. I am a strong independent woman who finally said, enough. I will never be a victim again."

"I don't know that I will ever forgive him! He didn't teach me anything!" Sean said with disgust.

"You are wrong. You learned what a bad father is. You will never be like him when you have children. Because he controlled me and kept me home all the time taking care of you two, you learned by my example what love and respect are. That was a gift. You treat Tia with respect. Do you think for a minute she would have looked at you twice if you were not the man you are today? Your childhood shaped you. There are blessings in every situation and lessons to learn. You have to identify them. Whatever you do, learn those lessons the first time, so you do not have to repeat the situation to learn them again!"

The table remained quiet until Cyndi served their food a few minutes later.

"Enjoy. Let me know if you need anything else. I will be back in a few minutes to see how your food is," Cyndi said.

Jeannette could tell Sean was thinking about what she said. The frown on his face gave it away. Sean finally spoke up.

"Okay, mom. I know I will never love him, and I am not sure I will acknowledge him as my father, but you are right. Lessons were learned."

"I feel the same way as Sean," Tyler chimed.

"Well, I do not know the man, nor do I want to, so . . . .I don't care!" Zach said. "What I do care about is this omelet!"

"Thanks for your input, Zach," Jeannette said dryly. That raised a chuckle from everyone at the table.

Mark leaned close to Jeannette and said, "As I said before, you are a wonderful mother."

The pool gathering was more fun than Mark had known in a long time, maybe ever. For years he has worked seven days a week. There was no time for fun. Later that evening, he and Tia learned what shake chick is. It was hilarious! Everyone had a coating of flour from head to toe — almost as much as the chicken did. Mark was holding his sides he was laughing so hard. Thank God they did it outside this time. Irma would not have been happy to see such a mess.

When Jeannette took over the chicken, she presented a towel to each person. They wiped as much flour off as possible from their bodies and hair. Then it was a cannonball contest. Zach was the expert cannon-baller. His title was upheld.

"Okay all you drowned rats, dinner is ready!" Jeannette yelled from the patio. "Get it while it's hot!" The group did not hesitate to race to the table.

There was no talking. The boys ate like they had been starved for days and cleaned up every morsel of food. No leftovers from this meal! It was just as well; the young people would be leaving to go back to school. Jeannette and Mark will head to Chicago tomorrow afternoon.

After dinner, the swimmers were relaxing when Tyler handed Jeannette her guitar. He said, "I heard through the grapevine you have a few new songs for Clay. Would you play one? Please?"

"I guess I could play one." Her right arm was bare, and the group noticed her scars from the attack. She realized she was being stared at, so she quickly put on a cover-up.

"My arm is not ready to play a lot, yet. But here is a knee slapper for you." Jeannette was true to her word. There was not one face that did not have a smile. "Well? What did you think?"

"Oh, I liked it! Is it one of the songs on Clay's new album?" Tia asked. "You wrote that?"

"Yes, to both questions. Clay's album will be on the shelves in about four weeks. You will hear it along with two others I wrote for him."

"Wait a minute. I have only heard two. You wrote a third?" Mark asked.

"The third one is a slow tune. I was told it is one that can be felt deep inside your soul. It is about broken hearts. I was in a sad mood when I wrote it. Now is not the time for sadness. You will hear it, just not now," Jeannette explained.

After the visitors had gone, and Jeannette's children (all four of them) had said goodnight, she and Mark cuddled together on the couch with a glass of wine.

"What do you think of Oregon? Did you have a good time?" Jeannette asked.

"Oregon is a magical place. I observed families doing things together. It is laid back — no hustle and bustle. I could see myself living here. I see why this place is so important to you."

"People think I am crazy about having a business in Chicago and traveling back and forth. Maybe I am slightly unbalanced, but I see it as having the best of both worlds. I can't say I enjoy flying all the time, but everything has its pros and cons. I have become friends with some of the flight attendants. I visit with them, so the flight is not so boring. Sometimes I work on my laptop."

"May I be rude for a minute and ask you if I can come back to Oregon sometime?" Mark asked and made Jeannette laugh.

"That is not rude. Of course, you can! I expect you to. The more, the merrier. This house has seen a lot of love. It started with the first owners, and the love is still here. This house is happiest when there are people and children laughing together. I can feel it. The atmosphere changes. It is hard to explain."

"You do not need to explain. I think I felt it, too. I love my family, but we never had fun like yours does," Mark said, smiling as he recalled the events of the day.

"What good is life if you can't laugh and have fun? I don't believe God put us on this earth to be sad and grumpy. He put us here to enjoy life. For several years after Robert passed away, I was in a deep depression. I wanted to do something about it, but I didn't have the energy to try. I realize that sounds crazy. There is no other way I know how to explain it to you. Then you came along and changed everything. Thank you," Jeannette said.

"You are most welcome. I am glad I could be of assistance. Would you mind if we changed the subject and talk about our wedding? When do I get the honor of marrying you?"

"I was thinking about either January with lots of snow, or April in the spring when everything is waking up from a long winter," Jeannette suggested.

"I like the idea of January. Starting the new year, with a new life together," Mark said.

"January it is. We can decide on a specific day later if it is okay with you? I'm tired. Let's go to bed," Jeannette said through a yawn.

"Wait a minute. I forgot to ask you how the phone call went with Tia's mother," Mark inquired.

"Tia was right. She had excuses. Her mother didn't commit to attending graduation, and the guest list wasn't started, but she will get to it soon. I am hoping she will at least attend the wedding of her only child. Carol does not realize how she is hurting Tia. I feel awful for that young woman. I know what it is like having a narcissistic parent. She needs to know what it is like to have love from a parent who is interested in her accomplishments. She has supported herself since she was eighteen years old. That is another reason why I think a car is perfect for a graduation gift. She has earned it."

Mark was quiet while he processed what Jeannette had just told him. Then he said, "Thank you for sharing that. I am beginning to understand. You have become her mother with more love than she has ever known. I am sure her parents loved her the only way they experienced love. Is her father coming to the wedding to give her away?"

"I haven't asked. I thought Tia and I should deal with one parent at a time," Jeannette said.

"You are a mother to a lot of young people!" Mark declared.

"I take a lot under my wing, yes. They seem to gravitate towards me. Young people make me happy. Happiness can be contagious if you are open to it. Loving them comes naturally to me."

"I have no experience with young adults or children. I do not know what kind of father I would have been. I want to think, a good one," Mark shared his thoughts out loud.

"Well buckle up, buttercup! You are going to be a father in January to a ready-made family! After watching you today, I know you will be a good dad."

Sunday was a day for goodbyes. Jeannette watched her children drive off, but not until each one received a hug and kiss from her. Mark was surprised when he had arms thrown around him by the young adults. It was acceptance. His eyes welled up with moisture, threatening to spill out. Jeannette could feel it, without looking at him.

Jeannette leaned into him and said, "They approved of you and demonstrated their love. It is what a parent feels like when a child returns your love. It melts your heart."

"If I had known what it was like to be a father, I would have tried to be one a long time ago. Well, we need to be leaving for the airport within the hour. Come on, Mom, let's get our bags packed," Mark said. He put his arm around her as they entered into a quiet house.

Lesson Learned: Forgive those who are in your life, even if they are not sorry for what they have done to you. Although, with time they very well could be sorry. If you hold on to hatred, it only hurts you, not them. Forgiveness is powerful. Your life will only get better with forgiveness.

4

Graduation day was two days away with a lot of activity leading up to it. Jeannette was helping make arrangements for Sean and Tia to move into her house while they took finals. Jeannette arranged for a moving truck, and a storage unit needed to be secured. She also procured a graduation celebration at the Blue Bucket the following Saturday after graduation. The final thing on the arrangement list was with the Chevrolet Dealership to bring the cars to the Blue Bucket with big red bows on them.

Jeannette flew home to Oregon on Wednesday to make sure everything was in place. Mark was not able to accompany her to Oregon this time. There was a convention in town three blocks away that was going to make *My City* extremely busy. He would not trust anyone to handle it, but himself.

Friday morning, Jeannette drove to Eugene. Five hours was a long drive. The hotel was easy to find with the college in plain view. She had just enough time to shower before meeting up with Sean and Tia. Tyler and Zach will see them at graduation on Saturday.

"Mom! Over here!" Sean shouted, waving across a grassy area.

Jeannette hurried to them for hugs and kisses.

"You and Tia look wonderful! So mature and ready for the world. I am bursting with pride. Tia, I hope you realize I already consider you, my daughter. You have one mother present and cheering for you at graduation, and I do mean cheer, literally."

Tia looked at Sean as if to say, *'oh no.'* Sean looked at her with a big smile and said, "This is what you are marrying into, so get used to it."

They spent the rest of the afternoon and evening reminiscing about earlier times. Tia could not stop laughing.

Jeannette asked, "Tia, you must have some good memories to share?"

"Nothing even close to what you have. Most of my memories are of my dad helping him with a landscaping job. There was nothing funny about planting a shrub or a tree. When Sean and I have children, I want them to have memories like Sean has."

"Well, that's okay, Tia, because we are going to make lots of great memories. We have already begun. Did you enjoy yourself in Clark City?"

"Yes! It was so much fun. Now I understand the term shake chick. What a mess! Did you use to do that in the house? Oh, no. When our children make it, we will take them outside to shake! Changing the subject, Mark is not with you. Will he make it to graduation?" Tia asked.

"I am afraid not — big convention. The restaurant will be too busy for Mark to leave. He sends his love and congratulations. I am hopeful he will make the celebration next weekend. Tia, have you heard from your mom and dad about attending the ceremony tomorrow?"

Her expression changed from happy to almost sad.

"No. I have not talked to them. I sent them an announcement, so they know when it is."

"Maybe you should think about giving them a call tonight to remind them. I am looking forward to meeting your parents. In three months, we are going to be related. I want to meet them before the wedding. Speaking of the wedding, will you ask your mother once again about a guest list? Sorry, I don't mean to nag. You still need to pick out a design for the invitations! We need to get them in the mail as soon as possible!" Jeannette exclaimed.

"I promise I will call her tonight. Do you want to bet on what she will say?" Tia asked.

"I don't think so. Let's hope your mom surprises you." Jeannette paused to yawn. "Excuse me. The drive wore me out, so did all the laughing. My cheeks ache. Listen, kids, I am fading fast. The hotel bed is calling me. I will see you tomorrow. I love you both."

Graduation was full of pomp and circumstance, as expected. Sean and Tia walked to the stage together. When they appeared Jeannette, Tyler and Zach stood. They cheered and applauded as loud as they could. Tia had a smile as wide as her face knowing someone was proud of her. It made for a good photo-op with her face lit up like a light bulb.

Sean gave the valedictorian address, making Jeannette even more proud. The speech was peppered with things she had taught him through the years. It made her a very proud mother.

She whispered to Tyler, "He was listening." Tears of love and pride fell from her eyes.

"Of course, he did, mom. We both did. You taught by example, too," Tyler said.

At the end of Sean's speech, he shared these words; "In conclusion, I would like to recognize a special teacher and to thank her for making me who I am today. She did not have the opportunity to go to college, but she is smarter than anyone I have ever known. Teacher, you say? No college? How is it possible to be a teacher without a college education? For this woman, it came naturally. She became a CEO literally overnight with no experience and has become a very successful woman. Now I am not standing before you, telling you not to go to college. Ninety-nine percent of the population needs a college education for success in life. There is one person here today that has taught me anything in this world is possible. If you dream it, there is a reason why. Dreams can come true with persistence and a positive attitude. She taught me integrity, honesty, strong ethics, how to survive adversity when faced with insurmountable odds, and the most important thing she taught me was how important family is. Without the support of my family, I would not be standing here delivering this speech. This special teacher's name is Jeannette to all of you. To me, I call her Mom. Please stand up so I can show you off? Thank you with all my heart," he threw her a kiss and gave a bow toward Jeannette then returned to his seat next to Tia.

The audience broke into applause as Jeannette rose, waved to the crowd, and threw kisses to Sean. She held her head high with tears of joy and pride streaming down her face. That was her baby, making her so proud to be his mother. While she stood facing her son and an audience of thousands, she thought, *"All the struggle during the early years was worth every second. I see now this was the reason for it. It was a gift to be able to stay at home with my boys and be allowed to teach them the important things in life."* On stage, Tia was on her feet applauding also with tears running down her face.

After the ceremony, Jeannette held her firstborn so tight he thought he might not survive.

"I love you too, Mom, but could you lighten your grip a little? I can't breathe."

"I can't help it! You have made this mother the proudest parent in the history of parenting! I have done something right in my life. I love you so much."

"I love you, too. I hope I can be half the person you are," He declared as he hugged her with closed eyes. He pulled back to say, "Enough of the mushy stuff. Let me strike a pose for pictures!"

Sean started posing and had them all laughing. Jeannette hugged Tia amid Sean's silliness and told her how proud she was of her.

Countless photos were taken marking this important time in their lives. A male voice came out of nowhere.

"There you are! I have been wading through a sea of people to get to you," Ed, Tia's father, said. "Tia! Look at you. All grown up with a degree."

"Hello, Dad. I didn't know you were coming today. It is nice to see you," Tia said, acting a bit uneasy.

She attempted a hug but was unsuccessful. Before she could get close enough, Ed turned to Jeannette and introduced himself. Sean saw the hurt on her face and pulled her close to him.

"It is nice to meet you, Ed, finally. Did Carol make the ceremony?" Jeannette asked.

"She was here but had to get back to the hospital. She asked me to relay a message to Tia...congratulations!" Ed said.

"I wish I could have met her. I do not want to take attention away from graduation, but do you have a guest list you would like to invite to Tia and Sean's wedding? It will be Labor Day weekend," Jeannette informed him.

"Um, my girlfriend, Alicia, was supposed to put together a list. I will check with her when I get back."

"I would appreciate it. The invitations must be sent out as soon as possible. Have Alicia email me the list. Here is my card. I have two email addresses listed. One is work the other is personal. Either one is fine. We are going to get something to eat. Would you like to join us? It will allow us to get to know each other," Jeannette suggested.

"I wish I could, but I need to get back to finish up a job. I left my employees with instructions. It makes me nervous not being there. Tia congratulations!" Ed said and kissed her on the cheek.

"Ed, before you go, I want you to know Tia is a wonderful young woman. She is smart and responsible. I will be proud to call her my daughter-in-law," Jeannette told him. Ed nodded his head and scurried off.

Jeannette wanted to bring a smile to Tia's face.

"Tia! They both came to see you graduate! That is wonderful! They are just not vocal like I am. Smile, it is a good day! Now, let's get something to eat. Since Sean was so long-winded with his speech, I am starving!"

"Hey! That was a good speech!" Sean moaned.

"You know I was kidding. It was a phenomenal speech," Jeannette said to boost his ego. Tyler and Zach were laughing at Sean's moan of disappointment. "Tyler, don't make fun of your brother."

"I can't help it, Mom. He WAS long-winded. I am just glad I didn't say it to him," Tyler joked.

"Just wait until both of you graduate!" Sean warned.

They teased and laughed through dinner. It was a beautiful day. Now the focus will be on the celebration scheduled for next Saturday. Sean and Tia will be home on Monday with bags in hand and a truck filled with everything they own. Tyler and Zach will be home and offered to help unload the truck at the storage unit. Everything was in place.

In Chicago on Monday, Jeannette frantically worked at catching up on paperwork. Thursday morning, she was headed back to Oregon.

Bridgett's voice came through the intercom, "Jeannette, Greg has requested you go to the sound booth. He has something for you to listen to."

"On my way." In the sound booth, Greg was turning dials and looking very busy when she walked in. "What is it, Greg? Is there a problem?"

He pointed to the sound room. She looked through the glass window that separated them. Clay and The Band were waving at her. She immediately went into the sound room and hugged Clay.

"Hey, Pretty Lady! We just finished recording one of your songs. I want your approval before we move on," Clay requested.

"Give me a minute. Greg, have you got Clay's song cued up? Great. Let's give it a listen." She made no expressions throughout the song. When it was done, she pulled her guitar from the closet and went into the sound room.

"I have a suggestion. Where the bridge comes in, it should sound like this." Jeannette demonstrated.

"Play it with us one time from the top?" Clay asked, then gave Greg a wink. He counted them down, and the music began.

Of course, Greg was taping it. When the vocals came in Clay motioned for Jeannette to sing harmony. She obliged. Before the song ended, she was singing the lead.

"You have not lost your touch, Jeannette. The music always sounds better when you play with us. Hey, Greg! Did you get that?" Clay asked. Greg shook his head, yes. "What do you say we all take a break and listen to it?"

"I should have known you would tape it. Okay, let's hear it." Jeannette said.

The music stopped. She turned to Clay with a surprised look on her face and said, "It is perfect even if I am singing and playing! It is going to make the charts! Greg, save it. I have two suggestions. The first is, we release this as a single. Greg, can we start production on this right away? Monday I will announce that the single will be hitting the stores in two weeks. We will get the radio to play it. The second thing is, I am going to call Mark to ask him if we can do this song at *My City* tonight or tomorrow night. Can you all make it? Wonderful! I will go to my office and give him a call. I will be right back. Don't leave."

Jeannette made the call to Mark. He agreed to it. A group of executives has reservations this evening, and this would impress them. The two were helping each other, business to business.

"We are all set for this evening. I made arrangements for us to have an early dinner before we played. Dinner is on *Windy City*. Greg, you need to be there, too. Clay, bring Amy and Greg, bring your wife. Band, if you have a special someone, bring them. We will make it a party. Poor Mark, he has no idea what he is in for" Jeannette said and shook her head. Everyone else chuckled. "Be there at six sharp! We play at nine." Jeannette stopped by Bridgett's desk and asked her to come along, too.

David took Jeannette to *My City* at five o'clock. She wanted to help set up to take some of the pressure off Mark and his staff.

"Darling, it is not necessary for you to help. That is what I have a staff for," Mark said.

"I know, but I sprang this on you at the last minute, so it is only fair for me to pitch in. I can set the tables. I assume you want us in the back?"

"Yes. I think it would be for the best. Have I told you today that I love you?"

"No, and it's about time, Mister!" Mark pulled her close and kissed her. "You need to let me go so I can go to work. You have things to do, too. Will you be able to join us for dinner?"

"Yes. So set one more place setting."

"Will do. The bill for all this goes to me. *Windy City* is picking up the tab. It is a client dinner, and well worth the money. I think this song is going to be a chart-topper! The best thing about it is, I wrote the song and recorded it with Clay today!" Jeannette squealed with excitement.

"Simmer down, Honey. You will have no energy left to perform on stage!" Mark said, laughing at her.

The *Windy City* group filled the room after bringing in their equipment. They ate, drank wine, and generally enjoyed themselves.

Mark stood on a chair and announced, "May I have your attention? The orchestra on stage is now taking a break, so you have space and time to set up. Let's show these people what good music is." The room cleared immediately.

Fifteen minutes later, Mark stepped to the microphone.

"Good evening, ladies and gentlemen. Our orchestra will be back in a few minutes. In the meantime, *MY City* has a special band joining us this evening for your enjoyment. I know you have heard and seen them. It is my honor to introduce Clay and The Band!" The audience broke into applause.

Clay took over the microphone.

"Thank you very much. Tonight, we are going to play a brand new song, no one has heard before, so maybe you can let us know if you like it. It will be on our new album coming out soon, and we will be releasing this song as a single in approximately two weeks. The pretty lady standing on my left with the guitar wrote this song. Here we go!"

He counted them down, and the song took off. The audience began to clap in time to the music. Mark did not see one person without a smile on their face. Mark's daily diner, Sam, was enjoying the music so much he put down his utensils and clapped along. That was entirely out of character for him. The music ended, and the audience erupted into applause.

Clay winked at Jeannette who was smiling from ear to ear.

Talking into the microphone again, he said, "Thank you, thank you. Does that mean you like our new song?" The applause started along with a few whistles. This upscale restaurant had never heard such a loud crowd. "Would you like to hear one more? Mark, is that okay? Which one do you want to do, guys?"

It was suggested the new slow haunting tune. Clay looked at Jeannette for an okay. At first, she shook her head no. Clay pouted, so she reluctantly agreed.

"We are going to slow it way down with this one. It is another new one that will be on our album written by the same pretty lady. Sing it, Jeannette."

A pin could be heard dropping in this crowded room of five hundred. Couples held hands a few ladies sniffled, and the consensus was, it touched their hearts.

Mark had not heard this song. It was the one Jeannette told him she would play for him one day. Today was the day, along with all his patrons. He knew when she wrote this one. It was when he hurt her.

The song was over, and no one moved a muscle. The silence was deafening. Jeannette froze with a look of terror on her face. Was the song that bad?

Clay had a blank look on his face and turned to Jeannette. No one knew what to do. Finally, a gentleman in the middle of the room stood to his feet and began to clap. It was contagious. The entire place erupted and was on their feet for a standing ovation. The group bowed several times before the applause grew quiet.

"Thank you, ladies and gentlemen. Thank you for being our test audience tonight. Don't forget to buy our album. Goodnight," Clay said and unstrapped his guitar.

The audience began clapping and shouting, "One more song!"

Clay had a look on his face that Jeannette had never seen before. It was a look of surprise. He looked at Jeannette as if to say, 'what do I do now?' Mark came out on stage and asked Clay if he would consider playing one more. He and The Band agreed.

One last time Clay took the microphone, "Ladies and gentlemen you have humbled us to our core with your appreciation of our music. It was not our intent to take over the stage from the orchestra. Since you asked so nicely, we are going to do one more! This one I know you have heard."

It was the second song Jeannette had written for Clay and a big favorite. At the conclusion, there was more applause as Clay, The Band, and Jeannette walked off stage.

Mark was waiting for Jeannette. He held her close and whispered in her hear, "Sweetheart, I now know how you felt. I am so sorry I caused you so much pain. I know I have said it time and time again, but I don't think I will ever be able to say it enough. I am sorry. I am so fortunate to have you by my side. By the way, the songs were wonderful. I am so proud of you!"

"I love you, too," Jeannette whispered.

"I don't mean to break up at this moment, but, I want to thank you for this evening, Mark," Clay began. "It takes a special friend to let us come in at the last minute and end up taking over your stage. Honestly, we only planned on one song. It snowballed."

"No apology necessary. My customers loved you! It was like giving them a private concert. I am here to keep them happy. Your music did the trick. It was great. I will listen for comments as well as instruct my staff to ask their customers what they thought about the entertainment tonight. I need to be on the floor, checking on the wait-staff, and especially my group of executives. I will see if they have anything to say. I love you, Honey. Stay for a while, please?" Jeannette nodded as he hurried out.

"Well, Jeannette, I think you were right. We might have a hit on our hands, maybe two!" Clay said. "What do you think about that?"

"I am not sure I can think. As the owner of the company who is producing this, I am ecstatic, and my mind is whirling about thinking about the advertising. As the author, I am at a loss for words. It is going to take a while for me to wrap my head around it," Jeannette confided.

"These songs, Pretty Lady, are going to make you and me rich!" Clay exclaimed.

"Excuse me. I need to sit down and put my head between my legs before I pass out. To think I just toyed around with writing songs, thinking it was a good pass time. In my opinion, my songs were never good enough for anyone to hear. I never, in my wildest dreams, thought this would happen. I have been blessed and deserve a good cry."

"I have a big shoulder you can use," Clay said as he held her in his arms. "Amy, what did you think? Did you like the new songs?"

"Oh, Honey, they were wonderful! You have a winner. Jeannette, Sweetie, why are you crying? The crowd loved the new songs. You should be proud," Amy said.

"I am. I am crying with joy and feeling very blessed, also relieved. I was nervous about presenting these to the public. Especially the slow one. When no one applauded, I thought I would pass out. The thought of it being so bad when no one acknowledged it at all, was such a horrible feeling, and I wanted to curl up in a ball and die right there on the stage. Thank God they finally clapped," Jeannette shared.

"It was so good you left the audience in awe. I also agree with the audience. I forgot to clap myself! I'm happy the one man stood up and shook everyone back to reality. The song expressed the hurt of a broken heart. We have all been through it at some point in our lives. You put words and music to what we felt. No one has ever done that quite as you did," Amy encouraged.

"Thank you. I needed to hear that. Okay, my crying is out of the way. Now it is time for the CEO to kick in. Greg. I am glad you are still here. We have got to get that single on the shelves right away. Tonight, we have succeeded in creating a buzz. We have to strike while the iron is hot, and fresh in their minds," Jeannette said.

"No problem, boss. Starting tomorrow morning, I will give it everything I've got. Since I am doing such a great job and this is going to make a lot of money, do I get a bonus?" Greg asked with a big smile.

"We will talk about it later. I am going to see if I can help clean up the room we used and pay the bill. It has been a great night. I Hope you had a good time. See you tomorrow!" Jeannette said and waved as she walked away.

"That is one special lady. I love her like a sister. Well, let's get our gear out to the truck," Clay said.

Jeannette was too wound up to sit. She helped in the kitchen with plating salads, putting orders together for the wait-staff to deliver, and assisting the chef with anything he needed. Mark made an appearance in the kitchen and saw Jeannette busy as a bee.

"Jeannette! What are you doing?" Mark asked.

"I am helping! I thought they could use a hand. I have an apron on, and I haven't put a finger in anything, I swear!"

"This is not necessary. The staff does this every night, and they know what they are doing." Mark explained.

"The kitchen can always use help. I know that from experience. Chef, do you want me to leave? Am I in your way?" Jeannette asked.

"You are not in my way. She is a big help! Tonight, we need it. There must be an overly packed house out there," Chef said.

"Yes. Not one empty chair. We had to bring in a few extra chairs for a couple of tables. That reminds me, I asked the executives what they thought of the entertainment tonight. They raved about the music. One asked if you had a contract with a recording company and if you needed a manager. He was disappointed when I told him about you. He said he would have invested in the group. Sweetheart, you have made Clay and The Band stars!"

Jeannette jumped in his arms with joy and said, "We will have to celebrate later, I have work to do, and you should be on the floor with the wait-staff. Go! We've got this!"

"I love you!" Mark said.

It was midnight before Jeannette sat down. The adrenaline had finally worn off, and exhaustion swept over her. Mark found her sitting on a crate asleep by the cooler. He gently tapped her shoulder and stroked her cheek.

"Sweetheart, it is time to go home. Come on. I will take you."

"Hey, Mark! Let her come back anytime. She was a big help," Chef shouted across the kitchen.

Mark helped her to her feet. They walked arm in arm to his car.

"I have not been this tired in years! Not since the boys were little. It was such a wonderful night. I did not want it to end. Thank you so much for letting us perform tonight. You are a good fiancé," Jeannette said with her eyes half-open.

"You were great for business. There was not one bad review. Speaking of review, one of the executives having dinner was from The *Chicago Town News.* He wants one of his journalists to interview you."

That woke her up with a jolt. "No, kidding? Wait 'til I tell Clay! You would think with the job I have, I would not be surprised and should be used to giving interviews, but this has to do with me. It makes all the difference," Jeannette said.

"I told him he could reach you at *Windy City.* I hope you don't mind. He will call you tomorrow."

"Wonderful," Jeannette said while yawning.

"My poor baby. Hello Sid. I will be back in a minute. I am going to see Jeannette to her door. She might fall asleep in the elevator as exhausted as she is," Mark explained.

Sid tipped his hat, and Jeannette gave him a little wave.

The next morning, the first thing Jeannette did when she got to her office was call Clay and tell him about the interview. He was just as excited as she was. There was no way the interview would take place if Clay were not involved. She reiterated that to Clay and planned to tell the reporter the same. She had just hung up with Clay when the reporter called. An interview was set up for 1:00 with the pair.

The interview took an hour. The journalist brought a photographer along to take pictures. It was a positive experience leaving them feeling good about it. The reporter informed them it would run in Sunday's paper before he left. Jeannette would be in Oregon, so she instructed Bridgett to make sure she buys two or three newspapers for her. If it turned out to be a good article, she would have it framed.

Jeannette was extremely busy with securing advertising for the new single. Several radio stations were set to start playing it next week announcing when it will come out and where it can be purchased.

She was finally able to relax on the plane bound for Oregon with Mark. They talked about the reaction his patrons had for the group. Mark suggested maybe once a month Clay and The Band could play a couple of songs. Jeannette agreed to talk it over with Clay but doubted they would be available every month.

On Friday she made all the final arrangements for the Graduation celebration the next day. Her house was busy, now that everyone had moved in. Tia helped with the celebration preparations as much as Jeannette allowed her to. Tia needed to be a little surprised tomorrow. After all, it was in honor of her and Sean.

Mark went with Jeannette to the Chevrolet dealership to pick out the colors of the cars and to pay for them. Of course, she negotiated a better price. After all, she was purchasing two cars. Mark watched her bargaining with the owner and had a smile of pride.

At 6:00, Mark suggested they all go to dinner at The Blue Bucket, knowing Jeannette would have a few questions for them about tomorrow. That way, he figured he could take care of two things at once: food and arrangements. He was correct. Jeannette excused herself several times to talk to the manager about arrangements.

The celebration went off without a hitch. There were at least two hundred people in attendance. It was a success in making the couple feel honored and happy. Now, it was time for the main event, the cars.

A microphone had been set up to make announcements and toasts to the graduates. It was Jeannette's turn to speak. "I would like to raise a glass to this wonderful young couple. Sean is my first born. I still think of him as my baby boy with an apron on, standing on a chair and helping me cook. Tia is going to be my daughter-in-law on Labor Day weekend. In my heart she is my daughter already. We are going to make wonderful memories in the coming years. Before I finish, I want to tell you a few things about these exceptional young adults. What you probably do not know about my kids; while they attended college, they both had a job to pay for their expenses, classes, and books. Nothing was handed to them. They EARNED their degrees, Tia in business law and Sean in business. I am so proud of both of them, and I love them so much. Okay I have to stop, or I will start crying. To my kids, may the rest of their lives be happy, blessed and give me grandchildren! Salute!" Jeannette shouted and the audience joined her and applauded.

"We have one more surprise for the graduates," she said. Mark whispered in her ear the cars had just arrived. "We will need to blindfold Sean and Tia first. Zach and Tyler will you do the honors? Be nice about it, not too tight. Ready? Boys, will you guide them to the door, please?"

No one knew what was going on except Jeannette and Mark. Jeannette's excitement built with each step closer to the door. Mark swung both doors of the restaurant wide open. The crowd gasped. Sean and Tia quickly took off their blindfolds. In front of them were two beautiful cars with a large bow on the roof of either. There was a dark blue one for Sean and a white one for Tia. Each was four-wheel-drive mid-sized automobiles.

Sean jumped in the air and yelled "Yee-haw!" Then he picked up his mom and spun her around.

Tia was speechless. She stared at the car with her hands cupped over her mouth. "A...a...Car? Are you giving me a car? I can't accept this! It is way too much!"

"Tia, you deserve this car. You have supported yourself since you were eighteen, you worked hard, got a degree, and you need a nice, reliable car. You are an attorney now and need to look like one. Tia, you are my daughter. Take it in the spirit it is given, love. The keys are in it. Take it for a spin!" Jeannette told her.

Tia's hands were shaking so hard she didn't know if she could drive, but she was going to do her best. Her body sunk into the leather seat. The new car smell was intoxicating.

Sean pulled away from the curb like a shot. Tia followed his lead. Jeannette got the reaction she was looking for. Surprise and happiness.

"Oh, Mark, the cars made them so happy. I don't think Tia's parents ever splurged on her. Neither one gave her a graduation gift that I know of. There are times I would like to grab her parents and shake them until they open their eyes to see what kind of a woman she has grown to be. It certainly wasn't because of them being such wonderful parents, that's for sure!" Jeannette spouted off.

"Okay, honey. Settle down. Tia has you for a mom now. Things will be different. Sean and Tia have the world by the tail. There is no telling what the two of them will accomplish together," Mark said.

Sunday morning the house slept in until ten. As usual, Jeannette was the first one up and making coffee. Mark followed, hoping the coffee was ready.

"Mark, can I ask you a question? Are you truly happy? I mean with stepping in as a father, marrying me, back and forth between Oregon and Chicago? Can you handle all of this? Tell me the truth. Is all of this going to be too much?" Jeannette asked.

"Why are you asking me this? All of this is worth it to be with the woman of my dreams. It is awesome to be part of a family again. After all, there is not another family like yours! I love it. That's the truth. You know, we have been so busy, you haven't met my family yet. We had to cancel the last time. When would you like me to set it up?" Mark asked.

"Definitely NOT this week. I will be too busy with the single we are releasing next weekend. The week after should be just fine. Go ahead and set it up, and I will make it work. Now, how about a cup of coffee?" Jeannette asked and handed Mark a mug of coffee.

"You are a lifesaver. Thanks, Honey."

Jeannette's phone rang. "Hello?"

"Hey, Pretty Lady! How was the celebration?" Clay asked.

"It went very well. Everyone had a good time. So, Clay, why do I have the pleasure of a call from you on a Sunday morning?" Jeannette asked.

"Well, I am sitting here with the newspaper in my hands reading it, when I ran across our interview."

"I am putting you on speaker so Mark can hear. Okay, go ahead," Jeannette said.

Clay went on with the conversation, "I just finished reading the article. It was excellent. I read every word, and there was no attempt at making us look bad at all. Nothing negative. The reporter wrote, and I quote:

'The sound that this group makes is phenomenal. The author of some of their music was written by Jeannette, the CEO of Windy City Publishing and Recording Company. Do not take this journalist's word for it, judge for yourself. A new single by the group is going to be released in the coming week.'

"What do you think about that? We even got free advertising! I believe this is worthy of a frame," Clay said cheerily. "You can read the entire article when you get back to Chicago and maybe we can have a glass of the good stuff."

"How did the picture of us look? Did he pick a good one?" Jeannette asked.

"It looks just like us. It is pretty good, I think," Clay told her.

"I can't wait to read it! I will be in Chicago tomorrow. Come see me this week so we can talk more strategy." Jeannette said.

"I will be in the sound room recording two days this week. Check the schedule and come to the booth. Have a listen. You can tell us if something needs to be, in your words, tweaked," Clay invited and gave a chuckle.

Jeannette and Mark's Sunday was spent lounging by the pool enjoying each other and the family. Jeannette began thinking about Sean and Tia's wedding. She was making lists in her mind of things that had to be done right away.

"Tia, have you talked to your mother about the guest list?"

"No."

"Do you have any idea who she wants to invite? Or how many?" Jeannette asked.

"I don't. I haven't lived in Portland for five years. I don't know if she has any friends," Tia said.

"How about your father?"

"I have not heard from him, either. I will call him right now." Tia walked away to make the call.

Jeannette saw her talking on the phone but could not hear what was said. She told Mark, "I hope Tia is getting somewhere with him. I wonder if he is going to give her away."

Tia cheerfully said, "Dad said Alicia is putting it together and is almost done. She will email it to me this evening. I am on a roll, so I am going to call my mother." Again, Jeannette could not hear what was being said until seconds before she hung up. Tia's voice got louder.

"Well, the same thing, as always, from mom. I told her to get it done tonight! That I wanted it in my email this evening. I am not going to mess around anymore. We have to get invitations out!"

"Yes, we do. Calm down. At least Alicia is doing her job, that's a step in the right direction. Before I forget, you need to pick out invitations, so the printer can get them printed for you. Put that on your list of things to do tomorrow. Sean is familiar with the printer. I am not sure how many we need to order. I wish I had their list. Sean, if you have friends you want to invite, make sure you get their addresses. Keep a list. I need to know how many guests we expect for the benefit of the caterer. Now that I think of it, order two-hundred-fifty. If we need more, we can have another batch printed. Before I forget, the contractor will be here on Wednesday to start the gazebo," Jeannette said.

"Honey, does your brain ever shut off?" Mark asked. "Relax. Give yourself some downtime. It will all get done. I promise."

"Okay. One more thing, then I will relax. Tia, do you want to buy your dress in Oregon or Chicago?" Jeannette asked.

"I have a choice? Really? Um, I don't know. Let me think about it," Tia answered, looking a little surprised at the prospect.

"Have a look at the bridal shop in town and Carson City. It will help you make a decision," Jeannette suggested.

Jeannette settled down to relax. The sunshine felt so good on her skin before she knew it, she was asleep.

5

That week at *Windy City* was hectic, to say the least. Meetings, luncheons, advertising agents, photo sessions, radio interviews, and also trying to coordinate wedding plans with Tia. It was Friday, and Jeannette was exhausted. She had been running on adrenalin all week.

`The single was expected to be out on Monday. Jeannette had produced hundreds of singles, but none has made her more nervous.

"Greg, how does everything look for the launch on Monday?"

"Everything is a go. The city will be flooded with singles. The following week we start shipping to other cities. The big chain stores have large orders we need to fill. I have stayed on top of shipping. They are working hard to get things done. We all are." Greg stopped for a second and looked at Jeannette. "Are you alright? Are you sleeping at night? Have you eaten anything today?"

"I am having a hard time shutting off my brain at night. I am exhausted. Eat? What time is it?" Jeannette asked.

"Almost three in the afternoon! Sit down right now!"

She did what Greg told her to do then Greg called Mark and told him how worried he was about Jeannette. Mark showed up twenty minutes later in the sound booth with a bag filled with her favorite foods.

"Jeannette, Honey. Let's go to your office so you can eat." Mark put his arm around her as they walked.

While Jeannette ate, Mark talked, almost to the point of scolding her about not taking care of herself.

"Jeannette. The single is finished. It is a masterpiece. You are killing yourself." Jeannette opened her mouth to speak, but Mark held up a hand to stop her. "I am not going to listen to excuses or what you need to get done. I am taking you home, and you are going to bed."

"Now who is the bossy one?" Jeannette asked.

"I learned it from you. Now let's go. We can tell Bridgett on the way out that you are leaving for the day, and you will not be in the office until Monday," Mark instructed, firmly. She was too tired to argue.

The single was released and was selling as fast as it hit the shelves. Jeannette's job was a roaring success for promoting Clay and The Band. The song was climbing the charts. In two weeks, the new album will be released. It had all the signs of being a big seller and possibly be a gold album. Clay was right, they had a hit, and Jeannette wrote it.

It was time to go home to Oregon for a rest before the album came out. Tia needed Jeannette's help with wedding plans. She hadn't been very much help lately. This week we work on wedding planning.

Mark was not able to take an entire week away from the restaurant but planned to follow on Friday. It was nice for her to come home to family anxiously awaiting her. Each of them was vying for her attention. Jeannette plopped in a chair. They stopped talking and looked at her.

"Thank you for realizing I needed all the conversation to stop. One by one, I promise, I will help with the solution to whatever problem each of you is having. May I ask one of you to take my bag to my room for me? One of you get me a glass of wine, please? Finally, one of you tell me what Irma is cooking?" Jeannette asked as she doled out jobs.

Tyler came back from talking to Irma with a report, "She is making ribeye steaks and baked potatoes for your dining pleasure." He then clicked his heels together and bowed like a butler. Jeannette laughed. She couldn't stop. That was just what she needed, a good laugh, from her silly son.

"Thanks for the laugh, Tyler. Hug me. You always know when and how to lighten my mood," Jeannette said.

Tia handed her a glass of wine and said, "I believe this is your favorite. What else can I do?"

"Not a thing, Sweetie. I say we chow down on steaks. I could use a good home cooked meal," Jeannette told her. "Did you finally get a guest list from your parents?"

"I received my dad and Alicia's. Mom is still giving me excuses. I don't know what to do. We picked out the invitations and picked them up yesterday. They are ready to be addressed," Tia said.

"We will work on those tomorrow. As for your mother, I will give her a call. Don't worry. It will all come together. Look at those steaks! They look delicious," Jeannette declared. "Oh, I almost forgot. Tia, how did your interview go with Mr. Baker?"

"I got the job! I start after the fourth of July, and I am taking the bar exam at the end of July. Then I will be a full-fledged lawyer," Tia said proudly.

"Congratulations, Tia! How about you, Sean? Any prospects for a job?"

"I have two interviews next week in Carson City. I would like to work for either company. I am qualified and would be an asset to each one," Sean said, almost bragging.

"Very nice, Sean. Tyler, what is going on with you? Did you go back to work at the warehouse?" Jeannette asked.

"No, I didn't. I am working with an architect in the office next to Mr. Baker. How about that? I can learn a lot and earn a little bit of money while I am at it. He liked some of my designs I showed him," Tyler said, showing pride in himself.

"That is wonderful, son! Irma, your turn. What is going on with you?" Jeannette asked.

"Most of my time is spent keeping an eye on this brood," She laughed. "Of course, I am kidding. These young people are terrific. Tia helps me when she is not glued at the hip to Sean. Tyler is not here most of the time. Of course, Zach spends time here. He is always hungry. I don't know where that boy puts it all."

Irma went on to catch them up on the local gossip.

It was Wednesday morning when Jeannette called Tia's mother, Carol. The conversation started with introductions and small talk. Then Jeannette got to the reason for the call.

"Carol, I called to see if you have your guest list done. We are running out of time to get the invitations sent. We have already dropped one-hundred-fifty in the mail. We need your list."

"I understand what you are saying. My work takes a lot of time away from personal activities. I have not had the opportunity to put the list together. I will get to it," Carol said.

"Excuse me, Carol, but you have told Tia that several times. Tell me, are you even planning on attending your only child's wedding? It is Labor Day weekend in case Tia forgot to tell you," Jeannette said.

"I can't believe you are talking to me like this!" Carol gasped into the phone. She regained her composure and said, "Tia is living with you now. She is your responsibility. I am done! No. I will not be attending the wedding, and I will not be sending you a guest list!"

"There it is — finally an answer. You have been stringing your daughter along for weeks. She has held out hope you will be here on her wedding day. Believe it or not, it is a big deal. You are missing out on so much. Picking out a wedding dress, helping with planning, giving her advice on the big day, helping her get into her dress and all the things that a mother and daughter should do together. Unfortunately, you do not know your daughter. She is a wonderful young woman despite you." Jeannette hung up without letting her get a word in. Now the hard part. Telling Tia her mother will not be at the wedding.

It was challenging to break the news to her now adopted daughter. She took it well. Jeannette decided she already knew her mother never intended to come to her wedding. Jeannette will gladly step in and take her place.

The invitations were completed and mailed. Before Jeannette went back to Chicago, R.S.V.P.'s was already arriving. It looked like every person who was invited planned on coming. It was turning out to be a huge wedding.

Sean interviewed for both jobs. He was offered a position for each company. He picked the one with higher pay, of course. He was expected to start the following week.

Jeannette loved the new gazebo. It was what she pictured. On Thursday, she took Tia shopping for a wedding dress in Carson City. They found the perfect dress. A trip to Chicago was not needed. While shopping for the dress, Jeannette got a call from Clay.

"Hey, Pretty Lady. Have you heard the music news? We have the number one song on the chart! Jeannette? Are you there?"

Her face lost all color. Her legs wobbled. She dropped into the nearest chair.

"Um, I think so. I have my head between my legs. I need blood in my brain to think. Would you repeat that?"

"We have the number one song on the chart! We are a hit!" Clay yelled with excitement.

"That is what I thought you said. Oh, my goodness, Clay! How does it feel to be famous? You are a star!" Jeannette laughed.

"It hasn't sunk in, yet. How about you? That is your song, and you are playing and singing it! So, I will ask you the same question, how does it feel to be famous?"

"I don't know. The CEO kicked into *Windy City* mode. I do not have time to feel, for now. Listen, Clay. I am going to take a red-eye tomorrow night. I will be in the office on Saturday. I want to talk about the album. Call me, and I will unlock the door for you. Also, I am going to put you with one of our talent managers. You are a star now. Let him do all the work. You concentrate on the music. The cost of my songs just went up! One last thing, Congratulations!" Jeannette heard Clay cringe at the new cost of more songs before she hung up.

She told Tia about her conversation with Clay. The girls were giddy with excitement.

"We are going to the Blue Bucket for dinner to celebrate! I will call Tyler. You call Sean. Have him meet us there at six," Jeannette instructed.

She talked to Tyler, he promised to be there, and of course, he will be bringing Zach. No surprise. It would not have been normal if he were not there. Jeannette also called Irma and invited her and her husband to dinner. She gladly accepted.

The girls finished their shopping chores with just enough time to make it to dinner on time. Nervous laughter was the mood of the girls as they traveled to Clark City. The giggles did not stop at dinner.

After announcing her news about having a hit song, Jeannette looked across the table at her boys and asked, "What do you think about your old mom writing a hit song?"

"I always knew that one day, you would have a hit. You are too good not to have a number one song! That was evident since I was little. The songs you made up for us were great. When I have children I will teach them their grandmother's songs," Tyler said.

"It all started when you decided to sell a song to Clay. Now you have made him a star with another song. You need to charge him more from now on!" Sean said.

"I already broke the news to Clay that the price has gone up! He cringed, I laughed. I am taking a red eye tomorrow. I need to be at the office. There will be a lot to do!" Jeannette said, still giggling.

Zach said between bites, "We heard the song playing on the way here on 98.3. I could hardly believe that our local radio station was playing it."

"I do not gossip about anyone at this table, but with this news? I am spreading it everywhere!" Irma said.

"This is gossip I approve of!" Jeannette said.

Saturday Clay met Jeannette at *Windy City* as planned. Jeannette picked the right manager for Clay. They immediately hit it off. The meeting went on for two hours working on strategy and a list of places Clay's new manager suggested on booking concerts. They also discussed releasing another single before the album, but before that was decided for sure, they would consult with a professional strategist.

Mark did not fly to Oregon as planned on Friday. It was just as well. He would have had to turn around and go back to Chicago the next day. Business at the restaurant was getting busier all the time. It picked up after Clay, and The Band performed. Mark was still getting a lot of positive feedback from his patrons about that night and asking if they were going to play again.

Over the next six weeks, things were happening at a breakneck speed. The song stayed at number one for two weeks, then dropped to number two. *Windy City,* Clay, and Jeannette were making a lot of money from the singles. When the album hits the shelves, it could easily go gold or platinum.

Jeannette hired another person to assist Bridgett. The company was growing. It was good the company was growing, in most ways, and not so good in other ways. *Windy City* has two sound rooms and sound booths that are booked all the time. Jeannette could not get to Oregon as much as she would like. The wedding was getting close, and she needed to be there for Tia. She did not want to hire someone to do her job at *Windy City*, but it was going to be necessary, for at least a month, maybe six weeks.

The first person she asked was Greg to see if he was interested in taking the helm while she was away. He thought hard about it before he told her yes.

"Wonderful! You know how everything around here works. Now the only thing I need to teach you is the contract side of things and Bridgett will help you with that, too. We are going to need someone to fill your spot while I am gone. Do you think Tom could handle your job? You work with him every day. You would know best." Greg nodded his head. "Okay, he gets a temporary promotion. Now we are still one person short for the sound booth. I will call the employment agency right away and have them get me a list of candidates. As soon as I hire someone, you will be here with me while you learn my side of *Windy City.* Does it sound like a plan to you?"

"I think you have a handle on it, boss. I will tell Tom," Greg said.

"One more thing, Greg. While you are doing my job, you will get a temporary bump in pay. I think you will be very pleased." Greg left the room smiling from ear to ear.

Jeannette and Mark had dinner that evening. She told him what her plan was. He agreed that she put together the best strategy. It made her feel good since he had college under his belt. She had none.

Mark started a new topic during dinner, "Sweetheart, we have not discussed our wedding at all. Both of our businesses have been getting in the way, not to mention Sean and Tia are getting married soon. You are helping her from here and making arrangements for their wedding, and we haven't talked about our own." He paused for a moment while he put his thoughts together, then continued, "There is something important we need to discuss. My attorney wants you to sign a pre-nuptial agreement."

Jeannette got quiet. She had not thought about it.

"I guess that would be a wise idea. Have your attorney draw one up. I will talk to my attorney about it tomorrow. I plan on going to Oregon in two weeks and staying until after the wedding. When do you think you can get away?"

"I hope to be able to fly there at least by the second week of August for a few days and back to Chicago. I will fly back to Oregon a couple of days before the wedding. It will have to be the last week of August on Thursday. The weekends are getting too busy," Mark told her.

Three weeks before the wedding, Jeannette asked Tia, "Did you ask your father to give you away? We will need to fit him for a tux."

"I asked him. He said he would like to, but my father is not sure if he will make it in time. He did say he would be at the reception," Tia said sadly.

Jeannette needed to say something positive.

"You know, all eyes are on the bride anyway. He wouldn't be noticed. He probably would not be able to come here to get fitted for a tux either. One thing out of the way. If you want someone to walk you down the aisle, I will volunteer!" That brought a smile to Tia's face. "You can ask anyone you feel close to you. It does not need to be your father. Mark would walk you down the aisle if you asked him. Or you can always make an entrance and walk alone. There is nothing wrong with that. It is all about what the bride wants to do. Think about it. Okay? No worries."

She managed to smile. "What is on the list for today, Jeannette?" Tia asked.

"We need to finalize the menu with the caterers and pay them. Next on the list is the florist. We need to pay for the flowers and the rent on tables and chairs. The photographer will be expecting us to drop off a check, go over the final details and what time he wants to start. We need to pay the bakery for the cake, and finally, you have a fitting for your dress. I am tired from just reading the agenda. By the sound of it, we are spending a lot of money today," Jeannette said.

"Thank God it's Saturday, and these places are open. Now that I am working it puts a cramp in the arrangements. I am so glad you are here. I would never be able to pull this off without you," Tia said and threw her arms around Jeannette.

"Sweetheart, I love helping with your wedding. I didn't have a daughter until you came along. It is going to be a gorgeous ceremony, and we are going to have fun. I love you." She pulled back and held Tia at arm's length to say, "The tuxes! Sean, Tyler, and Zach are supposed to get fitted today! Have you seen those boys?" Jeannette said almost in a panic.

"I am going to give you some of your advice. Relax. No worries. They are already on their way to the boutique. That's right. I repeated YOU back to YOU! Oh, that's funny!" Tia cracked herself up.

"Oh, you are hilarious, Tia," Jeannette giggled. "Let's get on the road. We have twenty minutes before we are supposed to be at the caterers. Like the cowboys say, load up!"

While Tia was getting her wedding gown fitted, Jeannette looked for a dress to wear. She thought it would be easy to find a black and white dress. It turned out that it was not an easy find in a bridal shop. There were all colors of the spectrum, but black was missing. Tia was almost finished when Jeannette spotted the perfect black and white dress. It was floor length with white insets in the skirt from the knees to the floor that made the hemline flare. The neckline was square with beading for accent. It had long, sheer black sleeves that gathered at the wrist. It was a perfect fit. She bought it and told Tia it was one more thing to take off the list.

Tia's colors were black and white with a touch of lilac. The maid-of-honor and bridesmaids dresses were black. The neckline was straight across the top of the bust. The shoulders were bare except for spaghetti straps attached to the dress. The design was a simple empire waist and a straight skirt with a slit to the knee. Just under the bust line were two thin ribbons, one white one lilac tied together in a bow. A small round headpiece with white tulle flared out six inches in the back to finish off the dresses with elegance. They carried a small bouquet of white roses and lilac baby's breath tied with a black ribbon.

The men were wearing white tuxedoes, white shirts, a black vest, black ties, and black shoes. They would contrast perfectly with the women. The boutonnieres had one white rose, and lilac baby's breath tied together with a black ribbon.

At first, Jeannette thought black and white was a bit odd for a wedding, but when it was all put together, the wedding party looked nothing short of elegant.

6

The big day had arrived. Jeannette had been trying not to cry all day. As long as she was giving directions, she had no time to think that her firstborn was about to be married. The wedding was scheduled to begin at 7:00 p.m., making it approximately the time the sun sets. By the time the bride and groom reach their spot on the gazebo The sky should be golden creating a beautiful glow for the couple.

Jeannette checked on the men and their photoshoot. Mark was acting as director and had the photographer and the boys laughing. Sean was jittery with nerves, and the entertainment was helping to distract him. She left before they saw her and spoiled their fun.

The girls should be ready. To ease Jeannette's mind, she needed to check and see how they were coming along. Mist from hair spray was heavy in the room, three different perfumes were clashing against each other, and last-minute makeup was being applied. They had completed their photoshoot earlier, so this was touch-up time. Jeannette was pleased that two of Tia's friends from college agreed to be her bridesmaids. Together, the three were stunning.

"Ladies, you are gorgeous," Jeannette said as tears welled up in her eyes.

"Jeannette, I have no one to give me away," Tia began. "You said I should ask someone who means something to me. The only person other than Sean is you. Would it be too weird if I asked you to walk me down the aisle?"

The question shocked Jeannette. With wide eyes, she answered, "Sweetheart, I would be honored. This is the last straw. I can't hold the tears back any longer." She gave Tia a big hug and whispered in her ear, "I love you, Tia." They shared several minutes in a touching embrace and let the tears escape their eyes. Jeannette pulled away to dab her eyes and said, "Now it's my turn to do some makeup touch up."

The music began signaling the men to take their places for the ceremony. Jeannette held her arm out for Tia to place her arm on top of Jeannette's and waited for the girls to take their positions. The wedding march began. The bride and mother-in-law walked down the aisle while trying not to let their emotions fall from their eyes. Sean was waiting in awe at the gazebo. He wobbled at the sight of his bride. Tyler discreetly steadied his big brother to keep him upright.

The minister asked, "Who gives this woman to be wed to this man?"

Jeannette answered, "Her father and mother do, and I love and accept this woman to be joined to my son." She turned to Tia, kissed her on the cheek, and then took her seat next to Mark.

The ceremony proceeded under a thousand tiny white lights that covered the gazebo. Roses were used from the landscape as well as white calla lilies from the florist to form an arch of an array of colors where the couple stood.

The ceremony concluded. Sean and Tia were married. Walking down the aisle as man and wife, guests threw flower petals, rice, and birdseed. Tia looked around the sea of faces searching for her father. He was nowhere she could see.

The gazebo became the dance floor under the tiny lights that formed the ceiling. Romance was in the air. Jeannette had tears of joy that kept threatening to fall from her eyes as she danced with her son. Tia's father did not come to the wedding or reception. Mark immediately saw her looking like she was about to cry from embarrassment because she had no one to dance the father-daughter dance. Mark quickly stepped to Tia, bowed, and held his hand out, asking her to dance. She accepted his hand. He waltzed her around the dance floor like she was a princess.

Sean and Tia left the reception at ten to catch a plane bound for Hawaii. It was nearly midnight when the last guest left. It was over.

Sunday was a day of rest. The wedding had taken a toll on everyone. Jeannette rolled out of bed at 10:30 a.m. and made coffee. Mark slept until he smelled coffee then appeared in sweatpants, a t-shirt and bare-footed.

"Good morning," Mark said with a yawn.

"Morning. I am still tired. Are you?" Jeannette asked.

"Exhausted. How about I take you to brunch somewhere?"

"I would love that. I will wake Tyler up to see if he would like to go," Jeannette added. "Tyler. Tyler, are you awake?" Jeannette asked while tapping on his bedroom door. There was no answer, so she quietly opened his door far enough to check on him. He was not there and hadn't been all night. Tyler did not sleep here! She rushed to the kitchen.

Jeannette anxiously spit out, "Mark, Tyler is not in his room and hasn't been all night! I don't know where he is! Should I call the police?"

"Tyler is a big boy. He doesn't have a curfew. He's a good kid. Probably spent the night with a girl," Mark responded without thinking.

"Excuse me! With a girl?" Jeannette screeched.

Mark's head snapped up, realizing what he had said without thinking.

"Can I take that remark back? I didn't mean to be flippant. Jeannette, your youngest son, I am sure, has been with a woman before. You just do not know about it. Now, don't take that the wrong way. He is in college, away from home, hormones are on high alert, it happens. There is nothing you can do to stop him from experiencing sex. Let it go. Talk to him when he gets home," Mark said, holding Jeannette.

"My boys cannot be this old. I now have a daughter-in-law and a son who stays out all night. I don't like them growing up," Jeannette told him. "I am going to call him and ask if he would like to go to brunch."

The phone rang five times before a sleepy Tyler answered, "Hello?"

"Tyler, its mom. Would you like to go to brunch with Mark and me? We are going to the Lodge in about thirty minutes."

"I could eat now that I am awake. Could I bring a friend?" Tyler asked.

"Male or female?" Jeannette asked

"Female, of course."

"That would be fine. See you at the Lodge," Jeannette answered. "Mark, Tyler is bringing a girl to brunch. He has never brought a girl to eat with us before. Hum."

"Don't read anything into it. It is just brunch," Mark said.

There was no shortage of customers at the Lodge for a mid-morning meal. Jeannette forgot it was a holiday weekend marking the end of summer. Quite a few events were going on around the area such as boating on the Columbia River, a Junior Rodeo, live music in the park, a classic car show, a rock and gem show, and a Farmer's Market to name a few. New faces were everywhere and smiling at her. The hotels and motels were at capacity. They waited thirty minutes for a table. Tyler, plus one, arrived just as the waitress came to show Mark and Jeannette to their table.

"Hi, mom. Hi Mark. I want to introduce Tracy. I am sure you recognized her as being one of the bridesmaids yesterday. Tracy and I have known each other for a while. Tia introduced us," Tyler explained. He leaned into Jeannette to say quietly, "This is not the girl Zach doesn't like."

"It is nice to meet you, Jeannette, and Mark. The wedding was lovely, and your house is gorgeous," Tracy replied.

"Thank you. I have to say, Tyler, I was a little surprised not to find you in bed this morning," Jeannette said. Mark shot her a look that said, be careful. She changed the subject, "How long are you staying in town, Tracy?"

"I will be leaving tomorrow."

"Where is home for you?" Mark asked.

"Troutdale. It is a town that borders Portland. I was born and raised there," Tracy answered.

"What is your major?" Jeannette asked.

"I am going to be a teacher. At the end of this school year, I will have a Masters' Degree in education. Elementary is the age group I want to teach," Tracy explained.

Tyler wanted to change the subject to take the attention off of Tracy.

"Mom. You look tired." Mark's eyes widened and shook his head at Tyler. "I mean you should get some rest today. Maybe lounge by the pool. You have been busy for weeks, non-stop."

"Nice save, son. That is my plan; do nothing. We are headed back to Chicago tomorrow. Clay's album is scheduled to hit the stores, so Tuesday we expect to be very busy," Jeannette told him.

"Wait a minute," Tracy said. "Tyler, your mom is THAT Jeannette? You or Sean have never said anything about WHO she was, just that your mother is an amazing woman. I am sitting at brunch with a star?"

Jeannette's face turned red. She liked to be known as just Jeannette.

"Well, a star is a little over the top. I wrote several songs for Clay and The Band. I joined in on the recording, so I am on his new album. Although I have done at least one song on his other albums also."

"No, I mean it! They are calling you a star on the radio and several TV shows I watched. They say you are the new up and coming star!" Tracy told her.

This news took Jeannette by complete surprise. Her mouth opened as she looked at Mark in shock.

She whispered, "A star? Up and coming? What have I done? I...I...Didn't plan on being a star. Mark, what am I going to do?" Jeannette gasped with difficulty breathing.

"Do about what? This is wonderful! You are being recognized for your God-given talent," Mark told her.

"I think I am going to pass out!" Jeannette declared.

"No, you are not. Take some deep breaths. Now calm yourself. That's it. You are getting more color back in your face," Mark observed. "This is going to be a new experience. We are going to handle this together."

"Handle it? I need to call Clay," Jeannette said, trying to stay calm.

"You need to eat first. On the way home, you can call him, but for now you need to relax and enjoy your brunch," Mark instructed.

"I am so sorry, Jeannette, I did not mean to upset you. It is exciting for me to think I know someone famous. I promise I will not say a word to anyone about who you are," Tracy vowed.

"Let's remember that at school, too, Tracy," Tyler said. "Mom, I am very proud of you. It is an amazing accomplishment! It's about time people recognized your talent."

"Thank you, Tyler. My mission in life has always been to make my boys proud of me," Jeannette said. Her phone rang. It was from Sean. "Hi, Sean! You are on your honeymoon! Why are you calling me?"

"We saw you in the news. You were singing and playing with Clay and The Band. The music world is all abuzz about you! Did you know that?" Sean asked.

"Not until fifteen minutes ago when Tracy told me. We are at brunch. Tracy and Tyler joined us at the Lodge. The news about me being famous shocked me. I am going to call Clay on our way home. Listen to me. Get off the phone and get back to your honeymoon. We can talk about this when you get home. I love you and Tia," Jeannette said. Sean said goodbye and hung up.

"How was your brunch?" The waitress asked. "Can I get you anything else? May I say congratulations? I saw you on the news this morning. It's so exciting!"

"Thank you. I would like to order a mimosa, please. Make it a big one," Jeannette said. "Okay. I am going to have to get used to this. I'm fine. Everything will be fine. "She looked up and across the room. A table of patrons was holding their mimosas in the air to congratulate her.

"Mark, that table is saluting me."

"That is very nice of them. Smile and give the group a nod. All you need to do is acknowledge them. See? That was easy," Mark said.

Tracy leaned close to Tyler and quietly said, "Why does your mom get so nervous? She is a strong woman and CEO of a big successful company, or is that just an act?"

That statement ruffled Tyler's feathers. Sternly he whispered, looking Tracy directly in the eyes, "Look, my mom is a real down to earth person who is not used to being in the limelight. It makes her nervous. She loves her company and her music. It has only been in the last several years that she has allowed anyone, other than family, to hear the songs she has written. My father kept her away from people for years. He broke her down to a person who was scared of her own shadow. After she got away from him, she reinvented herself into a strong woman. She had to. She was on her own with Sean and me. If you knew the real Jeannette and her whole story, you would never ask if she were acting!" Tyler said on the verge of losing his temper.

"I didn't mean anything by it, Tyler. Her shyness just surprised me. I should never have said anything. I apologize. Sometime I would love to hear her story," Tracy said.

"Someday, maybe I will tell you," Tyler snapped.

Jeannette took another deep breath and regained her composure.

She said, "So tell me, Tracy, in what town are you thinking about teaching? Any ideas?"

"Clark City seems like a nice place. I have been looking around, but I have not made any decisions. I went by Clark City Elementary the other day. It is a very nice-looking school. I will need to check it out in person and online before I think about applying. I don't know if there will be any openings either. I have been looking into Troutdale Elementary also. I have at least six months before I start sending resumes out," Tracy explained.

"It sounds like you have a plan," Jeannette said. "What do your parents do for a living?"

"My mother, Denise, is a registered nurse. My father, Duane, is a veterinarian. I have a sister, Suzie, who is older than I by four years. She is a dental assistant. They all live in Troutdale," Tracy said.

"If you would like to come over today to swim in the pool you are welcome. I am sure Zach will be stopping by, too. For dinner, we are going to grill some burgers. Nothing fancy," Jeannette told Tracy. "Mark, I am exhausted. Are you ready to go? Tracy, it was nice to meet you. Bye Tyler, I love you," Jeannette said and kissed his cheek before they left.

As they walked the length of the dining room, several people congratulated her. She said thank you, smiled, held her head high, and walked with a show of confidence out the door.

"There's the woman I know. Self-assured and lovely," Mark told her, making her smile.

In the car, Jeannette called Clay. The first thing out of his mouth was, "Congratulations!"

"Clay! People are going to start recognizing who we are! That is great for you, but I am not sure I like it."

"You are right! I have already had a few people stop me and tell me they love our music! It was awesome! Please hear me when I tell you, there is nothing wrong with being known for the talent you possess. God gave it to you. He gave it to you for a reason. Your music is pleasing to the ears of millions. Your words are blessing them in ways we will never know. You saw the reaction to the broken-hearted song. People were touched because you put their feelings into words that they could never express. I believe this is the reason you were put in my path. You write special songs, and The Band and I play them. YOU are special," Clay tried to convince Jeannette.

"What I am about to say, I say out of love," Clay became serious. "Jeff caused you to be insecure about your abilities because *he* was insecure. Controlling you made him feel important. Like he was special. Jeff could make you do anything he wanted. He controlled every minute of your life with words, actions, and emotion. You are still carrying around insecurity and doubt that you are not good enough. Hasn't the reaction people are having proved to you that you are talented? When I see you like this...Well, I know you are better than this. How about seeing Dr. Lamb again to get this out of your life for good?"

Jeannette was silent. Her mind was trying to believe Clay that she possesses exceptional talent, but there was a little voice arguing with her. Jeannette suddenly realized it was the words Jeff and her dad used to control her with! She snapped out of it when she heard Clay attempting to get her attention on the phone.

"You are right! Jeff's words are embedded in my brain! He is still controlling me! This stops now! I am going back to Dr. Lamb and get these scars he left on the inside taken care of. Thank you, Clay, for telling me what I needed to hear. I admit I didn't particularly like it, but I needed to hear it. I love you too, my friend. I will see you at *Windy City* on Tuesday," Jeannette agreed.

Mark listened to Jeannette's side of the conversation as he drove, not saying anything.

After she hung up, he asked, "What did Clay say to you? I can see it had quite an effect."

"He told me I need to see Dr. Lamb and get rid of the insecurities Jeff caused. He is right. I could hear Jeff and my dad in my mind telling me I was no good. I had no talent, and I was fooling myself. Jeff told me once '*I needed to face it, that my dream would never come true, to get over it*'. He crushed me with that statement. I wandered around for years with no dreams whatsoever. Not even when I slept or tried to daydream, I could not dream at all. He took them all away. He told me I was ugly, and he was the best I would ever do. I proved him wrong. Now I have to get him out of my head! I AM talented!" Jeannette declared.

"Yes, you are," Mark said. "I will be with you every step of the way. If Dr. Lamb wants me to come with you, I will be there. Whatever it takes, I will do. I want you to be whole," he paused and kissed her hand. "Could I steer the conversation in another direction? When can we set a date and start planning our wedding?"

"That will be a good conversation to have by the pool. We're home, let's change so we can lounge by the pool and pick out a date," Jeannette suggested.

Lesson learned: The tactics that have been used to control a person, such as words, actions, threats, etc., leave scars in the mind and the heart. They need to be recognized and dealt with, or you are still under the control of the aggressor. NO ONE DESERVES TO BE OR SHOULD EVER BE CONTROLLED BY ANOTHER PERSON!

Whatever is embedded in the deepest part of your mind will surface at some point in your life. Maybe several times until you recognize it for what it is. The negative things that are deep within can impact you in many ways, thus giving it enormous power over you. Reprogram your mind to provide yourself with positive thoughts about yourself. If you change your mind, you will change your life.

7

Clay and The Band had become stars overnight, and *Windy City* was flooded with potential clients. Several had asked or begged Jeannette to write them a song. She very politely refused. In her mind, she would say, *"The only one I will write for, is Clay."*

In the midst of all this, she had put off meeting Mark's family. Wednesday night is dedicated to the meeting, and she promised she would have dinner with his family. Jeannette had been seeing Dr. Lamb twice a week. She was feeling much better than she had in a long time. The panic attacks had stopped. The last one she experienced was several weeks ago. Meeting his family was going to be the test to see how she handles a different kind of stress.

She arrived at *My City* a little early to help Mark if he needed it. He was prepared, so they had some alone time and a glass of wine before the family arrived.

"While I have you all to myself, maybe we should decide on a venue for our wedding? We decided on January 2nd, right?" Mark began. "Off the top of my head, I can think of three places. The first is here. I planned on being closed on the second anyway. It should be tranquil after all the celebrating on the first. The next choice is your house in Oregon. It is beautiful and would be especially romantic with snow on the ground. The final suggestion is someplace in the mountains. There would be snow on the ground, a pine scent in the air, and all the sounds of nature. What do you think?" Mark asked.

"Oh, I like the idea of the mountains. I know of several gorgeous places in the Blue Mountains of Oregon. Tomorrow I will make a few calls to see if anything will be available at that time of year. The next time we are in Oregon we will have to explore," Jeannette said.

"Ahem. Am I disturbing anything?" Mark's father cleared his throat to get their attention.

"Dad! Of course not. Dad, I would like to introduce you to Jeannette. Jeannette, this is Ken, my father. This lovely lady is my mother, Shannon. Mom, this is Jeannette."

"It is so nice to meet you finally. You must be very proud of your son. He has done a wonderful job with his restaurant," Jeannette said.

"Yes, we are proud of him. He is a good son," Ken answered with no emotion and a slight abruptness. "Mark, is Skylar going to make it?" Ken asked.

"I am behind you, so I would say I made it," Skylar announced.

"Hi, Skylar!" Mark chirped. "Skylar, let me introduce you to Jeannette. Jeannette, my sister, Skylar."

"So, this is the woman that finally made my brother think of something other than a restaurant. It is very nice to meet you," Skylar said, shaking Jeannette's hand.

"Would anyone be interested in a glass of wine before dinner?" Mark asked. He was showing signs of nervousness.

Shannon spoke up, "I would love a glass. Mark said you are from Oregon. I have heard that it is a beautiful state. I would love to visit one day. Tell me, what do you do for a living in Chicago?"

"I am the CEO of *Windy City Publishing and Recording.* I own it." Jeannette said proudly.

"The big recording company a few blocks from here?" Shannon asked, looking surprised. "Mark didn't tell us much about you or what you did. I always worry that he might get involved with a woman that only wants him for his money. You know? A gold digger."

"Mom! As you can see, Jeannette is not like that!" Mark gasped.

"It is okay, Mark," Jeannette said, putting her hand on his arm. "Shannon, I have two boys, and I would worry about the same thing. Rest assured, I am not a gold digger. Should I worry that you are a gold digger, Mark?" Jeannette said with a giggle. "Sweetheart, you know I am only joking."

"Whew. I am glad we got that cleared up," Mark answered with a chuckle.

"What would you like to know about me, Shannon? Ken? Skylar? I am sure you have some questions. Just ask. I will answer you truthfully. We are going to be in-laws in a few months. We should get to know each other," Jeannette said.

Skylar started with, "How did you meet?"

"A mutual friend introduced us one night when I was having dinner with them here in *My City*. I was immediately smitten with Mark. He kissed my hand, and I felt a spark. That was that."

Ken asked the next question, "You said you have two boys. Were you married before?"

"Yes, I was. The father of my boys was my first husband. He was not a nice man. He was running around with other women and mistreated me. We divorced when my boys were young teenagers. My second husband . . ." Ken and Shannon had the same look of shock on their faces.

Jeannette was cut off by Shannon. She gasped, "You were married twice?"

"Yes, I was. Five years after the divorce, I met my second husband, Robert. He was a wonderful man. He had a heart attack and passed away several years ago. I have not dated since he passed, nor did I want to. I was not interested until I met Mark," Jeannette explained and looked lovingly at Mark.

"Thank you for your honesty. I have to say I am astonished. Mark, you knew about this?" Ken asked.

"Of course, I did. Neither marriage ended because of Jeannette," Mark added.

"But son," Shannon began, "She already has children. Is this the way you wanted to have children?" Shannon questioned.

"Mom, I have met her boys. I will be proud to be their stepfather. They are not your normal rich kids. They are down to earth, well mannered, educated young men. I attended her oldest son, Sean's wedding. Wait until you meet them. You will understand. Besides, when do I have the time to have a baby? She and I have very demanding businesses," Mark explained.

"I, for one, would like to have a baby to spoil! Oh, my goodness! When you marry Jeannette, I will be an instant grandmother!" Shannon exclaimed.

"When Sean and Tia have children, you will be a great-grandmother! That's where the babies come in. We can both spoil them," Jeannette encouraged with a big smile.

Skylar had been quietly laughing since the conversation started. She remarked, "Oh, this is great! My parents will finally be grandparents, and it is not because of me!" She paused to laugh, then carried on, "Thank you, Mark. Now they will get off my back about settling down and having a family" Skylar regained her composure before saying, "So how long will it be before I am an aunt?"

Mark spoke up, "We have decided on January 2nd. New year, new life." He looked at Jeannette with love and a smile.

Shannon and Ken still had a shocked look on their faces, and their mouths were open.

Ken finally pulled himself together to say, "Mark, are you sure about this? You are taking on a readymade family and a woman with two failed marriages. Have you thought about this?"

"Of course, I have! I have seen her ex-husband. I understand why he is no longer in her life. He left her. She had no say in the matter with Robert. He died. Jeannette has not dated ANYONE except me after his death. Mom, Dad, she is a wonderful woman. Give her a chance," Mark requested.

Shannon cleared her throat and said, "This is a lot to take in. I wish you had talked to us first."

"Well, I, for one, am totally on board with this marriage. I will be there with bells on!" Skylar declared. "I make a living designing clothes. Jeannette, I never ask this, but would you allow me to design your dress?" Skylar questioned.

The offer took Jeannette's breath away. She looked at Mark, then at Skylar.

She was tongue-tied for a moment but managed to spit out, "I would love that! I have never had a designer dress or any other piece of clothing by a designer, for that matter."

"Why not? I assume you have plenty of money?" Skylar inquired.

"Yes, I have an abundance, but I cannot justify spending the price that a designer charges. I am, what Mark calls, frugal, and my boys call me the queen of frugal. In my earlier years, I had to be. I had to save up to buy my sons an ice cream cone. The scarcity of what we had will stay with me forever. By the way, Mark's attorney wants me to sign a pre-nup. I have agreed. He needs to be protected even though I am not the kind of person who marries for money. I have my own," Jeannette explained.

"Since you are going to be my sister-in-law, I will only charge you for time and material. Is that frugal enough?" Skylar asked.

"Yes! A thousand times, yes! Mark! I am going to wear a designer dress!" Jeannette squealed.

"Where is this wedding going to take place?" Shannon asked.

Mark took the lead and said, "We are thinking about a lodge in the Blue Mountains of Oregon."

"Oregon? Really? That far away? Why not Chicago? Your friends and family are all here!" Shannon sounded horrified.

"Well, there is another place we have not discussed. We could have it right here at *My City,*" Mark told them.

Jeannette spoke up, "Mark, I am fine with having our wedding here. I agree with your parents. I can fly my children here. My family will not be coming anyway."

Ken asked, "What about your family? Your mother and father? Do you have siblings?"

"My father passed away a year ago. My mother is still alive, living in the same house where I grew up. I have three siblings, Beth, Leroy, and Rose. They will not be attending the ceremony for too many reasons I don't care to talk about," Jeannette informed them. "Mark, let's have it here. I already have ideas whirling around in my head."

"If that is what you want, My Love, and then it is settled. The wedding will take place at *My City* on January 2nd."

Skylar chimed in, "I have a few ideas also. We need to put our heads together, Jeannette."

"Great! I want it to be a forties theme. If that is okay with you, Mark? It will go perfect with the décor," Jeannette said.

"I had the same idea. Great minds think alike," Mark said.

With a worried look on his face, Ken said, "Mark, I don't think I approve of this wedding. How well do you know her?"

"Dad, that is just rude! She is sitting right here!" Mark exclaimed.

Shannon saw a possible fight brewing. She said, "Honey, we are just not sure she is the right one for you. How do you know she is telling the truth? Have you checked her out? Is Jeannette really who she says she is?"

Mark opened his mouth to speak, but Jeannette stopped him.

"Shannon, I am an open book. I am hiding nothing. Mark knows all about me, the good and the bad. To make you feel better, I will pay for an investigator. You pick one. It is your choice. Do not tell me his name. That way you cannot come back and say I paid him off to say good things about me, so will that satisfy you and put your mind at ease?"

"Are you kidding me?" Mark exclaimed, loudly.

"I have no problem with this. The last thing I want to do is enter a marriage with in-laws that do not approve of me, that look down on my sons and me and do not trust me. I want them to be comfortable with your wife," Jeannette said confidently. She took her checkbook out and wrote a check for $5,000.00 made out to Ken. "Here is a check to cover the expenses. If the expense is more than that, let me know." Ken accepted the check and put it in his pocket.

"Jeannette you are so cool under pressure," Skylar said. "I wouldn't do what you just did. I am going to like having you as a sister! Can you come to my store on Friday? I will email you the address. You can give me an idea of what you are thinking about the design, and we can take some measurements."

"Skylar, I will see you on Friday afternoon at about 1:00. Here is my card with email addresses on it," Jeannette told her and stood. "Sweetheart, I have listened to enough disapproval and anti-marriage for one night. Tell your attorney to get the papers to me. I will have my attorney look them over before I sign. I want us both to be protected. Ken and Shannon, it has been, let's say, interesting to meet you. Skylar, I love you. We are going to have fun being in-laws. Goodnight My Love." She turned on her heel and left.

When Jeannette was out of earshot, Mark yelled with a red face, "You have humiliated me! How could you be so rude? You talked around her as if she didn't exist! How dare you! Then you accept her check for a private detective!" Mark jumped to his feet and yelled, "My God! What is wrong with both of you?"

"Mark, lower your voice. We are your parents. Like it or not, we are going to have her investigated," Ken informed him.

"I am a grown man! Do you think I am stupid? I would like you to leave my restaurant! I cannot look at either one of you any longer. I will think about sending you an invitation, but for now, I am finished with you!" Mark yelled, not caring if his wait-staff heard him. He left his parents seated at the table with their meals half-eaten and Shannon gasping at his rant.

Skylar followed him to his office. She found him pacing.

"Good for you for standing up to them and defending Jeannette! It is about time you put them in their place. I think Jeannette is a wonderful woman just by observation. I am going to be an aunt!"

"Thanks, Skylar, but I am not in the mood for your cheeriness. They said they didn't like her! They ignored her! Rude! Rude! How could they treat her like that? I don't know if I will ever forgive them for this! I pray this isn't a deal-breaker for Jeannette," Mark barked.

"I understand and agree with you. Jeannette strikes me as a person who will come through this with flying colors, although I am not sure she will like our parents after tonight. The only thing we can do is wait and see," Skylar said.

"You're right. I am so angry with the way they treated her! I am calling Jeannette and apologizing for them treating her so horribly," He announced. "Hi, honey. I am glad you answered. I want to apologize for my parents' crude and unforgivable actions. I have never seen them like that."

"I guess I brought it out of them," Jeannette said jokingly. "You are right. They were rude to me. As a parent, I can understand their caution, although it could have been said privately to you and handled differently. I am hoping they will change their mind about me after the investigator gives them a report. There is nothing to find out. Honey, I am going to hang up so I can get some sleep, okay? I love you, goodnight," Jeannette told him.

"I love you, too," Mark replied.

"She is one cool cucumber. I am impressed," Skylar said, leaning against the door jam.

"Jeannette is an amazing woman. Wait until you get to know her," Mark promised.

"I have seen enough to know she is one astonishing woman. She is good for you," Skylar confided.

"One night we had dinner here. I was needed on the floor, so I left her for a bit in my office. When I came back, she was not there. I couldn't find her. I went into the kitchen, and there she was, helping my chef. She told me she *wanted* to help. There was a full house, and they were swamped, so she grabbed an apron and dug in. Not many women would do that. Most would expect to be treated like a queen since they were dating the owner. Not Jeannette," Mark recalled.

"Okay, brother of mine, I am leaving. Good luck with mom and dad. Let me know what the report says. Bye," Skylar said as she left.

On Wednesday the next week, Mark had the pre-nup for Jeannette to sign. He gave Jeannette a call.

"Hello, you beautiful woman of mine," Mark said.

"Hello, handsome. You are such a sweetheart. I have a meeting in ten minutes, so I cannot talk long," she informed him.

"I just wanted to let you know I have the pre-nup. I have a few minutes later, I can drop it off if you want me to," Mark suggested.

"Sure. Has either of your parents got back to you about the report from the investigator?" Jeannette asked.

"Nothing yet, but I am not surprised after I yelled at them and told them to leave my restaurant after you left," Mark said.

"Oh, honey. You did that because of me? The last thing I want to do is come between you and your parents!" Jeannette exclaimed.

"Don't worry about it. It has been building up for years. I finally blew. They had no right to act like that!" Mark snapped.

"Calm down. It is over. We still love each other, and I love your sister. We have fun when we are together. I will see her again on Friday. She has a sketch of a dress for my opinion. I am going to have to hang up. I have a meeting. I love you."

"I love you too," Mark said. The thought of his parents irked him. He was all worked up again.

He heard a timid tap at the door. "Come in," he said.

Shannon peeked around the door. "May we come in? Please?"

"Speak of the devils. If you are here to make more negative or derogatory remarks about Jeannette, you can turn around and leave the way you came!" Mark fumed.

She opened the door wide enough to walk in with Ken following closely behind.

"We are here to apologize. We got the report back from the investigator. She is a wonderful woman. We jumped the gun and judged her too quickly. Did you know she is worth millions?" Shannon said with surprise.

"Mom! I don't care about her money! I am not marrying her for her money! I am marrying her because I am madly in love with her. The pre-nup is in my hand for her to sign. I am taking it to *Windy City* as soon as you leave. For your information, MY attorney drew it up. She wants BOTH of us protected! It was not HER idea. It was mine!" Mark shouted.

"Shut the door, Ken. We don't need the help hearing this," Shannon said. "Calm down, Mark. I know you are upset. We just wanted to make sure she is who she says she is. The only way to know was to have her investigated. We are not ashamed of it," Shannon stated.

"You should be! My God! Jeannette gave you a check to get it done, and you took it!" Mark exploded.

"She can afford it. We can't," Ken added.

"How can we make this up to you and Jeannette?" Shannon asked.

"I don't think you can! She is much more forgiving than I am. Skylar accepted her immediately. Why couldn't you?" Mark asked.

"Well, your sister has not always been the best judge of character. She has proven that several times," Shannon said with sarcastic undertones.

"You have just proved YOUR character assessment leaves something to be desired, also! Say it! You don't trust my judgment either, do you? The proof of my judgment is in that report you received. If I was not good at judging character, how would I have built this place? How could I hire a good staff? I have a brain. I am not going to argue anymore!" Mark shouted and grabbed his keys. "I want to show you Jeannette's business. Let's go have a tour," he said sarcastically. "She calls her employees her *family*. Believe me, they are. Everyone knows she is the boss, but they can go to her with any problem. She listens and will offer help or advice. They help each other as a team with work or personal. She does not have ANY turnover. No one quits. She truly cares for every one of them. She has a driver named David. I want you to talk to him and get his opinion of her," Mark paused for a moment to hold up a hand for Shannon to close her mouth. "This is not a request, mother. I am going to introduce you to some of her employees. You are going to ask them questions about what kind of boss and person she is. Let's go! I will drive myself. You have the address. I will see you there in ten minutes!" He looked directly at them, and pointing his finger, he roared, "Be there!"

Mark stormed out of his office. He was going to make his parents eat crow while he watched. He made a quick call to Skylar to invite her to attend. She dropped what she was doing with excited anticipation of seeing a showdown. Skylar was out the door before she hung up. This was going to be an event she did not want to miss.

Mark drove like a mad man to Jeannette's office. Max, from security, was standing by the door when he saw Mark stomping toward the building. He opened the door for him.

Max greeted him with, "Hello," looking concerned at Mark's attitude.

"Is Jeannette in her office? I'll ask Bridgett," Mark said anxiously.

"Mark, is everything alright?" Max asked.

"Just peachy. Bridgett, is she in?" Mark inquired again.

"She is just finishing up with a client. She should be free in about five minutes. Can I get you some water? Anything? You are flushed," Bridgett observed.

"No, thanks. I am sorry. I have never been more upset with my parents in my life! They had a private investigator check out Jeannette to make sure she is above board and not a gold digger."

Max overheard the conversation and shook his head in disbelief. Bridgett was shocked and gasped.

"They got the report and came by to apologize. They need to eat crow, and I am going to see that they do! I told them to meet me here and ask anyone here what they think of Jeannette. Don't hold back. Tell them the truth. As soon as they get here, I will take them to the sound booth and introduce Greg and Tom. From there, we will make our way to Jeannette's office. Give Greg a heads-up that he will have visitors. They just pulled up."

Shannon and Ken entered the building with frowns on their faces. Mark motioned for them to come to Bridgett's desk where he was standing.

"Bridgett let me introduce my parents, Shannon and Ken. This is Bridgett. She is Jeannette's right hand. Go ahead. Ask her what she thinks of Jeannette."

"Mark, this isn't necessary," Shannon said, looking a little embarrassed.

"Yes, it is!" Mark hissed.

"Very well. Bridgett, what kind of boss is Jeannette?"

"She is like no other boss I have ever had. I had quite a few jobs before I came to work here. Jerry hired me before Jeannette took over. As I got to know her, the things I discovered about her are she is understanding and caring, both as a boss and a regular person. I love and respect her. There is nothing I wouldn't do for her. She has proven she would do the same for any of us. This is my last job. I will be here until I retire," Bridgett told them.

"Thank you, Bridgett. Our next stop will be the sound booth." Mark stopped at the door and waved to Greg to ask if they could come in. He gave them a nod.

"Could we take a minute of your time, please?"

"Of course. What's up? You look a little out of sorts." Greg observed.

"First of all, these are my parents, Shannon and Ken this is Greg. He runs the sound booth and produces the talents' recordings. Shannon has a question for you."

It just so happened Clay was in the sound room recording. Greg hit a button to turn the sound on in Clay's headset so he could hear what was going on.

"Really? You are going to keep this up, Mark?" Shannon asked.

"Yes! I want to make sure you know what the investigator reported about Jeannette was truthful. Go ahead."

"Wait a minute," Greg said. "Investigator? What is going on? Did you investigate Jeannette? Whatever for?"

"They wanted to know all about her and make sure she was who she portrays herself to be. They wanted to make sure she is not a gold digger," Mark spewed.

"Whoa, wait a minute. Gold digger? Jeannette?" Greg laughed. "Money is not what Jeannette is all about. She is the most frugal person I have ever met. Jeannette shops sales and uses coupons. I have watched her haggle over the price of an office chair until she got the price she wanted. She is kind and cares about her family at *Windy City*. We have each other's back. Mark and Jeannette went through a rough patch, and I was ready to punch him in the nose. No one is going to hurt our Jeannette. She is more than a boss. She is family, and we love one another. She has made us a team that cares," Greg explained.

Mark saw movement to his left. Skylar had joined them at some point without his noticing. She gave Mark a wink and a smile.

"Excuse me, Greg. I would like you to meet my sister Skylar. Greg is in charge of the sound booth."

The sound room door opened and out walked Clay.

"Greg, buzz Jeannette and have her come to the booth. You say you hired a private investigator to look into Jeannette? You wanted the true story? Who do you think you are?" Clay asked.

"They are my parents. Clay is one of the artists that has a contract with *Windy City*, and has a number one hit that Jeannette wrote! She has written several songs for him and performed on each of his albums. He is also her friend. My parents, Shannon and Ken, want to make sure Jeannette is good enough for me to marry," Mark informed Clay.

"You have that turned around. The question should be, is Mark good enough for our Jeannette? We were skeptical of him at first. She has been to hell and back and survived. Did you not see in the news about her attack? Or were you living in a cave? It only made her stronger and more caring. She has not let ANYTHING harden her heart. Believe me. A lesser person would be bitter and angry at the world. Not Jeannette. Speaking of her, hello, Pretty Lady. We were getting to know these people. Get your guitar and let's show them what we do here. No buts," Clay demanded and held his hand up to stop any protests.

Greg passed the guitar over the sea of heads to Jeannette. "Thanks, Greg. Hi Honey. Skylar! I didn't see you hiding over there," Jeannette said.

"We are burning time, Jeannette. Come on," Clay said.

The doors closed, headsets on, and Clay counted down a knee-slapper Jeannette liked. They never recorded this song before now. She forgot all about who was in the booth with Greg. She was in the world of music until the song ended. Clay hugged her and whispered in her ear, "Good luck with that group!"

Greg's voice came through their headsets. He said, "We got it. Jeannette, Clay come and have a listen."

Skylar gave her a smile and a wink. Mark gave her a kiss and a hug. Greg played back the tape. Shannon started to say something, and Jeannette shushed her. Shannon looked appalled.

When the tape finished, Jeannette said, "I think that was as close to perfect as we are going to get. This is a single, right? It could make the charts. Nice job, Clay. Greg, as usual, you were amazing. Why don't we take this little gathering back to my office?"

"So, Mark, did you bring the pre-nup?" Jeannette asked. "Did it take the whole family to deliver it?"

Ken started the explanation, "No, it didn't. Mark insisted we have a tour of your company. We received the investigator's report. We owe you an apology for doubting you. The truth is, we discovered that you are an amazing woman. We couldn't ask for a better person to be Mark's wife."

"Thank you for the apology," Jeannette acknowledged. "I assume that means we have your blessing?"

"Absolutely. What can we do to help?" Shannon asked, smiling as if this ugliness had never happened and was excited to get started.

"Nothing, thank you. Skylar, you have been smiling since you got here and have not spoken a word. Did you tag along for fun, or is there something you need to talk to me concerning my dress?" Jeannette questioned.

"Oh, I tagged along to watch the show," Skylar answered. "I have wanted to see my parents put in their place for years! Sorry mom and dad, but it is time someone stood up to you. Our family has always been middle class, but you act like you are royalty, always looking down your nose at others, believing they are beneath your station in life. It is time for you to get over yourselves. I love you, Jeannette! Thanks for doing what we were unable to do."

"Please, understand I had no intention of splitting your family or causing any problems. I fell in love with your son. It is that simple. You should never judge someone before you know the facts. It would be even better if you didn't judge at all. I am sure you have skeletons in your closet. Maybe I should have you two investigated? Unlike you, that is something I would never do. My sons have accepted Mark as their stepfather, and their opinion matters to me. Investigating Mark was never a thought," Jeannette paused to shake her head.

"I had no idea I was facing an inquisition. Knowing Mark, my opinion was that he came from a good family. Not this family. Let me reassure you that I will be a good wife to Mark. I will be faithful, he will always be a priority, I will take care of him, and most of all, I will love him until my last breath. One last thing I need to inform you, my oldest son, Sean, just got married. I hope they make me a grandmother very soon, which will make the two of you great-grandparents! One more thing. Did the investigator cost more than $5,000.00?" Jeannette asked with a little sarcasm in her voice.

"As a matter of fact..." Ken started.

"Dad!" Mark yelled and rubbed his face with his hands.

The shocked look on Shannon and Ken's face was priceless. Skylar laughed out loud and said under her breath, "You go girl! This is the best entertainment I have ever witnessed. I will have to remember to thank Mark for the call."

Jeannette put her arms around Mark and kissed him passionately without caring that his parents observed without a word. She pulled away only to see Mark smiling with love.

Over the intercom came Greg's voice, "Jeannette, I need you to listen to a recording. It needs your tweaking."

She acknowledged him over the intercom then turned to her soon to be in-laws and said, "If you don't mind, I need to excuse myself. I have work to do. I know you have seen my financials, and now you see how I EARN every penny. Mark, I will be having dinner with you at seven. Skylar, I will see you on Friday. Shannon and Ken, maybe I will see you at the wedding," Jeannette said, turned on her heels and walked out.

Not one more word needed to be said. Jeannette walked to the sound booth with a smile on her face — no panic attacks. For the first time since she was seven, she was beginning to feel normal. She stood up for herself with confidence.

Mark's family stared at the door where Jeannette exited. Mark broke the silence.

"Isn't she amazing? I hope you have learned something today. My soon to be wife is a confident woman who will not be degraded or shamed by anyone. In the future, watch what you say to her and how you treat her. I don't think she will be this nice to you next time."

"She is overbearing! Does she tell you what to do? Is she forcing you to marry her?" Ken asked with worry.

"Did you NOT learn anything at all? She is NOT forcing me to do anything! No, she does NOT tell me what to do! We have mutual respect and a lot of love for each other! No one is going to get away with treating either of us in a manner like you did! I will always choose Jeannette over anyone. That includes you, Mom and Dad!" Mark shouted.

"Okay, we get it," Shannon turned to her daughter and asked, "Skylar? Is this how you saw us all these years? Do you hate us?"

"Hate is too strong of a word. I love you, but I dislike you. Over the years, I have watched you operate. It hasn't been a pleasant sight to watch as you cut someone into ribbons with your tongue. Jeannette just gave you some of your own medicine. How did that feel?" Skylar asked. "Mark, thanks for the call. I wouldn't have missed this show for the world. I have to go back to work. If it is alright with you, I will join you and Jeannette for dinner tonight."

"Okay. See you at seven," Mark said to Skylar. "Mom, Dad? You probably have things to do. I will show you the way out."

The group filed past Bridgett and Max. Both shook their heads at Shannon and Ken in disbelief of their actions toward Jeannette.

At dinner that evening, Jeannette asked Mark about Thanksgiving. "What would you like to do for Thanksgiving?"

"I hadn't thought about it. What did you have in mind?" Mark replied.

"I have two suggestions. We could have dinner in Chicago at my apartment, or we could go to Oregon. Now that I think about it, we should probably go to Oregon. We are going to want to be in Chicago for Christmas. It will be getting too close to the wedding to leave," Jeannette suggested.

"Oregon sounds wonderful. It's settled," Mark decided.

Jeannette looked at Skylar and asked, "Would you like to join us? I can introduce you to my sons and daughter-in-law. I promise I am a good cook. My treat. I will purchase your plane ticket when I get ours."

"I would love to go! I usually go to some friend's house for dinner. Our mother has not cooked dinner in years unless she did and didn't invite us. This is wonderful! When do we leave?" Skylar asked anxiously.

"I think Tuesday before Thanksgiving," Jeannette replied. "I will have Bridgett check on flights. If we need to take a red eye on Monday, will that be alright with you?"

"Anytime will be fine. I will make sure of it! Thank you for inviting me," Skylar said.

"We are almost family. You need to get to know my children. You are going to be their aunt," Jeannette told her, placing her hand on Skylar's.

The rest of the evening was wedding planning and discussing what needed to be accomplished, right away. Three-hundred invitations needed to be printed ASAP and sent. The decision for a photographer has to be decided out of a field of four. The conversation included Mark when it came to the menu, and he was ready. He pulled a list of choices from his pocket. Jeannette agreed with what he chose.

"Oh! I almost forgot. Would you be my bridesmaid? Of course, I would pay for the materials and time for your dress just like we agreed on my dress. We will need one more dress for Tia, my daughter-in-law. I am going to ask my best friend, Judy, to help me get dressed and cut the cake . . ." Jeannette said but was interrupted by Skylar.

"Jeannette, slow down. I would love to be your bridesmaid. Woman, you need a chill pill or something. Do I need your approval on the design of the dresses?" Skylar asked with a gleam in her eye.

"Yes! I will have the final say. So do not go too wild. Tia is pretty conservative."

"Honey, you need to eat," Mark said with concern. "You haven't touched your food. You are going a mile a minute and need fuel. You have plenty of support. Talk later, eat now."

"I know you are right. My mind has so many things whirling about, and I need to get them out or I will explode! As usual, I have my lists, and I know what I have to do. There is so much going on right now, that I have trouble shutting off my brain. Business is crazy busy since Clay became our new resident star. Music! I have forgotten about music!" Jeannette exclaimed.

"Settle down. My orchestra will be here. See? We can take care of things, too," Mark told her. He squeezed her hand.

"Did you decide on colors?" Skylar asked.

"Yes. A medium red, nothing too dark, and white."

"That will be perfect with the design of your dress, although a deep purple would look good also. The purple would make it look rich. I will make two drawings, one with red, one with purple then you can choose," Skylar told her.

"Honey?" Jeannette asked, turning to Mark. "Have you decided on two ushers? The week after Thanksgiving, they need to get fitted for a tux. That reminds me, I would like the men in white tuxes with short jackets and tails. Sean's ushers looked so nice in white, and I would like to do the same. The difference will be in the length of the jacket and the tails."

"I have not asked anyone, yet, but I am sure the two I have in mind will say yes. I will take care of it. Please, stop worrying for at least the rest of the evening? I have made arrangements for *My City* to be closed on January 2nd. I will have most of my waitstaff working our reception and, of course, Chef will be cooking. Now I need to ask you something personal. Are you going to help me pay for this?" Mark meekly asked.

"Of course! It is OUR wedding. We share everything, even the expenses of the wedding. Just because this is your restaurant doesn't mean I expect you to pick up the tab. Work up some figures for me. Give me the total of what it will cost, including paying the employees and chef with a generous tip. We will split it. Is that acceptable?" Jeannette asked.

"Completely acceptable. Thank you," Mark said with relief.

"You two are a hoot to watch," Skylar giggled. "Neither wants to step on the others' toes. You always come to a mutual decision that is beneficial. I hope I find a husband one day who will be as good and thoughtful to me as you two are. In the meantime, I will be entertained by both of you."

Mark smiled and said, "I live to entertain you, Skylar."

"I have another question for you, Jeannette. Are you going to let mom help with anything?" Skylar asked.

Jeannette thought a moment before answering.

"I probably will. I do not hate them. I told her the truth as I saw it. I planned to have her feel what it's like to be on the other end of her judgmental attitude. I hope I didn't cross the line and sound mean. I understand that they want to protect their son, but they could have gone about it differently. Spend time with me. Observe what I do and say. Actions speak louder than any voice. Of course, that's my opinion."

"Mark, I will repeat; Jeannette is a good choice!" Skylar declared.

Lesson learned: People who judge others and find fault in them are blind to their own shortcomings. Sometimes the flaws they see in others mirror their own.

You should never be impressed by how much money someone has, their title, or how educated they are, or how many times they have been married. The things that should impress you are integrity, kindness, humility, and generosity. These traits are not spoken but can be observed.

Do not judge until you know the facts. It is better not to judge at all.

8

Jeannette, Mark, and Skylar took a red-eye to Oregon on Monday before Thanksgiving. They had three seats together and talked the entire way. Mark was not out of the loop. He sat in the middle and added his opinion from time to time.

Skylar watched the mountains below. "Oh. Wow. The mountains are so vast and beautiful. Do you live in the forest?"

Jeannette giggled and answered, "No, but it is beautiful where I live. We should be landing very soon. I think you will like my house, don't you, Mark?"

With a huge grin, Mark remarked, "I don't think she will complain."

Twenty minutes later, they were on the ground and headed for Jeannette's home. Skylar took in as much as she could see through the window of the back seat.

When the car came to a halt at the front door of Jeannette's house, Skylar asked, "Why are we stopping here?"

"This is my home," Jeannette replied.

Mark opened Skylar's door and asked, "Are you going to sit in the car all day or get out and look around?"

Her mouth dropped open. When she caught her breath, she walked around, not believing what she was seeing.

"Jeannette! Mark!" Irma shouted, standing in the doorway. "Boys, Tia, your mom and Mark are here! Oh! Who is this?"

"Irma, this is Mark's sister Skylar. It is her first visit to Oregon. Skylar, this is my oldest son, Sean and his wife, Tia. This is Tyler, my second born and this is Irma my friend and housekeeper." Irma and Tia hugged her, and the boys shook her hand. "Now that I have made the introductions," Jeannette went on to say, "Irma, what did you make to eat?"

"I made one of your favorites, ham and cheese quiche, with hash browns and toast. Coffee is waiting for you," Irma reported on the menu.

"You are a dream. Tyler, would you show Skylar to the lavender bedroom? It has a private bathroom. Thank you. As soon as you do, we can eat!" Jeannette said.

Skylar fit right with any of the conversations. She was right in the middle of them with her opinion or a story about the topic. She announced, "I am going to love being a part of this family!"

Sean tapped his glass with a spoon to get the group's attention and stood.

"I have some news. Mom? You said you couldn't wait for grandchildren?" Jeannette put her hand over her mouth. "Well, you will have to wait seven more months for our little addition to the family."

Jeannette jumped to her feet. Tears were streaming down her face. She hugged the expectant couple.

Through sobs, she said, "I am going to be a grandma! I love you both so much! A little June bug. That makes me so happy! There will be a baby in the house again! A year from now at Christmas, it is going to be so much fun!"

Skylar burst into laughter. Every eye was on her. She caught her breath and said, "That makes our parents great-grandparents!

Oh, this is wonderful! Please let me be the one to tell them?" She could not stop laughing. Mark smiled and chuckled.

Sean and Tyler looked confused. Jeannette explained Shannon and Ken do not have any grandchildren, and now they will be not only grandparents but also great-grandparents.

"I do not think Shannon is going to like it. You will understand after you meet them," Jeannette said. "Oh! Skylar! Dresses! Baby bump. Hers can be styled a little different than yours, but must be the same color," Jeannette instructed. "Tia will you be my maid-of-honor? You are going to have a designer dress if you say yes."

"You bet I will! I would say yes, even without a designer dress."

"Meet your designer, Skylar. This is what she does for a living. Maybe while we are here, you girls can come up with a design. We can go into town today to get a sketch pad. I have to get all the ingredients for dinner anyway. We will make it a girl's afternoon and have lunch at the Blue Bucket after shopping," Jeannette suggested.

"Well, Grandpa, what do you think about all this? You hit the jackpot! In six weeks, you will be a father, six or seven months later you will be a grandpa. Wow! That's some fast work, Buddy!" Skylar joked.

Mark looked at Jeannette with love and said, "I am going to love every second of it." Looking at Skylar, he told her, "You are going to be an aunt and a great-aunt. Did you think about that?" Mark teased. She stopped laughing. Her face formed a frown. "Is that too much for your brain to compute?"

"At the moment, yes, it is."

"Okay, ladies, let's get the dishes cleaned up so we can get our shopping done. Boys, and Tia, if you have someone you want to invite to Thanksgiving dinner, that's fine, just let me know before I go shopping. Tyler, before you even say anything, I always plan on Zach. Dinner would not be the same if he were not here," Jeannette told him.

As they cleaned up, Jeannette noticed Irma seemed a little down. "Irma, would you and your husband like to join us for Thanksgiving?" Jeannette asked.

Irma's face brightened. "Oh, Miss Jeannette! We would love to! Our children are not going to come home this year. It was only going to be my husband and me. Thank you for the invitation."

"You are always welcome at family functions and dinners. After all, you are part of this growing family," Jeannette told Irma and hugged her.

At Jeannette's last count, possibly twenty would be attending their dinner. She felt blessed.

Mark began, "Now that the women are out of our hair, we can have some guy time. Let's go sit by the fire pit." Sean and Tyler followed. "I want you to know, I already feel like you boys are my sons. I love you two, and I am very proud of you both. I wish I could have been with you in your early years, as you grew to be such special young men. I know your mom had something to do with it, but ultimately it was your decision on which path to follow. Sean, would you please be my best man and stand with me as I marry your mother?"

"I would be proud to, Mark," Sean said with a lump in his throat.

"And Tyler, would you be my usher and also stand with me as I take my vows?"

"Absolutely!"

All three stood and wrapped their arms around one another and felt bonded as father and sons. This moment was special. It was their private moment. It was going to be kept between them as a father-son time of bonding.

"By the way, I need to tell you your tuxes will be white with tails. Before you say anything, you cannot back out now. You have already committed," Mark teased.

"Tails?" Tyler asked. "What are tails? Like a dog?"

Mark and Sean threw their heads back and laughed out loud. When Mark regained his composure, he explained what the tails on a tux were. Tyler was a little embarrassed but laughed along with them.

The ladies felt bad after shopping, thinking about the men having to fend for themselves. Tia called to invite them to lunch. Tyler had just made a sandwich which he gladly set aside at the prospect of lunch at the Blue Bucket.

For the first time in years, it snowed on Thanksgiving. It was wonderful. The snow made the atmosphere cozy. They had a crackling fire in the fireplace when the guests arrived. Each one gravitated toward the fire to warm up. Jeannette's heart filled with gratitude for her beautiful family.

"A toast!" Jeannette shouted. "To family! May we all be blessed and as happy as we are right now! Salute!"

They all shouted, "Salute!" in unison.

Skylar did not want to go back home to Chicago. She enjoyed being with the family Jeannette had created with love.

This designer felt blessed and thankful they accepted her into their family. Skylar wondered what life would have been like if she had been part of a family like this. Someday she might have her own. She will raise them with love.

Their time in Oregon came to an end, and it was back to Chicago. Skylar and Tia successfully designed dresses for the wedding over the holiday week. It was a wonderful Thanksgiving.

Lesson learned: Do not ever be afraid to start over. There is a reason why the opportunity has come about. Make it an adventure. You can accomplish amazing things if you take a step forward.

9

The Christmas season was upon them. Sean, Tia, Tyler, and Zach arrived in Chicago on December 23rd. David met them at the airport, ready to congratulate the happy couple.

"Hello, David. It is good to see you. Merry Christmas! We brought you a little something from Oregon. We took a chance that you like whiskey. This bottle is distilled in Carson City, close by where we live. It is quite good. Enjoy," Sean said.

"Sean! That is so nice! Thank you. Yes, I do drink whiskey. I will be opening this tonight. You are a thoughtful young man. A chip off the old block," David gushed.

"David, this is for you. It is a hat from Oregon State University where I attend college. That is a beaver. It is our mascot. I guessed on the size, and this is a scarf for your wife from OSU. Merry Christmas!" Tyler said.

"My wife is going to love the scarf, and I certainly like my hat. It fits! Thank you, Tyler! These gifts were not expected but greatly appreciated," David told them.

Their mother's apartment had Christmas decorations everywhere she could squeeze one in. It was her favorite time of year. When the young adults arrived, she and Mark were in the kitchen baking cookies. It was more like she was baking, and he was keeping her company while drinking a glass of wine.

"Merry Christmas! We are here!" Tyler yelled.

"In the kitchen!" Jeannette yelled back.

One by one, they got a hug and a kiss. Tia got a little more attention because of the baby. She had a baby bump which Jeannette bent down and kissed.

"This baby is going to recognize grandma's voice before it gets here. Zach! I see you snitching cookies! You will spoil your dinner!" Jeannette laughed.

"Oh, come on, Mom!" Zach said.

"You know nothing spoils his appetite. Let's put our bags away then maybe mom will let us all have a cookie if Zach hasn't eaten them all," Tyler said.

Before dinner, they relaxed in the living room while they talked and watched the snowfall through the big windows.

Finally, Jeannette said, "I need to tell everyone, Mark and I invited his parents and Skylar over for dinner tomorrow night. I expect all of you to be on your best behavior. They are going to be your new grandparents, and I want to show you off. Of course, you get along just fine with Skylar, but take Mark's parents with a grain of salt and don't let them get to you. Deep down, I think they are nice people. There are just a few quirks you have to get past."

Mark felt he needed to explain, "My parents are not touchy-feely people, and sometimes they can be judgmental. Don't let them get under your skin. I am hoping your mother will rub off on them. Jeannette and I will run interference if they start to get out of hand."

"Even though they are not accustomed to being hugged, go for it! Show them how we say hello! We have got to break them in sooner or later. It might as well be now," Jeannette said with a giggle. She turned to Mark to say, "This is going to be fun. The looks on their faces are going to be priceless! We have got to have a camera ready! I hope Skylar is here early. She is going to want to see this."

"Hey, enough talk!" Zach said, sounding impatient. "When do we eat? I am starving! Whatever is cooking smells wonderful. I can't take it any longer! Can we please eat?" He moaned.

"I have a roast in the oven, and it should be ready by now. Okay, Zach, let's eat!" Jeannette announced.

The next morning, Jeannette started cooking, early. The stuffing had to be prepared, the turkey needed to be in the oven by eleven, and side dishes had to be put together. The pies, one pumpkin, and one coconut custard were made the day before. (Jeannette had to keep an eye on Zach, so he didn't eat the pies.) Tia jumped in to help. That afternoon the apartment smelled heavenly with the scents of Christmas and last-minute gifts were wrapped and placed under the tree.

The family had gathered in the kitchen for lunch consisting of sandwiches made by their own hands. Jeannette was not going to stop what she was doing to serve them. They were capable of making a sandwich.

No one left the kitchen after eating. Funny stories were told about experiences of Christmases past while Jeannette prepared a feast. It was nice, she thought, keeping her company so it suggested time went by quickly.

Skylar was the first to arrive with a bottle of white wine as a gift for the hostess. "Merry Christmas!" Skylar shouted when Mark answered the door. "Where are my nephews and niece? Auntie brought you a gift." She handed each one an envelope it had a card and a one-hundred-dollar bill inside. She knew Zach would be here, so she made sure she had an envelope for him also. He was her adopted nephew. They showed Skylar their appreciation with hugs and kisses on her cheeks.

"I am going to like being an aunt," Skylar beamed.

Tia held her money and said, "This is baby money."

The doorbell rang, and the room hushed. The new grandparents had arrived.

Mark opened the door and said, "Merry Christmas! Come in. Let me introduce you to your grandchildren. Sean is the oldest."

Sean stepped forward and gave Shannon and Ken a hug. Shannon had no idea what to do. She looked stunned. So did Ken.

Mark went on, "This is Tia, she is married to Sean, and I believe Skylar told you she is expecting." She stepped forward to give hugs.

"This is Tyler Jeannette's second son." He stepped forward and hugged them.

"This is Zach, not a biological son, but an adopted family member."

Zach held his arms out and said, "Grandma, Grandpa, great to meet you!" He did not hold back. He gave each one a bear hug.

Jeannette had to turn away so a giggle would not escape. She knew Zach was going to do something unusual. That's just who he is.

The couple looked like they were in shock from being accosted by the group of young people.

"Well...I...um..." Shannon could not get her mind to function or her mouth to form words. She could not think of a word to say.

Skylar could not hold back any longer. She burst into laughter. "Mom, it was only a hug. Remember what that is?"

"Yes, well, Merry Christmas," Shannon said. A half-smile garnished her face for a split second then the frown came back. She straightened her dress as if the hugs had wrinkled it.

Ken said with a small smile, "Merry Christmas. Dinner smells wonderful."

"Thank you, Ken. I will take your coats. Please, make yourself at home. Mark will pour you a glass of wine. Excuse me," Jeannette said and left the room with their coats.

"So, tell me a little about yourself, Sean. I understand you just graduated from college. What is your degree in?" Ken asked, trying to start a conversation.

"My degree is in business. I was valedictorian of my class. I am working for a company in Carson City, Oregon. I oversee three states of sales representatives. Tia, why don't you tell them about what you do?" Sean suggested.

"I have a degree in business law. I am an attorney, and I work for a law firm in Clark City, Oregon. That is where Sean and I live," Tia told them. She saw their eyebrows raise in response.

Tyler added, "I have not graduated, yet, but I will be an architect when I do graduate."

Zach raised his hand and said, "Me too. I will be an architect, too."

Ken cleared his throat before saying, "Ahem. Well, that is impressive."

"Speaking for the group," Sean began. "We would like you to know we have worked very hard at getting an education. That goes for Tia also. She was on her own at the age of eighteen. We had nothing given to us, and we did not spend our time partying. We all had jobs since the time we were young teenagers. We held down a job through college to help pay for classes, books, and miscellaneous living expenses. Mom taught us, just because she has money now, nothing has changed. Money can be gone in an instant, but family will always be by your side to help you get back up. You can count on family. They love you no matter what. Money is not important. Family is."

Shannon and Ken looked at each other without words as Mark and Skylar stood by and observed. They were not going to interrupt this enlightening conversation.

Jeannette quietly returned while Sean was giving his speech. When he finished, she said, "Son, you make your mamma proud. With what you just said, it proves I am a success. Now, before I cry off my makeup, dinner is ready. Mark, will you sit at the head of the table, please? Shannon and Ken, please sit to his right. Skylar can sit next to me, and everyone else sit wherever you like."

After everyone was seated, Jeannette clinked her glass with a spoon for attention. "I would like to propose a toast to the first gathering of our new family. May we always have happiness and love. Salute!"

Mark took Jeannette's hand, squeezed it, and said, "I love you more every minute." He leaned in and kissed her.

"Oh, come on!" Zach moaned. "Save the mush for later! Carve that bird! I'm starving!"

In unison, they all said, "You are always starving!" They all burst into laughter, breaking the awkwardness felt by all. Now it felt like a family meal with everyone talking at once and food making its way around the table as Mark carved the turkey.

It had been so many years since Shannon and Ken attended a family style dinner, they were clumsy with what to do, at first. As soon as dishes started being passed around, they remembered.

This Christmas was an entirely new experience for the new grandparents. They were not sure what to do or say. Skylar observed her parents throughout dinner with a smile. Spoken words were not necessary. It was a learning experience for Shannon and Ken, where the younger people were doing the teaching to the oldest.

After dinner, the family gathered in the living room for coffee and dessert. Tia and Skylar helped Jeannette bring in plates of pie and a carafe of coffee.

Before serving, Jeannette said, "Shannon and Ken, we have a gift for you." She handed them an envelope. Inside was an open-ended airplane ticket for two to Oregon, first class.

"We left it open so you can use it whenever you choose. It is from all of us. Everyone pitched in. We hope you will use them."

Tears flowed down Shannon's cheeks, and Ken's eyes were misty. The tables had turned to surprised expressions on the faces of Mark and Skylar. They had never seen their mother let her guard down and cry, let alone their father. Seeing tears from the couple proved the tickets to be the perfect gift. The family had succeeded in melting their hearts.

"Ahem...I don't know what to say," Ken began. "Ahem. Thank you. We apologize for not having brought gifts. We were not sure what to do. Next year will be different. Our family will be different. Our family changed today." There was not a dry eye in the room after that.

Jeannette thought it was time she reached out to Shannon and included her opinion of her choices for the wedding.

"Ladies, let's go to the other room and show Grandma what we have put together for our wedding ceremony."

Jeannette hooked her arm through Shannon's as she steered grandma down the hall, hoping it made her feel included.

"Our colors are deep purple, mauve, and white. The men are wearing white tuxes, white shirts, purple vests, and mauve ties. Tia and Skylar are wearing deep purple dresses with mauve accents, and the material has threads of silver woven through it, so they will sparkle as they walk down the aisle. The dresses are strapless so since it will be cold out, she designed a cropped shrug in purple with mauve colored fur trim. Instead of carrying flowers they will wear a muff to match the fur trim of the shrug. Here is a drawing of what they will look like. You will notice the dresses are styled slightly different, giving Tia a little extra room for expansion. These dresses are designed so they can be worn again. Not a one and done kind of dress."

Shannon had never paid attention to Skylar and her designs. When she saw the drawings, she reacted by saying, "YOU drew these? Did you design these? They are beautiful! I had no idea you were so talented. Now I understand why you went into designing. You have a gift."

Skylar's eyes filled with tears, once more as she hugged Shannon. She had never received a compliment so heartfelt from her mother before.

"Now let me show you MY dress," Jeannette said. She pulled the drawing from a hiding place so Mark could not see it.

Shannon gasped and put her hand on her chest. Regaining her voice, she said, "This is stunning! How do you come up with all these ideas?"

"I have to admit I collaborated with Jeannette on the design of this one. She wanted something in the style of the thirties or forties. One dress, in particular, stuck in her mind over the years after watching an old movie. This is the closest design we came up with to what she saw."

"Since it is not her first marriage, she can wear colors. The main dress is made of white lace over mauve-colored satin. The dress has long sleeves made of lace. It is simply straight to the knees and flares from the knees down so she can dance. It has trains of lace which are attached just under the bust line that will flow to the sides as she walks revealing the dress beneath. The trains are about two feet longer than the dress and will be hooked around the bottom of the dress later for dancing. The trains are three pieces, one in the back and one on either side so they will look like Jeannette is floating when she walks down the aisle."

"The coat she will wear during the ceremony is deep purple velvet with white fur trim. The sleeves are oversized bell style with white fur trim. It has an oversized hood that will be pulled over her head until the Justice of the Peace says Mark can kiss her. At which time Mark will push the hood down. It has two hooks at the neck so that the weight of the coat does not pull it off her shoulders as she walks down the aisle. The long train of velvet at the back can be detached so she can wear it again. You will not be able to see where it attaches underneath. As you can see the coat is much longer than the dress and trains so it will drag behind as she walks and opens in the front, again revealing the dress beneath. There are separate panels at the back that can be detached, and shorter ones replace the long ones so it can be worn again. Instead of a bouquet, Jeannette will carry a white fur muff. What do you think?"

"Stunning. Absolutely stunning. Is it done?" Shannon asked.

"I have the bridesmaids' dresses finished, but we have one more fitting for Jeannette," Skylar answered.

It was clear Shannon wanted to be present for the fitting.

Jeannette asked, "If it is okay with Skylar, would you like to come to my final fitting Wednesday at four? I would love to have your opinion."

This time Shannon was the one hugging Jeannette. "I cannot think of any place else I want to be more, than with you girls," Shannon said. It turned into a group hug.

Mark and Ken thought they should check on the women. They heard a lot of chatter and a few giggles and then silence. They were astonished at the sight of a sobbing group of women hugging.

Mark spoke up, "Mom? Jeannette? Is everything okay in here?"

"Sweetheart, I am so proud of you. Jeannette is a rare gem. I see why you love her. Ken, our daughter, is exceptional in design! Do not make any plans for me on Wednesday at four. We have a fitting for Jeannette's wedding gown!" Shannon announced. She dabbed her eyes, stood up straight, and said, "Ken, I have had enough emotion for one day. Jeannette, do you need help with the dishes? I am willing to give you a hand if need be."

"We have it covered, Shannon, but thank you for the offer. I have some leftovers for you to take home if you would like them.

Turkey is always a tasty sandwich the next day," Jeannette offered.

Shannon glanced at Ken, not knowing for sure what to say. She had never been offered leftovers before.

Ken answered her, "I don't know about Shannon, but I would love some. You are a good cook."

"Wonderful! I have them already dished up for you. I threw in a couple of pieces of pie, too," Jeannette said, looking at Ken. She smiled and gave him a wink.

It turned out to be a lovely evening after they got through the awkwardness. Skylar stayed to play a board game with her nephews and niece, eat more pie, laugh, and in general enjoy family time.

Jeannette and Mark bowed out. She was exhausted from cooking for two days. They sat in front of the most prominent window and watched the activity going on below and the snow gently falling. Jeannette placed her head on his shoulder. In a quick minute, she was asleep.

Mark did not mind. He kissed the top of her head then whispered, "Thank you for showing my parents what family time is all about. You have won their hearts."

Lesson learned: The mind is a powerful thing. If you fill it with negativity, that is what you will get, more negativity. If you fill it with positive thoughts, you will attract more positive. Your life will change for the better.

Love others. Show your love toward them. Everyone needs love and kindness. It can melt a hardened heart.

10

It was time for the final fitting of Jeannette's wedding dress. The excitement was building from outside the fitting room. Shannon and Tia were anxiously waiting, sipping on champagne for Shannon and water for Tia, to see the bride make her appearance.

Jeannette announced from behind a curtain, "Okay, here I come!" The audience of two was on the edge of their seats. Jeannette walked out with Skylar's help. Shannon's hands covered her mouth in awe.

"Well, ladies, what do you think?" Skylar asked.

"I am dumbstruck! The only word that comes to mind is stunning. The dress, the coat, the muff is gorgeous, but the ensemble doesn't make Jeannette beautiful. Jeannette is what makes all of it beautiful," Shannon said.

"That is the nicest compliment I have ever gotten! Thank you!" Jeannette declared.

"She's right. Stunning is the word for it. Mark is going to get weak in the knees when he sees you," Tia added.

"That is exactly what I want! I want to make an impression on him," Jeannette said.

She turned around to see the back, turned to the right and then the left. It looked perfect.

"Skylar, you are so talented! I guess now would be a good time to tell you what I have done. I had handouts printed, something like programs, to be given out to every guest who attends. It will have the names of everyone in the wedding party, including the justice of the peace, and the order in which the ceremony will unfold. I had a special paragraph put in about you. It says you designed my gown and the bridesmaids' dresses. It gives the address of your shop, phone number, and email address. One more thing, the Chicago Town News is sending a reporter and photographer to cover the wedding. The only reason I agreed to let one newspaper attend was to give you some exposure and free advertising. People need to know how good you are!"

"I would hug you, but I can't get to you! There's too much coat in my way!" Skylar cried out. That got a laugh from them all. She noticed a few women were trying to see what was going on through the windows, so she rushed Jeannette to the changing room before anyone saw her design.

"Sorry to rush you, but no one sees this dress until January 2nd. You and the dress will make a debut when you walk down the aisle. Now I am excited!"

"Do you want me to take the dress home? Or do you want to keep it under wraps and bring it yourself to *My City*?" Jeannette asked.

"If you don't mind, I would like to keep it locked up in my office for safety. I will wrap it all up and bring it myself to you the day of the ceremony. Is that agreeable with you?" Skylar asked.

"That would be a load off my mind. One less thing to do! Okay, help me get out of this so you can lock it up," Jeannette said. "I think we should have dinner at Mark's restaurant tonight. What do you think? We have rehearsal dinner tomorrow night, the next night is New Year's Eve, and so if I plan this right, I won't have to cook for a couple of weeks! I'll call Mark."

When Jeannette came through the curtain, she found Tia and Shannon talking and laughing.

"It is nice to see you two are getting along! I called Mark. We are having dinner at the restaurant. I also called the boys and Ken. I sent David to pick them up. He will drop them at the restaurant then pick us up. That will give Skylar time to close. Is that agreeable with the both of you?"

"Fine with me! I am going to have to eat something light, or I will not fit in my dress!" Tia said. "This baby makes me so hungry. I want to eat all the time! I am going to weigh a ton if I keep on stuffing my face!"

"We have been there. Just don't starve yourself. The baby needs food to grow. The weight, you can lose after the little June bug gets here," Jeannette said.

Shannon spoke up, "Maybe Ken and I will use our plane tickets to come to Oregon as soon as the baby is born. I am starting to look forward to being a great grandma. Whoa. I am getting better at calling myself that. I usually cringe," Shannon said with a laugh.

Jeannette saw David pull up. "Let's go, David's here. Did Ken drop you off, Shannon?"

"Yes. Will I be able to ride with you or should I hail a cab?" Shannon asked.

"Of course, you can ride with us! There's room. I will sit up front with David. Come on, Skylar! Let's go!" Jeannette yelled.

"I'm coming! I had to make sure your dress was locked up. I don't want my design to be stolen or copied. I am so anxious to see what the response is going to be! I have worked up a BIG appetite. I am having filet mignon for dinner," Skylar announced.

"Good evening, ladies," David greeted the four excited women.

"Hello, David. Shannon, if I haven't introduced you before, this is David, my faithful driver. He has been with me since I took over *Windy City*. Poor man. I call him at odd times of the day, and he comes to get me no matter where I am. By the way, David, Shannon is going to be my mother-in-law, and Skylar will be my sister-in-law. I will finally have more girls in our family, so I am not out-numbered anymore!" Jeannette said.

"It is very nice to see all of you. When I pick all of you up from dinner, I will bring the limo. I have wine in the limo," David told them.

"I wish I had a driver," Skylar said.

"After the wedding, you might be able to afford one. You are going to be busy with orders. I know it! I am having so much fun!" Jeannette giggled. "I don't think we need any wine tonight, David." She gave David a wink.

Jeannette talked to David as he drove, "I am so glad you and Raelene will be at the wedding! Do not forget to bring your invitation. Our people at the door will be checking for invitations. If you do not have one, they will not let you in. From what I have heard, everyone wants to come to our wedding. As a matter of fact, every table, and every chair are reserved. We are expecting a bit over five hundred guests! Can you believe it?"

"The buzz is your wedding is the event of the year!" David informed her.

"What? Are you kidding me? Now I am nervous," Jeannette confessed. "By the way, will you pick me up in the limo for the wedding?"

"Of course! I had already planned to."

"Bring your wife with you when you pick me up. There is no need to go back and pick her up. We can always use another giggling woman," Jeannette told him.

"Thank you, Jeannette. I will," David said with a smile.

"I almost forgot! We need a second limo for the men!" Jeannette gasped.

"Relax Jeannette. It is all taken care of," David informed her.

Jeannette turned slightly in the seat and asked, "Shannon, would you like to ride with all the girls to the wedding? We would love to have you."

"Oh, yes! Thank you so much for inviting me! I suppose ken will ride with the men?" Shannon asked.

"I am sure he will," Jeannette told her.

"We might need a third limo just for your dress!" Skylar announced. That made the group of females laugh the rest of the way to the restaurant.

11

Today is the day Jeannette will become Mark's wife. He woke her up with a phone call at 6:00 a.m. with the words, "I love you. I will be the handsome guy in a white tux standing on stage waiting to marry you. Do not be late!" He hung up, leaving Jeannette with a smile on her face.

The wedding was at six that evening. By noon *My City* was buzzing with activity. The wait-staff was setting tables, the florist was arranging flowers, Chef was giving instructions to the line cooks, and Mark was giving instructions to security and the head waiter.

"No one gets in unless they have an invitation, the newspaper people MUST show ID with their invitation. Only ONE newspaper has an invitation. The guests that are to be seated close to the stage are on this list. Everything else is self-explanatory," Mark explained.

Jeannette, Tia, Skylar and Shannon came in through the service entrance so Mark would not see her before the ceremony. A room had been set up for the girls to dress. On a table, there were bottles of water on ice, a large tray of cut-up fruits, yogurt, various sodas, cheese and crackers, and to finish it off was a bottle of Jeannette's favorite white wine.

The photographer began a photoshoot with the women at 3:00, then the men at 4:30. Time was passing quickly. The guests started arriving as early as 5:00. The orchestra began playing before the first guest was ushered into the dining area. It had begun.

Shannon had excused herself earlier to check on the men then slipped back into the room with the girls to see if they needed anything. She was carrying a small box.

She sat close to Jeannette, took her hand, and said, "I wanted to offer this to you earlier, but I didn't know if you would want it. This pearl broach was my grandmother's. She wore it on her wedding day. Their marriage lasted until my grandfather died seventy years later. I brought it in case you needed something old or borrowed."

"I would be honored to wear it! The broach is lovely. Skylar, would you help me put this on my muff? That way, everyone can see it. It is gorgeous, isn't it? I will make sure it gets back to you. Surely Skylar will want to wear it when she marries." When Jeannette said that Skylar rolled her eyes, thinking it will never happen. Jeannette said, "Thank you for this! Now I am crying! There goes my makeup!" Jeannette cried and laughed at the same time. The nerves had kicked in and she was beginning to shake. She calmed herself with deep breaths, like she always did.

"Okay, I have caused enough damage, so I am going to our table." Shannon stood to leave. As she approached the door, she turned to say, "Jeannette? I love you," and disappeared through the door. Jeannette's makeup was ruined one more time.

The music began for the procession to begin. Tia and Skylar's dresses made quite an impression on the crowd. They could hear positive whispered comments as they walked toward the stage. When Tia and Skylar had reached their designated spot on the stage, the orchestra played louder signaling it was time for Jeannette. When she appeared, comments and gasps immediately began at the sight of her dress. Several women started to clap. It was contagious. It was not long until the entire dining area was clapping. Camera flashes were going off everywhere. Even though all eyes were on Jeannette, she did not feel self-conscious or afraid. She was proud to be wearing such an elegant wedding dress and in love with the most wonderful man in the world who was waiting to marry her. Jeannette's focus was on Mark.

Skylar fought back the tears of pride for her design. The dress was a hit.

Mark saw only Jeannette as she made her way to him. His face drained of color. He went down on one knee so he would not pass out. Tia was correct when she said Jeannette would make an impression on Mark.

Sean and Tyler had quickly followed suit and went down on one knee, so it looked like it was planned. The girls also bowed, although not knowing why. Their poses suggested a queen had just arrived. When she reached the steps which led to the stage, Mark regained his strength and stood to his feet. The others followed his lead. No one was the wiser if it was not planned in the ceremony. Crisis averted.

Sean whispered to Mark, "Are you okay?"

Mark whispered back, "Yes. Your mother is so beautiful. I lost the feeling in my legs. Thanks for the cover-up."

"You're welcome. I know that feeling," Sean said quietly with a slight chuckle.

At the close of the ceremony, the bride and groom turned to the guests and was introduced as husband and wife. The guests erupted into applause. Shannon and Ken shot to their feet, clapping as loud as they could. Mark had made them very proud parents.

During the reception, Sean and Tyler danced with Shannon. They were gentlemen, and it was the appropriate thing to do. Ken danced the father-daughter dance with Jeannette since he was the closest father figure she had at the moment. If Clay could have made it to the wedding, Jeannette would have asked him.

The orchestra went directly into another song for the bride and groom to share a dance. Jeannette was no longer wearing her coat, and Mark waltzed her around the floor. The dress made it look like she was floating on air. She felt as if she *were* floating. The feeling of flying from her childhood was back! The real Jeannette was gradually coming back. She was truly happy.

"Mark, this is the happiest day of my life. I gave you my heart in every possible way today. I love you so much, and I am proud to call you, my husband. I don't want this night to end," Jeannette said to Mark as he swept her around the dance floor.

"You are the most important person in my life. You are everything to me. I have waited a lifetime for you. My one regret is we did not meet before now. This restaurant was my dream for so many years and meant everything to me until Amy and Clay introduced you to me. My heart was yours with the first kiss of your hand. I would give up this restaurant if you asked me to. I love you, wife of mine," Mark whispered in Jeannette's ear.

All that were in attendance enjoyed the reception immensely. Toward the end of the evening, Mark had Chef and his staff stand on stage for a round of applause. Chef stepped from the stage and asked Jeannette to honor him with a dance. It was an evening filled with romance that no one will forget.

The newlyweds said their goodbyes and excused themselves at about 10:30. They booked a room at the '*W*' for their wedding night. David, of course, was waiting outside in the limo which was decorated with crepe paper and balloons thanks to Sean, Tyler, and Zach. David had Raelene in the front seat with him.

"Jeannette, your dress was, I don't have the words to say how gorgeous it was!" Raelene gushed. "Mark, your sister really designed it? Wow. That's all I can say, wow."

"Yes. My new sister is very talented," Jeannette started to carry on a conversation but was stopped by Mark's lips crushing hers.

He pulled back from the kiss, and with a big smile, said, "Shut up, wife, and kiss me!" The car went silent. David pushed a button to shut the glass behind him, so the newlyweds had privacy.

Jeannette and Mark left the next morning for the Bahamas. Their honeymoon would only last four days. They needed to return to their businesses.

While the couple was off honeymooning, Sean Tyler and Zach surprised Mark by moving everything out of Mark's apartment, while Tia cleaned it. Some things were moved to storage, but some things they knew he would want were taken to Jeannette's apartment. Mark's new family was too big for his residence, so they made Jeannette's apartment their home in Chicago. Her living space was twice or more the size of Mark's, with a better view of the city, and extra bedrooms.

David picked up the couple from the airport. "My, my, my you two are tan!" David declared.

"Yes, we are. We took a lot of naps on the beach, drank a lot of fruity drinks at a bar in the middle of a swimming pool, walked along the shore, and did a little shopping. It was heaven," Jeannette reported and kissed Mark.

"I am glad you enjoyed yourselves. You look relaxed," David noticed.

"We are," Mark said, not looking at David. Instead, he kissed Jeannette.

"Before I forget, David, could you take us by my apartment, please? I need to pick up some clothes," Mark asked.

"No."

"Excuse me? Did you say no?" Mark was shocked.

"Yes. I said no. You do not live there anymore. So no," David told Mark. The town car pulled up in front of Jeannette's apartment and stopped. Four smiling faces were looking at them. David rolled down Mark's window.

"Surprise! Welcome home! Mark, we have moved all your things out of your apartment for you and Tia cleaned it. We brought over things we thought you would want or need. Everything else we put in storage. We hope that was, okay?" Sean said.

Mark was stunned. "David, you knew about this?"

"Yes, sir," David said with a big grin.

"You guys did that for me? I was dreading the job. Thank you!" He hugged each one and told them he loved them. Jeannette watched and beamed at her thoughtful children. "We will eat dinner at *My City* tonight. Sweetheart, would you call Mom, Dad, and Skylar and have them meet us there at seven? David, would you please take me to *My City*? Wait a minute. I have a car. I still have my car, don't I boys?"

"Yes, about your car," Zach began as he stroked his chin. "We found the extra set of keys. Did you know how fast that car is? Sean and Tyler did not want to drive it, so I did." Zach was looking pretty proud of himself.

"Zach! What did you do with my car?" Mark exclaimed. A vein was starting to bulge from his forehead.

"Nothing. It's in the parking garage for the apartment. We registered it so it won't get towed," Zach explained and enjoyed the reaction he raised from Mark. All the young people were laughing.

Mark let his breath out. "Zach do not do that again! David, I will drive myself."

The six went into their new family home in Chicago, arm in arm, as a family.

At dinner, Jeannette, Skylar, Shannon, and Tia were talking a mile-a-minute about the wedding. They all spoke at the same time. The men shook their heads in disbelief how women understood several conversations at once.

After a few minutes, Skylar was the only one talking, "There was a big spread in the society section of the newspaper on Sunday, with pictures of your wedding and the 'designer' dresses! The reviews were wonderful! They said I was the best designer that has come along in a long time, and to watch for my designs soon. They said I was going to take the world of fashion by storm and look out Paris! Can you believe it? I have had fifty calls from women since you have been gone wanting me to design for them! Some of them are famous!"

"Skylar! That is wonderful! You are going to have to hire at least two new seamstresses, take out an ad in the paper, and have an interview with . . ."

"Honey. Your CEO is coming out. Let Skylar handle her business," Mark said sweetly.

"Oh, I am sorry, Skylar. I didn't mean to take over and tell you what to do. Sometimes my thoughts fall out of my mouth," Jeannette apologized.

Skylar laughed. "I don't mind! You thought about the same things I did. I have an interview with the society reporter at the end of the week. My business has taken off like gangbusters thanks to you marrying my brother."

Mark's attention turned to a disturbance.

"Excuse me. I need to see what is going on." He came back to the table a few minutes later. "It was a group of five people who were insisting on seeing Jeannette. Apparently, they have been trying to get an appointment at *Windy City* but have been turned away because there are no more contracts available right now. That's what Bridgett told them. They have been at *Windy City* every day. I told them to leave, or I would call the police. They left; I think."

"They wanted to see me?" Jeannette asked. "Mark, something is telling me to go talk to this group. Please come with me?"

The group was standing on the sidewalk looking like they had lost their last friend.

"Excuse me. My name is Jeannette. Were you looking for me?"

"Oh, my God! It is you! We have traveled from the state of Washington to try and get a contract with *Windy City*. We have been turned away every day for the last week. Earlier today we spent the last of our money on something to eat. Now we are broke and have nowhere to go, no gas, and we don't know how we are going to get home."

"I see. Can you give me a quick example of your music right now?" Jeannette asked.

"Here?"

"Yes. If you have talent, you can sing and play anywhere, and I will hear it. So, give me a sample right here, right now. This is your audition."

"Okay! Karen and Shawn will be on guitar. Seth, you take the lead. Let's sing 'It Is Dawning.' My name is Johnny, and this is A.J. Okay, one, two, three, and four . . ." They began to sing and drew a small crowd.

Jeannette listened and watched the reaction of the crowd. At the end of the song, there was applause from the onlookers.

"You have a good sound. Here is my card. Jeannette wrote on the back: *'Bridgett, Let me know when this group arrives. Jeannette.'* Give this to the receptionist. Where were you staying? Do you need someplace to sleep tonight?"

"Last night we slept in our van," Johnny said.

"Okay. Give me ten minutes. I will be right back," Jeannette said. Mark followed her back inside.

"Jeannette, what are you doing?" Mark asked.

"I think this group has the possibility of making *Windy City* a lot of money with the right tweaking. But I need to get them in the booth to find out for sure. So, I am calling the hotel two blocks from *Windy City* and getting them a room for the night. Then I am going to ask your chef to make up five dinners. They need a good meal."

"Okay, I trust you."

Mark took care of the dinners while Jeannette was on the phone to the hotel. With bags in hand, Jeannette and Mark went back to the awaiting group.

"Okay. First of all, here is dinner for each of you. You look like you could use a good meal. Two blocks from *Windy City* is a hotel. I have written the name and address on this piece of paper. They are holding two rooms for you. I have already paid for them so don't worry about that. Here is a hundred-dollar bill for gas. Get a good night's sleep and come see me in the morning."

"I don't know what to say, except, thank you!" Johnny gushed.

"You are welcome. I am not going to promise you anything at this point. Remember that. I want to hear what you sound like in the booth before I make a decision. There is no repayment required for the hotel. Let's keep an open mind, and I will see you tomorrow," Jeannette told the group.

Johnny shook Jeannette's hand vigorously and said, "This is so kind of you! I hope God blesses you really good! We will see you in the morning! Thank you, thank you, and thank you!"

Karen threw her arms around Jeannette and cried into her ear, "I am so thankful for you. I knew in my heart of hearts if we could talk to you, good things would happen for us. I have no idea where I got that idea. I just felt it. I believe something led us to you. Thank you so much!"

Jeannette kissed her on the cheek, and of course, she had tears in her eyes. "Okay. Off you go. The hotel is waiting for you."

Mark put his arm around Jeannette and said, "Sweetheart, you are so sensitive. It is one of the many reasons I love you. But when you cry, it hurts me. I want to scoop you up wipe your tears away, and comfort you until the tears disappear."

"Oh, my love. Sometimes I wish I were not so sensitive, but this is not one of the times. Karen whispered in my ear. She said she believed they were supposed to find me. She confirmed what I was feeling. These are tears of gratitude. Each time I act on my intuition, it is like I am being rewarded for following it. I'll bet I am clear as mud, trying to explain this to you?" Jeannette tried to make Mark understand.

"I understand what you are telling me, but I don't know how it feels. I see what it does to you, and I will always be here to comfort you for as long as you live. I love you." Mark kissed her on the forehead. "Now. Let's go eat."

"I am starved! That took a lot out of me. Good things are coming for that group and *Windy City*. I can feel it!" Jeannette said with a smile on her face. "By the way, *Windy City* will pick up the cost of their dinners. What did you have the chef prepare?"

"Filet mignon, baked potato, salad, and for dessert apple pie."

"Perfect," Jeannette agreed.

"Mom, is everything okay?" Sean asked.

"Perfect timing. It looks like our dinner is still hot. Yes, Sean, things are wonderful. It turned out this group has been trying to see me for several days. They drove three-thousand-six-hundred miles from the state of Washington. They ran out of money, so they slept in their van. I asked them to give me a sample of their music outside on the sidewalk. If they were serious about their music, it wouldn't matter where they were to audition. I liked their sound, and I want to get them in the booth right away. I am going to sign them. Humph. Now, why did I say that? I had not decided that yet. I guess I just made the decision."

"What's the name of the group?" Tyler asked.

"I have no idea! I will let you know after tomorrow," Jeannette giggled.

Mark smiled with love and admiration for his wife. "I wouldn't worry about your mom's decision. Remember she has superpowers?" He leaned over and kissed Jeannette with passion.

"Gross! Old people are kissing," Zach said. "I'm eating over here!"

Jeannette pulled away from Mark to say, "You wait, Zach. The toast I am going to make at your wedding is going to be a doozy! Don't call me old again, young man. You will lose your pool privileges."

"Huh, oh. Zach's in trouble," Tyler laughed.

The next morning, Jeannette was at *Windy City* at 7:30. The group from the night before was waiting for her.

David saw five people standing around the door to *Windy City*. He went into protection mode.

"Stay here, Jeannette. I will take care of this."

"David! Wait! I asked this group to see me today. Not this early, though."

"Are you sure? I can make them leave if you are uncomfortable," David offered.

"I am sure," Jeannette said as she exited the car. "Good morning! You all look bright-eyed this morning. Much better than last night. How were your rooms at the hotel?" Jeannette asked as she unlocked the door. "Good morning, Max. This group is with me."

Max tipped his hat and gave David a wave and made him relax.

"The hotel was wonderful! They treated us like we were famous or somehow special. And dinner was delicious! That's the first good meal we have had in two weeks! Thank you, Jeannette, so very much," Karen gushed.

"You are welcome. Let's go right to the sound booth."

"You are going to record us? You?" Johnny asked with a look of disbelief.

"Of course. I know how all the equipment works. I used to produce music before I became the CEO. I need to hear what you sound like in a controlled area. You sounded pretty good on the street, but this is where we know for sure. Here we are. Go ahead and get set up while I get the equipment warmed up. Then put the headsets on."

The group worked quickly and was set up in five minutes. Jeannette pointed at them to start. After the song finished, Jeannette pushed a button and asked if they had another song prepared, a slow one. They had just played an up-tempo tune, and it was good. *"Now, what do they sound like with a slow song?"* Jeannette thought. The group played their favorite slow song, *"The moon is on the rise."*

"Okay, everyone come in the booth with me and have a listen to hear what you sound like," Jeannette instructed. After both songs were listened to intently, she asked, "How do you think you sound?"

They looked back and forth at each other. Finally, Johnny said, "We think our music sounds good."

"It does sound pretty good, but I would like to make a suggestion. It needs a tweak in the chorus. Karen, sing harmony. Start where the chorus has a tiny break. Let me show you what I am talking about." Jeannette got her guitar from the closet. She played and sang the chorus her way. "What do you think about that tweak?"

"I like it," Karen said. The rest of the group all nodded in agreement.

"Great! Let's try it, quickly."

Of course, Jeannette got it on tape. "Okay, pack up your gear and come have a listen." After the new recording of the song was concluded she asked, "Thoughts?"

"Oh, I agree with your tweaking! It felt better doing it that way." Johnny declared.

"Good. Sometimes that's all it takes to make the difference from the bottom of the charts to number one. Let's listen to the new recording," Jeannette suggested. Everyone went silent.

Jeannette applauded the group then asked, "What did you think?"

"That was so much better! It felt better to play and sing doing it your way. I think we did a good job," Karen said.

Jeannette looked beyond the group. Greg was coming down the hall to the booth. "Good morning, Greg. We were just finishing up. The equipment is all warmed up for you. Let me introduce this group of people. Starting from my left, this is Karen, Johnny, Shawn, A.J. and Seth. Group, this is Greg. He runs the sound booth and is our number one producer. You know who Clay and The Band is, don't you?"

"Of course! You would have to live under a rock not to know who they are," Johnny reiterated.

"Greg produces their albums and singles," Jeannette told them.

"And Jeannette tweaks them," Greg added with a chuckle.

"Well, we are done so you can have your booth back. Will you all please go to my office and wait for me while I talk to Greg? Thank you. Straight down the hall. It's a big door." Jeannette turned to Greg and said, "You have got to hear something." She cued the second recording to play. Greg listened. "Well? What is your opinion?"

"I want to know where you found this group. I like the new sound."

"I was hoping you would say that. I am going to sign this group. I found them on the street last night in front of *My City*. We were having dinner last night, and there was a disturbance. Mark immediately got up to see what the problem was. He came back to the table and said they were trying to get to me, but the head waiter would not allow them to pass. I felt I should talk to these strangers, so I did. Mark went with me. I had them audition right there on the street. I liked their sound, so I put them up in a hotel, gave them five filet mignon dinners, and told them to come to see me in the morning."

"Why did you do that?"

"Because I know they are going to be famous, and they were broke. This group of young people drove from the state of Washington to see me in hopes of getting a contract. I could tell they were hungry. Bridgett had turned them away every day. Before you say anything, I know all of our contracts have already been filled for the year. I am going to make an executive decision, just this once, for one more contract."

"Jeannette, how are we going to find the time to get them in the booth?" Greg asked her.

"Let me worry about that. Uh, oh. I better see what all the loud talking is. Bridgett. Bridgett, they are with me. I told them to wait in my office."

"Oh! I apologize," Bridgett said to the group and left the room with Jeannette following.

"Bridgett, I should have told you about this group. I am so sorry."

"You know these guys? Because I have turned them away every day for several days. I told them all the contracts were filled."

"Yes, you are right, they are. You did the right thing. But this group was persistent enough to come to *My City* and try to talk to me last night. Long story short, I listened to them on the street and liked what I heard. I told them to come see me today. Will you please type a standard contract? I am making an exception to the rule today. And please call the photographer we usually use. Ask him if he can come right away. I want this signing on film."

"Yes, ma'am. I will have the contract done by the time the photographer gets here."

"I apologize for the mix up this morning. That was my fault," Jeannette said as she walked into her office and shut the door. "What did you think about being in a real recording studio?"

"It was so cool," Karen exclaimed.

"Do you think this is something you still want to do? This is what you want to pursue? Let me warn you it takes a lot of work, practice, and traveling. Who writes your songs?"

"A.J. and Karen," Johnny told Jeannette.

"Both of you are talented. Keep it up. Do you have a good support group? Do your family and friends encourage you?"

A.J. answered, "We all do, except Seth." Jeannette looked at him, and he hung his head. "His family is not sure this is right for him. We make sure he has support from all of us. His parents will not stop him from making music, but they don't encourage him with music."

"I, see." Jeannette's phone rang. It was Bridgett. "Okay, bring it in. Ladies and gentlemen, I am making an executive decision. I am going to sign one more contract. I have never done this before. I want to sign you. What do you say?"

For a second the group was stunned. Suddenly Johnny threw his arms in the air and yelled, "Yee-haw!" The remaining group started to cheer, hugged one another, and Karen shed tears of happiness.

Jeannette asked when the group settled down, "Is this a yes?"

"Yes! A thousand times, yes!" Johnny shouted.

"Great! Would you like an attorney to look over the contract before you sign? I want you to be comfortable with *Windy City*. It is a life-changing moment." They weren't sure what to do. Jeannette went on, "I will go over the contract line by line with you and make sure you understand it. If there is something you do not like, we will stop and discuss it, and if need be, we will change it. Is that acceptable?"

Ten minutes into the contract, Bridgett buzzed, "Jeannette, the photographer is here."

"Good. Send in the photographer, please."

Karen asked with surprise, "Photographer?"

"Absolutely!" Jeannette exclaimed. "This is a red-letter day! I want a picture of this signing to hang on my wall right next to your framed gold album. Okay, we have gone over everything in the contract. Do you accept this contract?"

"Give us a pen and show us where to write our names!" Johnny answered.

The photographer started flashing pictures. Some they posed for; some were action shots they didn't see coming.

When the photographer left, Jeannette explained, "I want you to go home and practice. How many songs do you have ready right now?"

"Six."

"That's a good start. You need to prepare six more so we can cut an album. We will also cut a single from one of the songs to get your name and pictures out to the public. It will be the 'hook' song, as we call it. It will be the featured song on your album. It makes the public want to buy your music. In a month to two months, you will come back and start the work on an album. What's the matter? Everyone looks worried." Jeannette asked, "This is a happy day!"

"Oh, we are ecstatic. But we have a big problem," Karen informed her.

Johnny took over, "We don't have any money, and the only gas in our van is what you gave us last night. It will not go far, and we have no food or any way to buy food."

"Say no more. I will call the hotel you stayed at and ask them for one more night. You need to have a good night's rest before you start your trek home." Jeannette opened a wall-safe, took $3,000.00 out, and handed it to Johnny. "This should cover your expenses on your way home. I consider this an investment. Please call the office when you get home and let us know you made it safely. If there is any money left, split it between the five of you. Don't scrimp on food or lodging because you want to keep some of the money. It is important to get the rest you need and food for fuel to write and play your songs. Stay healthy."

"We will," Karen promised.

"One more thing before you go. Are all of you twenty-one or older? Wonderful! I always seal the deal with a shot of good whiskey. From this day on we are *Full Steam Ahead*! Salute!" The deal was done. Jeannette always felt good when she could help a new group.

The group left Jeannette standing by Bridgett's desk. Jeannette told her, "That band is going all the way. They are going to be famous. This is going to be a great year, Bridgett. A very successful year."

Lesson: Listen to your intuition or your gut feeling. It is telling you something. Act on it. If you don't, it might be a missed opportunity.

12

As the year went on, *Windy City* was more in demand than ever since Clay, and The Band became big stars. The company was experiencing severe, growing pains. They were already using all the space in their building. Jeannette thought long and hard to come up with a plan that would satisfy the company's needs. She talked to her accountant, attorney, and Mark when she had come up with an idea. She needed to go to Oregon. Her plan involved Sean, Tia, Tyler, and Zach. She called for a family time dinner the following weekend keeping the reason quiet about the purpose.

As usual, Irma had a delicious meal ready when Mark and Jeannette arrived. There was no shortage of conversation during dinner. When everyone had eaten, it was time to get down to business. Jeannette decided it was time to unveil her plan.

Jeannette whispered to Irma, "I will help with clean up as soon as we are finished in the office."

Mark stood and tapped on his wine glass for attention.

"I know you are probably wondering why we called a family meeting. Let's adjourn to the office since this is business. Okay, is everyone comfortable? Jeannette, I believe the floor is yours."

Jeannette began, "I have something we need to discuss. What I have to propose is business-related. You have heard me say, many times: *Windy City* is getting too big for its britches. Our client base has more than tripled. It is difficult to find enough time in our two recording rooms for the clients we have, and Greg and Tom are overworked. For that matter, everyone is. So, I want to expand. By expand, I do not mean, tear out a wall and build into the street. First, I have enough room in the building to make a third sound room and booth, which I have already hired a contractor to start building on Monday. That will help. Then I want to branch out even more and open another *Windy City* in Clark City. The Pacific Northwest talent is untapped. We have clients who come from all over the U.S. or want to come, but a lot of them are starving artists with no money to get to Chicago and stay for an extended time trying to land a contract with us. I feel we are losing money by *not* having a studio here. I think it would help ease the growing pains we are experiencing."

"That sounds like a great idea, mom, but I don't see where we come in," Sean stated.

"I would like to use you, Sean, on the business end of the company to keep it operating as it should by coordinating sales and advertising, etc. at the Oregon branch. Tia, I would like you to be our attorney at the Oregon branch. Tyler, I would like you and Zach to design the new building. Of course, we would pay you two for the design. I do not want any of you to accept my offer without thinking it through completely. You are either joining me 100% or not at all. It is your choice. Eventually, we might build another office somewhere else. For now, we are looking at just this one — Tyler I can see the concern on your face. First, let me finish, and then we will address your concern. I want you to design it so there is a second floor with office space for new businesses in the building. One of which would be for you Tyler, and Zach to open an architecture company. It would be a complex of sort. We are assuming you want to open your own company? Your choice," Jeannette explained. "Tyler, you are up! What worries you?"

"What about you, Mark, and your restaurant? Are you staying in Chicago? Are you going to sell *My City*?" Tyler asked with concern.

Mark answered, "Good question, Tyler. We figured by the time the new building for *Windy City* is completed, I should have a manager I can trust to run *My City* for me. Your mother and I would go to Chicago once a month instead of every other week. We might keep the apartment in Chicago, but this house is our home. We figured it would take at least eighteen months, maybe two years for *Old West Windy City* to be built and up and running. We are also talking about building a new restaurant in Clark City, sharing the parking lot with *Old West Windy City*. That would be project number two for Tyler and Zach to design. Do you think you can handle both projects, son?"

"You bet!" Tyler and Zach answered at the same time.

"Please give it a lot of thought before you give us an answer? It's a big life-changing decision. My advice to all of you is do NOT share this information with your employers even if you do decide to do this. Most of all, do not share this plan with anyone outside our family. There will be ample time later to give your employers notice and tell anyone else you want. Before this is a done deal, we have to present our plan to the City Council and the County commissioners to have their stamp of approval. Okay. We are finished with that — new subject. Sean and Tia, we have something to talk to you about," Jeannette said.

"It doesn't involve me," Tyler put in, "So I am out of here."

"I'm gone," Zach said.

"Mom, if this is about how long we have been here . . ." Sean began.

"Sean that is not what I want to discuss. I love that you and Tia are here. It is nice to come home and have someone here to greet us," Jeannette assured them. "You can stay as long as you want, you should know that."

"Now, the reason we wanted to talk to you. We know you and Tia are going to want to have your own place for your little family. What we are proposing is having a house built at the north end of the five acres. You would be close by, but not too close. The money you have been saving for a house would start the house, and I would take over the rest of the cost. The house would be all yours. We can have a one-acre parcel re-plated and transferred into your name so it would be all yours. I don't need all of the five acres on that side of the estate. There is plenty more property. The land already has a yard. It is not necessary to answer right now. I realize what we are proposing is another big step in your life. Sleep on it, talk about it, and we will talk about it again before Mark, and I go back to Chicago. We have given you a lot for you to discuss. If you are still on the fence about our proposal when we have to leave, we won't push, okay? Take all the time you need to make these life-changing decisions."

Tia was wide-eyed. "This IS a lot to take in! A job, a house, what next? Sean, is this real? I was going to ask if we could set up a nursery and change our bedroom to the basement. It would give us more room for our little June bug. A pretty small request after hearing your proposal."

"Absolutely! Do you agree, Mark?" Jeannette asked.

"It only makes sense. I agree."

"Thank you! Sean let's start moving things right now!" Tia suggested.

"Whoa, woman. You are eight months pregnant. You are NOT moving anything except maybe baby clothes. We will ask Tyler for some help. We could ask Zach, and he would probably help if we offered to feed him," Sean suggested.

"Great idea!" Tia cheered. They left to ask Tyler if he would help them start moving.

"Mark, I think we have made them happy. This makes up for all those years my boys didn't have anything. Sean and Tyler didn't know what it was like to have a yard until we moved to this house. I want to make sure our grandchildren have a yard and are able to come to grandma and grandpa's house whenever they want," Jeannette wished.

"Honey, you are going to be a wonderful grandma. It won't be long either," Mark reminded her.

A loud yell made them snap their necks toward the hallway. Mark and Jeannette ran down the hall to find Tia standing in a puddle of fluid. Tia had a look of complete terror.

"Jeannette, is that my water that broke? What's happening?" Tia asked in a panic.

"It is alright, sweetheart. Don't be afraid. Yes, your water broke. Do you have a bag ready to go? Good. Sean, call the doctor and tell him what happened, and that we are taking Tia to the hospital right now! Tyler! Come here! Irma, we need you!" Jeannette yelled.

"What's all the racket?" Tyler asked, coming out of his room.

"Miss Jeannette! What is it?" Irma asked.

"Tyler, get my car. The keys are by the door. We are taking Tia to the hospital. Irma, I am sorry to leave this mess with you to clean up, but we need to leave. Tia's water broke. We are going to the hospital. Sean grab her bag and several towels. Let's go!" Jeannette ordered.

"Ouch!" Tia yelled. "Oh, that hurts!"

"You are having a contraction. Sean note the time. We need to know how far apart the contractions are. Something tells me this little boy is not going to wait very long to make his appearance. Thank you, Tyler. Sean, give him your keys so he can drive your car to the hospital. Did you have the car seat installed, Sean? Good. We are ready," Jeannette said then looked at Mark behind the wheel shaking like a leaf. "Are you going to be able to drive?"

Mark pulled away from the house quickly and onto the road leading to the hospital. He then said, "Believe me, I need to drive! I have no idea what to do! Thank God you are here!"

Tia yelled in pain again and Mark jumped. Jeannette questioned, "How long was that Sean?"

"Three minutes, I think," Sean said with fear in his voice.

"Honey, everything is going to be fine. Keep holding her hand. She needs to feel the support. We will be at the hospital in less than five minutes. Have you picked out any boy names Tia?" Jeannette asked, trying to get her mind focused on something other than a contraction.

"Yes. If it is a boy, his name will be Jeremy. I have always liked that name. Jeremy Robert to be exact. Oh! Here comes another one!" Tia screamed, and Mark jumped like he was shot.

"Hang on, honey. We are pulling into the hospital right now. Sean run in and tell them we need a wheelchair. I will help Tia out of the car," Jeannette instructed. "Okay, Tia, easy now. Swing your legs out of the car. That's it. Here comes a nurse with a wheelchair. Can you stand up?"

"No! Another contraction!"

"Don't hold your breath, pant like a dog. Sounds stupid, but it will help. Good. Let's get you in the wheelchair before another one hits. The nurse and Sean will take care of you. I will be in the waiting room unless you need me!" Jeannette yelled as Tia was whisked off. She got in the car with Mark. He was slumped over the wheel, hugging it tightly.

"Mark? Mark, are you alive? We need to park the car and go to the waiting room. Honey?"

Mark slowly turned his head toward Jeannette. He looked like he had been drug through knotholes. He swallowed hard and said, "It's a good thing I didn't have children. I would not have lived through it, and it's a good thing you are bossy. Nobody knew what to do."

Jeannette started to laugh and said, "You and the boys are all men. Of course, you wouldn't know what to do. Scoot over, Sweetheart. You have been traumatized. Let me park the car. Then we will go in together."

Tyler ran up to Mark's window and knocked scaring Mark half to death. "What's happening?" He asked with a smile a mile wide.

Mark rolled down his window and snapped, "I am having a heart attack thanks to you scaring me! Good lord!" Mark shouted and made Tyler laugh.

Jeannette couldn't help but laugh. Mark was a mess.

Jeannette answered Tyler, "A nurse just took Tia in. Sean is with her. Would you do us a favor? Park this car then you can meet us in the waiting room. I don't think Mark is capable of driving one more foot. Before you leave, I need Tia's bag. Thanks."

Mark leaned on Jeannette as they walked through the emergency entrance. Tyler joined them before they reached the waiting room. She helped get Mark settled with a cup of tea when Sean came sprinting around the corner.

"Mom, Tia wants you with her!" Sean gulped.

"On my way. Mark, I am going in with Tia. Tyler is here with you," Jeannette told him and kissed him on the top of his head.

She hurried to Tia's side. "I am right here Sweetie," she said in a soothing voice. "Nurse, is the doctor here?" Jeannette asked.

"Yes. Dr. Chris just checked her. She is almost ready. She is dilated to nine. It won't be much longer. Is this her first? She is going to deliver quickly. Normally with the first, it takes quite a while. She is fortunate."

"Did you hear that? You and Sean are going to be parents very soon! You can do this. So, you are going to name your son Jeremy Robert? That is very nice. I like it," Jeannette said.

Sean added, "If it is a girl we decided on, Marcy Jeannette."

Jeannette's head popped up. "My name? Oh, honey. My name? The doctor didn't tell you what Tia was having?"

"No. We wanted to be surprised," Sean informed his mom.

"You will not need the girl's name. Jeremy will be here shortly," Jeannette said, smiling at her son.

"Oh! I need to push!" Tia screamed.

"Don't! Not yet! Pant. Sean, get the nurse. Tell her she needs to push! They will send the doctor right in. Until he gets here, you cannot push. Focus on me and pant through the urge. That's it."

Dr. Chris rushed in, putting on gloves.

"Well, little miss, you think you are ready to meet your little one? You are right! We have a crown. Nurse, are you ready? Do you need to push? Okay, Tia. Give me a big push. Good. Relax. Now this next push, you are going to push the head all the way out. Ready? Push! Hard! Push! Push! Push! We have the head. Dad, you should see this." Sean stepped to Dr. Chris and saw for the first time his son's face. He was stunned.

"Here we go, Tia. Huge push! Keep pushing! Okay, relax. This next push will be it. Ready? Okay, push! Keep pushing! Don't stop! Don't stop!" Tia heard a big gush of water and felt relief. "It's a boy! Dad, would you like to cut the cord?"

Sean looked at Jeannette, not knowing if he should say yes. She gave him a nod. He took the scissors and cut as the doctor instructed. Little Jeremy Robert laid on Tia's chest. The new parents had tears of joy and pride streaming down their faces. Jeannette slipped out to tell Mark and Tyler the news.

Mark had his head down with his arms resting on his knees. Tyler was playing a game on his phone and did not notice Jeannette enter the room. She sat by Mark and put her hand on his back.

"Mark," she said quietly. "We are grandparents. Tyler, you are an uncle. Did you boys hear me? Tia had the baby. It is a little boy. His name is Jeremy Robert."

Tyler looked up. Mark said, "What? She had the baby? I am a grandpa? Well hot damn," Mark said quietly in shock.

"I'm an uncle! It's a boy! I can teach him things! How to ride a bike, how to annoy his parents, talk to him about girls," Tyler planned.

"You need to cool your jets, young man. Sean will teach him most of those things. We will give them about ten minutes to get things cleaned up and then we can see the little guy. When I left the room, he was screaming at the top of his lungs," Jeannette reported.

"We can see him?" Mark asked.

"Of course! You can even hold him."

Mark stopped in his tracks and said, "Oh, I don't think I should. I have never held a baby. I might drop him or break him."

Jeannette laughed. "You won't break him. Babies are stronger than you think. I will be right there helping you. Don't be scared."

Sean was holding Jeremy as they walked into the room. Jeannette snapped a picture with her phone and sent it to Shannon and Ken titled great-grandparents.

Sean moved to his mom and asked, "Do you want to hold him, Grandma?"

"You have to ask? Give him to me! Tyler, look at your nephew. Isn't he sweet?" Tyler bent and kissed his little head. "Grandpa, do you want to hold him? You can do it. Support his head. There you go," Jeannette encouraged.

Mark had tears falling from his eyes. This tiny little person had stolen his heart. He looked at Jeannette with an expression on his face that told her everything she needed to know about how he felt. He loved Jeremy. He will protect him and be a wonderful grandpa.

"Could I have my baby back now?" Tia pleaded.

Mark put one foot in front of the other very carefully to ensure there was no possibility of tripping or dropping the perfect little bundle. Jeannette had taken a picture of him holding Jeremy for the first time without Mark noticing. It will be one for the baby book, for sure, she planned on putting together.

"I think we should leave the new family to get acquainted. Sean? I love you, Daddy. Thank you for making me a grandma. Tia, you did a great job. I love you." Sean gave Jeannette a big bear hug and cried into her shoulder with happiness.

Tyler hugged his big brother and said, "Congratulations! Your car is parked close to the entrance. Here are your keys." He kissed Tia on the cheek and, once more, kissed his nephew on the head before leaving.

As they sauntered out of the hospital, Mark told Jeannette, "He is so tiny but perfect! It is a miracle. When will she and Jeremy come home?"

"Most likely tomorrow. Did your mom call? I sent her a picture of Jeremy," Jeannette inquired.

"Holy crap! Mom! She called earlier, but I ignored," Mark dialed his mother. "Mom, or should I cut to the chase and call you G-g-ma? Short for great grandma. He is perfect. I held him! Yes, he is early, but he is healthy and beautiful. She wants to know if he has ten fingers and ten toes. I didn't count them! He did, didn't he?" Mark nervously asked Jeannette.

"Yes, Sweetheart, they are all accounted for. Tell her he weighed 7lbs. And his name is Jeremy Robert," Jeannette suggested to Mark.

Mark gushed with emotion about the new life for a few more minutes with his mother before hanging up.

"I never knew it was possible to love a brand-new little person so much! We just met, and I want to protect him from the world. This experience was made possible because Clay and Amy introduced us. I have to send him a bottle of the good stuff. So much has happened in such a short time! My whole world has changed for the better. My parents have changed! They are nice people now. I am so thankful I followed my heart. I love you, Grandma," Mark marveled.

Jeannette said, "That is too bad about Tia's mom and dad, not wanting to be around her. They are missing out on so much! I am going to send her parents a quick text to let them know they are grandparents."

"Are you sure about that?"

"Yes, I am," Jeannette said, and she did just that.

Their response? "Thank you for letting me know," *click*.

"*It is so sad*," Jeannette thought.

Lesson learned: Generosity warms the heart and can change another's heart.

A new life is a miraculous gift.

13

It was the holidays again. On the 10th of December Jeannette received a call from Rose. "Hello, Jeannette, this is Rose."

Jeannette answered with a vague emotion of pleasantry.

"Hello, Rose. Is someone dying, or did you just want to chat?"

"No one is dying. I wanted to reach out and ask you if you were interested in a family gathering for the holidays. Maybe dinner?" Rose asked meekly.

"I am not sure. What are you up to, Rose?"

"Before mom passes away, I thought we should all get together and mend fences," Rose suggested. "I am sure you have plans during Christmas, so maybe we could have dinner on the 20th? Before you answer, my other question is, could we have it at your house? It is the only place big enough to hold all the family members."

"Well, hum. I am not going to give you an answer right now. I need to talk to Mark and my boys first. I will call you back with a decision tomorrow. Thanks for calling, Rose. Good-bye."

Jeannette sat in her office staring into space, and thinking, "What is going on, God? Is there a lesson in this? I don't know if I can be around them or if I want them in my house. Although Rebecca is a great-grandmother and Leroy, Rose, and Beth have never met my boys or Mark. Tyler and Sean have never met their cousins. I don't know if I could face another hurtful situation from them. Or is this going to be healing? I have to talk to Mark." Jeannette dialed Mark with a shaking hand.

"Hello, my beautiful wife," Mark said.

"Hi, honey. I just got a strange call from my sister, Rose and I need to talk to you about it. Can we have lunch today? I want to talk to you in person," Jeannette asked.

"This sounds serious. Of course, we can have lunch. What time?" Mark asked.

"Can we make it early? How about in an hour at 11:30?"

"Okay. I will have the private room set for you and me," Mark agreed.

"See you then. I love you."

"Bridgett, will you call David and have him pick me up in forty-five minutes, please?"

Jeannette sat in a dazed state at the shock of Rose's request.

"Jeannette, David is here," Bridgett's voice sounded over the intercom.

Jeannette jumped about a foot off her chair. She fumbled with the phone but realized it was the intercom. She pushed the button and said, "Thank you. I will be right out."

David greeted Jeannette with his usual smile and cheery attitude, "Hello, Jeannette. Where would you like me to take you?"

"*My City*, please. I need to see Mark."

From behind the wheel, David asked, "You look troubled. Is there anything I can do?"

"Huh? Oh, sorry, David. I am arguing in my head over a proposal my sister asked me about this morning. A part of me says to do it. The other part says no way. I am hoping Mark can break the tie and help me come to a decision," Jeannette tried to explain.

"It sounds like quite a dilemma. I wish I could help, but I know you will make the right decision. Here we are."

"Thanks. Would you pick me up in an hour-and-a-half?" Jeannette asked as she exited the car.

"I will be here."

Mark met Jeannette at the door with a concerned look on his face.

"Honey, what's wrong? You are frowning. That is not normal. What did Rose say to you?"

"Can we sit down before I begin?" Jeannette asked.

"Of course, sweetheart. Our lunch is ready. I thought you might like a bowl of clam chowder and rolls — comfort food. It sounded like you needed it. By the looks of it, I was right. Now tell me what Rose proposed," Mark inquired.

"For the first time in a long time, I am shaking. Rose wants to have dinner with all my family at our house on the 20th. That means Beth, Leroy, Rose, their children, and Rebecca. She says she wants to mend fences before Rebecca dies. Rose asked if we would host it at our home. Of course, the estate is the only place large enough for everyone. I don't know if I want to do this. Am I being set up for one more way they can hurt me? Mark, what do you think?"

"I need a minute to think about this. Let's eat our soup," Mark suggested.

They ate in silence. When Mark and Jeannette finished lunch, they sipped a glass of wine.

Jeannette began, "Well? What are your feelings about this dinner?"

"To begin with, I have never met your family and only know about them from your stories. They sound much worse than my family. But since Warren died, maybe they have mellowed? Maybe Rebecca has mellowed? Perhaps they do want to mend fences? You told me you forgave Warren, and maybe it is time you do the same with the rest of the bunch?" Mark suggested.

"I do promote forgiveness, don't I? And I have held on to this pain for a long time. It is not hate that I feel toward my family. It is hurtful and unacceptance. Since I was seven years old, I have felt like I did not belong in that family. Rose is a lot younger, and she was not around when I used my intuition. I used to rock her to sleep at night. My parents let her scream and it kept the family awake. I would sneak in and get her and sing to her until she fell asleep. I digress. I pushed my intuition away as much as possible, and Rose probably isn't sure she believes the stories of my '*knowing*' or if anyone has told her about them. I was born this way! I couldn't help it! I am not the devil! Oh, Lord. Listen to me. Just talking about this has freaked me out. I know this is something I should face, I need to face, but I don't want to. Do you think we should say yes?"

"Sweetheart, you are not the devil. In my opinion, you were born perfect. I think you have already decided to tell Rose, yes. Deep within you, your little voice is telling you to try one more time. Show our family to your family. Let them see what a real family is. Maybe this will change their hearts? I will be by your side, and so will Tyler, Zach, Sean, and Tia. You have support," Mark told her gently.

"I know you are right, but I am wrestling with it," Jeannette told him. They sat quietly and finished a glass of wine. "Mark, I am going to call the boys. I will tell them what Rose proposed and see what their reaction is. I am also going to tell them you and I agree to accept. Is that correct?"

"Yes. What day do you want to fly to Oregon?"

"How about on the 17th? I am going to have to cook, so I need the time to go to the grocery store and prepare. But let's spend Christmas in Chicago. We can fly our children and grandchild here. I might need to put distance between my family and me depending on how dinner goes. Does that sound like a plan?" Jeannette asked.

"Yes. I will mark myself off on the calendar," Mark told Jeannette.

"Thanks, honey. I love you. I am stronger with you beside me."

Sitting at her desk, Jeannette made a conference call with the boys. "Hello, boys."

"Hi, Mom," Tyler said.

"Hi, Mom. What's up?" Sean asked.

"Well, I got a call from your aunt Rose this morning."

"Who died?" Sean questioned. "That's the only time she calls."

Jeannette giggled. "I asked her the same question. Nobody died, this time. She wants to get my family, meaning my siblings and Rebecca, together for dinner on the 20th at our home. Of course, that includes you guys because you are part of me. Your cousins will be there that you have not met. She said we needed to mend fences before Rebecca dies. I am not saying Rebecca is dying. She's just old. What do you think?"

"I say screw them!" Sean said with his voice raised.

"Oh, Mom. I don't know if this is a good idea. They have always treated you so awfully. Do you really want to do this?" Tyler asked. "I am not sure I can be nice to them."

"Well, Mark and I have talked about it. We think we should give them one more chance to mend a fence or two. Besides, I want to show off my boys and my grandson. I want to show them what a family should be," Jeannette explained.

"You actually want to do this?" Sean asked with surprise in his voice.

"Let me put it this way: I don't want to, but I need to. I forgave my father. That was one thing. This gathering is to heal from the hurt I have endured over the years. If they really want to mend fences, I think we need to try. So? Are you two in?"

"I'm in, Mom," Tyler said reluctantly.

"I guess I am in, too. But if anyone gets out of hand, I am going to let your family know how I feel about them and throw them out!" Sean promised.

"Okay, Sean, cool your jets for now. I am going to call Rose back and tell her we will have dinner on the 20th at our home. Mark and I will fly to Oregon on the 17th so I can prepare. Also, we want to have Christmas in Chicago. Of course, we will get your plane tickets. I might need some distance between my other family and me. I guess I should ask, do both of you want to come to Chicago for Christmas?" Jeannette asked.

"I need to check with Tia before I say yes to Chicago. Jeremy would probably like the plane. I will let you know tonight or tomorrow," Sean told her.

Jeannette had put off calling Rose long enough. She bit the bullet and dialed.

"Hi, Rose, it's Jeannette. Our answer is yes. We want to host dinner at our home on the 20th."

"Oh, Jeannette, that is fantastic news! We do not plan on exchanging gifts, so don't get anyone anything. We want to come and enjoy dinner and visit, that's all," Rose instructed.

"That is fine with me. Why don't we have dinner about 3:00? Does that sound okay with you?" Jeannette asked.

"Three was the time I was thinking. We will each bring a side dish for dinner. I assume you will be making the main dish. Do you know what that will be?"

"I haven't given it much thought, but probably prime rib and turkey," Jeannette told her.

"That sounds good. Okay, dinner at your house on the 20th at 3:00. Remember, no presents."

"I will not forget. No presents. Goodbye, Rose."

The next call was to Mark. "Hello, Honey. I called Rose. We will have dinner at 3:00 on the 20th."

"Okay. Are you all right with this?" Mark asked Jeannette.

"My stomach is a little tight, but I am, for the most part. Maybe this time it will be better."

"It will be my love, because I will be with you," Mark encouraged.

Jeannette blew out a big breath of air and said, "Yes, you will. I am going to hang up now. I am in planning mode, and I need to call Irma and the boys. See you at home."

Sean and Tyler were Jeannette's next call. They did not sound pleased about seeing their aunts and uncle along with their cousins. But they supported Jeannette if she wanted to try one more time at getting along with her siblings and mother.

"Irma, this is Jeannette. I am going to host a dinner for my siblings, mother, nephews and nieces on December 20th at 3:00. Could I enlist your help with cooking? Of course, it will be extra pay for you. Oh, thank you, Irma. I planned on prime rib and turkey. The others are supposed to bring side dishes, but I want to have a couple ready just in case. Okay. We are ready. Goodbye."

December 16th came too fast for Jeannette. She wrestled back and forth about canceling dinner. She came up with several excuses, but she couldn't bring herself to do it. She had to face this. It is a 50/50 chance it will work out for the better.

Jeannette had a terrible time sleeping that night. She was too wound up, knowing she had to fly to Oregon in the morning. Suddenly at four a.m., she was hit with a strong urge to go to *My City*.

"Mark! Mark! Wake up! We have to go to *My City* right now!"

"Why? It's four in the morning!"

"I don't know why. But I know we have to right now! Come on!"

Mark quickly climbed out of bed and grabbed his clothes and asked her, "Is your intuition telling you something? Did we get a call? What's going on?"

"I don't know what it is, but I know we have to get there. Yes, it is a knowing," Jeannette insisted.

Mark drove as fast as he could to the restaurant. All looked fine at the front door. They drove around back, and there was a small amount of smoke coming from around the door in the alley. Mark jumped out of his car to unlock the door while Jeannette called the fire department. He grabbed a fire extinguisher and doused the flames. The fire department arrived in a couple of minutes. By the time they got there, Mark had the fire almost out.

The firemen rushed in with hoses ready. They located Mark and sent him outside and finished putting the fire out. Mark was coughing from the smoke, so they put an oxygen mask on him for a short time to help him breathe.

"Oh, my Lord, Mark! Are you okay?" Jeannette cried out, rushing to Mark. "What happened? Where was the fire at?"

Mark took off the mask and said, "The fire was in the storeroom. I almost had it put out when these guys got here. Thank God for your intuition! We could have lost the restaurant!"

"I was so scared you were going to get burnt! Oh, thank the lord, you are fine. This is the second time my intuition has been that strong. The other time was Robert's heart attack. I was so scared something was going to happen to you!" Jeannette said and broke down crying.

The fire-captain asked, "Sir is this your place of business?"

"Yes, my name is Mark."

"Hello, Mark. What kind of business is this?"

"It is My City Restaurant. Why?"

"For my report. It looks like the fire started in the storage room. I have an investigator in there right now looking to see how it got started. How did you know there was a fire? Were you in the area?" the captain asked.

"No, just an uncanny feeling something was wrong. A hunch," Mark told him then looked at Jeannette and smiled.

"Well, that hunch paid off! You caught it early. If the storage room were left burning, it would have burned into the kitchen and spread throughout from there. Thirty minutes longer, and the place would have been a total loss. You were lucky. Hey, Ayden! Did you find the source?"

"Yes, Captain, I did."

"Ayden, this is Mark. It is his restaurant. What did you find?"

Ayden gave them a report, "There were no signs of the fire being electrical or any accelerants, so that ruled out arson. I believe this is the culprit." Ayden held up a cigarette butt. "Mark, are your employees allowed to smoke in the storeroom?"

"No! They know they have to go out here in the alley to smoke on their break. You can see the tall ash can with sand in it by the door they use."

"Do you smoke, Mark?" The captain questioned.

"Absolutely not!" Mark answered.

"Well, it looks like the fire is out. We will be out of here in a few minutes," the captain said.

Mark shook his hand and turned to Jeannette. She held him tight in her arms. They both were shaking.

"My, God, Jeannette! Did you hear the captain? Thirty minutes more, and we would have lost everything. I am so thankful for you being born with a superpower. Let's see how much damage there is."

Mark and Jeannette looked around inside the storage room to assess the damage. Some of the supplies were lost and would take a couple of days to replace. Mark was going to have to hire a cleaning crew to come in and clean the entire kitchen and wash the smoke from the walls. The dining area was excellent. There did not look to be any smoke damage in that area at all.

"I have to contact the insurance company and get them out here ASAP so I can get things cleaned and replaced," Mark told Jeannette. He looked at her with sad eyes.

"I already know what you are going to say. You can't possibly go to Oregon. I understand, honey. Do you want me to stay in Chicago and help you? I can cancel dinner," Jeannette said with hope.

"Sweetheart, you helped me by listening to your intuition and saving *My City*. Now you need to go to Oregon. The boys, Tia, and Irma will have your back. Come on. I will take you back home, and I can grab some work clothes. We will be closed for at least two, probably three days. I have my work cut out for today."

"I am glad this happened while we were here and not in Oregon. We would have come home to a total loss. I will miss you. I will be back on the 21st. David can pick me up at the airport. You will have your hands full."

"I am so sorry. I can't be there for you. Call me when you get to Oregon. I love you." Mark left.

Sean was at the airport to pick up Jeannette and Mark, he thought. "Mom! Over here!"

"There's my boy." Jeannette gave him a big hug.

"Where's Mark? I thought he was coming with you," Sean questioned.

"He was. There was a fire at *My City* early this morning. I had one of my knowing's we had to go to the restaurant at four a.m. I woke Mark, and we raced there. Smoke was coming from the door in the alley. Mark ran inside and put most of the fire out with an extinguisher. I called the fire department, and they were there in just a few minutes. They put out the rest," Jeannette recounted the story.

"Oh, Mom! That's horrible! Was Mark, hurt?"

"No, he is fine. He was coughing from the smoke, but he is fine."

"What caused the fire? What part of the restaurant was it in?" Sean asked.

"The fire started and was contained in the storage room. The fire investigator found a cigarette butt at the origin of the fire. It was the cause. Arson was quickly ruled out. The fire Captain said we were lucky we discovered the fire when we did. Thirty minutes later, and *My City* would have been a total loss. Mark had to stay in Chicago. He has to call the insurance company and notify the employees not to come to work. He will have to close for at least two but probably three days to get a cleaning crew in to scrub the walls and the storeroom. Then he has to itemize what was lost and restock the storeroom."

"I am surprised you didn't stay in Chicago."

"I offered. Mark told me to come to Oregon, and he would take care of *My City*. He didn't want me to cancel dinner. I tried to cancel. I am flying back on the 21st. It's a good thing we planned to be in Chicago for Christmas," Jeannette said with a small smile. "How is my little Jeremy? Is he growing like a weed?"

"Yes, he is. He is so busy and so cute," Sean said, beaming with pride. "How is *Windy City*?"

"Busy, very busy. I think we are going to have the most profitable year yet. I am so glad to be home! I wish Mark were here," Jeannette said. "Irma! I'm home!"

"Oh, Jeannette I am always happy to see you! Where is Mark?"

"Well, that is a story for dinner. Is Tyler and Zach here?"

"I heard my name! Hi, Mom! Where's Mark?" Tyler said, coming around the corner.

Zach was directly behind Tyler, "Hi! Thank God you are home! Now we can eat dinner!"

"Thanks, Zach, it's nice to see you too," Jeannette said with a chuckle. "Let's help Irma get dinner on the table, and I will tell everyone why Mark isn't here. But first I need Jeremy kisses. Where are you? Jeremy? There you are! I see you!" Jeannette picked Jeremy up and kissed him all over his face. Jeremy wiggled, squirmed, and giggled.

"Hi, Mom," Tia said, blowing a stray hair out of her eyes.

"Tia! Sweetheart, how are you? You look a little tired," Jeannette observed.

"That little guy wears me out! He never stops."

"His daddy was a busy one, too. Let's sit down for dinner, and I will tell all of you why Mark isn't here."

Jeannette repeated the story of events that took place just before she left Chicago. At the end of her story, Irma gasped.

"Oh, no! Was Mark burned?" Irma asked with horror in her voice.

"No. Mark is fine. He had a little smoke inhalation, but a fireman gave him oxygen at the scene. Health-wise Mark is excellent but upset that one of his employees started the fire, unknowingly. Somehow, he is going to flush him or her out who ever decided to have a smoke in the storeroom. Then Mark will fire that person. But first, he has to deal with the insurance, clean-up, and restocking before he can open again," Jeannette explained.

"Boy, I'm glad I am not the one who did it," Tyler spoke up. "Mark is going to tear him or her a new one! I don't blame him. Mom, your knowing paid off, again."

"Yes, my superpower was in full force, thank God. Let's call my sensing by its real name of intuition. I believe that is what made my father think I was the devil. He called me the devil once. Back in the time when I grew up, intuition was not considered to be 'God-given,' but something an evil person possessed. It was considered something that came from the devil. At seven years old, I innocently told my mother Leroy was hurt and he needed help. My mother and her friend freaked out. They rushed outside to find Leroy. But he wasn't anywhere they could see or hear. I can remember the look on Rebecca's face when she looked at me. It was a look of horror, fright, unbelieving, and questioning all rolled up in one expression. Her friend had the same look on her face. She asked me if I heard him. I told her no; I just knew he was hurt. It took a few minutes before they heard Leroy crying and being escorted across the acreage at the farm by a teenage boy. I was right. He hurt his foot. From then on, I think Rebecca and Warren were afraid of me. I don't know of any other reason for them to treat me the way they did all those years," Jeannette reminisced.

"Mom, I am so sorry you had to grow up that way. I don't remember you telling this story to us. We grew up just the opposite. You knew things. It was normal. We didn't broadcast it. You were our mom, and you had a superpower. I wish you had passed it down to us," Sean responded to Jeannette.

"Well, son, in this day and age it is accepted. It's a new age. I grew up in the 1950s and '60s. Compared to today, it was the Stone Age. My father considered himself a staunch pillar of the church, and to have this gift, it was evil. He tried to hide it from everyone. He believed the church might kick us out and label our family as 'antichrist believers' or something worse. That's the only thing I could come up with, and of course, this is only my opinion."

Zach broke the moment of silence, "Wow! I know a superhero! How cool is that?"

Everyone broke the awkward silence with laughter.

"Thank you, Zach. I needed a laugh. Now that I have told everyone this, do you look at me differently?"

"Jeannette, I always knew there was something special about you," Irma said. "I don't see you as a freak, and you are indeed the furthest thing from the devil I know of. Boys, to have a gift like that is a heavy burden. It seems like it would be a cool thing to have, but I am sure there are times Jeannette wished she didn't have it. But today she and Mark are very fortunate she does possess it. I, for one, thank God she does."

"Right now, I am so thankful for having the gift of intuition. You are right, Irma. It can be a heavy burden," Jeannette agreed. "If I could go back in time, I think I would tell myself to shut up and not tell mom about Leroy. I might have saved myself a lot of unhappiness. But then again, there was a plan afoot I didn't know about. God's plan. It shaped me into who I wanted to become. I spent a lot of years full of anger directed at my father. I finally gave it up. It took too much energy. Okay, enough of this talk. Is everyone prepared for dinner with my family?" Jeannette began to laugh.

Tia said, "Why are you laughing, Jeannette? How can you even think about having these people in your home?"

"Nervous energy. Like it or not, this is my family. I am going to try this one last time to get along with them. I expect all of you to be on your best behavior. Let's show them how a family should be. No hugging required. You don't have to greet them like you did Mark's parents. Be respectful and nice. I will handle the rest. Okay? If I start laughing, it is nervous energy. Oh, I already told you that. My nerves are hanging by a thread."

"Whatever you want, mom," Tia said with a concerned look on her face.

"Tia don't worry about these people. It will be okay. I promise — one more thing. They emphasized no gifts. You guys know me, I would probably have gotten a gift for everyone. But I agreed to no presents. I found it odd, Rose told me that two or three times. No worries. Irma, I am going to do the grocery shopping tomorrow so make me a list, please? Is everyone working tomorrow?" They all nodded, yes. "Does Jeremy go to daycare?"

"Yes," Sean answered.

"How about I pick him up after I get finished at the store and bring him home? Please call the daycare or tell them when you drop him off, his grandma will be picking him up. Otherwise, they might call the police on me," Jeannette told them.

"That could be funny," Zach said.

"No, not funny, Zach. Okay, I am exhausted. I have been up since four this morning. That is 2:00 a.m. Oregon time, I think. Irma, the dinner was delicious as usual. Thank you. I am going to bed. I love you all, goodnight.

Jeannette talked to Mark several times before she went grocery shopping. He was making headway at getting the fire disaster cleaned and sanitized. Two of the walls in the storeroom had to be torn down and rebuilt. The insurance company was being cooperative, which Mark was grateful for. The adjuster came to the restaurant the day of the fire. Mark had all the lists and prices of the cost of repairs, the cost of items that were destroyed, the cost of the cleanup crew, and the cost of lost business. The insurance agent paid him on the spot. Everyone is working as fast as possible so *My City* can open for business again.

Jeannette's issue with her family seemed small compared to what Mark is dealing with, and handling so well.

Jeannette thought as she shopped, "Mark has to be stressed to the max, but he sounds so calm when I talk to him. If he can undertake everything he is doing with grace, then I can too with a simple dinner for my family. They will surely be judging me. Yep! Bring 'em on!"

It was the morning of December 20th. Jeannette tossed and turned the night before, so she had a hint of dark circles under her eyes. Makeup took care of it.

"I am so thankful you are here today, Irma. With my stress level, I would mess up the prime rib for sure, I know it," Jeannette told Irma as they prepared the meat.

"You know I am always ready to help you. Why don't you have a glass of wine to quiet your nerves? Should I set out wine glasses on the table?"

"No, thank you, Irma. They don't drink. But it is not going to stop me from having what I like with dinner. I will have a glass of wine, and Rebecca will stare me down. That's okay. It is not unusual. By the way, I think they will start arriving around 2:30. That gives us just the right amount of time for these two chunks of meat to cook. Thank God for double-ovens. The turkey is in the oven, so I am going to take a shower and change clothes."

"Jeannette, remember we are here for you. You are not alone," Irma said. Jeannette reached out and hugged Irma.

At 2:30 on the dot, the first car pulled in. It was Leroy and his family. Jeannette met him at the door.

"Hello, Leroy. Did you have any trouble finding my home?" Jeannette inquired.

"No. I have GPS in my car. So, this is your castle."

"It's not a castle. It is my home. It's significant because my family keeps growing and I need the room," Jeannette told Leroy. "Please, come in. I will take your coats. It is warm by the fireplace. Sean, will you show your Uncle Leroy where we keep the fireplace? By the way, this is your Uncle Leroy. Thank you. Rose is here."

"Hi. We made it. Thank God for GPS! Come on, Mom. Let's go inside. I think Jeannette has a fire going. It will warm you right up."

"Auntie! We finally get to have dinner with you!" Laiklyn yelled. "We brought mashed potatoes and a chocolate cake for dessert!"

"That's my pretty girl! Merry Christmas! Laiklyn you are more beautiful than the last time I saw you, and taller! It has to be the chocolate cake that makes you lovely," Jeannette teased Laiklyn.

"Auntie, you are silly," Laiklyn said with a big smile and hugged Jeannette.

"Laiklyn, I think it is time you met Sean, Tyler, Tia, and Zach."

"Are those all your kids?" Laiklyn asked.

Jeannette laughed then said, "Sean and Tyler are my boys. Zach is my adopted son, and Tia is married to Sean. They have this cute little guy. His name is Jeremy. I am a grandma. That makes him your second cousin." Laiklyn looked a little confused. "Don't think about it too hard. All you need to know is he is related to you. Why don't you go into the living room with everybody else? There's a beautiful fire burning, and you can get warm."

After hanging the coats in the closet, Jeannette joined the group by the fire. She began introductions.

"Help yourselves to the coffee, hot chocolate, and finger foods to get your appetites started. I want to introduce my children. My oldest son, Sean. He works for a company in Carson City. He oversees three states of sales representatives. Tia is married to Sean and is an attorney for a law office here in Clark City. Their little boy's name is Jeremy. My youngest son is Tyler. He will graduate at the end of this school year with a master's in architecture. My adopted son is Zach. He will also graduate this year with a master's in architecture. I didn't legally adopt Zach, but he is with us more than he is with his parents, so for the last six years, I have called him my son. He is Tyler's best friend. One more person I do not want to forget, Irma. She is my right hand in our home. She takes care of my house and anything I ask of her. She is also my friend. She is a fantastic cook. You will taste her prime rib in a little while. Mom, would you like a cup of coffee?"

"No, thank you. I thought we were going to eat dinner and leave?" Rebecca said to Rose.

"If that is what you want to do, then let's go into the dining room. Sit wherever you want at the table. I will help Irma serve the food. Sean, Tyler, Tia, and Zach, why don't you get to know your relatives while I help Irma?" Jeannette suggested.

Jeannette went straight to the wine in the kitchen. She said to Irma, "Do you think they would notice if I just put a straw in the bottle and drank it that way?" Both women laughed.

"Okay, I think we have everything on the table. There are pitchers of iced tea, water, and soda on the table if you do not want wine. Sean, will you carve the turkey, please, and Tyler would you carve the roast, please?"

"You allow your children to drink wine?" Rebecca gasped. "Are you all alcoholics?"

"No, of course not! Wine helps digestion. There is nothing wrong with having a glass of wine during a meal, and I am not embarrassed or ashamed of it at all."

"Maybe you should be!" Rebecca said, sounding appalled.

Sean started to stand to say something to Rebecca, but Jeannette grabbed his arm to stop him.

"Why don't we enjoy this nice meal and not talk about wine?" She whispered to Sean.

"Auntie. Aren't you going to say the blessing before we eat?" Laiklyn asked.

"I am going to give that job to you today. Would you please say a blessing for the food?" Jeannette asked.

"Okay. We have to hold hands. Now bow your heads. Dear Lord, please bless our food and make everyone get along? Amen."

"Thank you, Laiklyn that was a sweet prayer. Dig in, everyone," Jeannette announced.

Things were tense. Nobody knew what to say, except Jeremy. He was having a great time with the mashed potatoes and cooked carrots.

"What is Beth doing today?" Jeannette asked. She knew Beth didn't want to come today, especially since the gathering was at Jeannette's home.

Laiklyn spoke before anyone had a chance to respond, "She's at home. She didn't want to come. I told her it would be fun at Auntie's house," Laiklyn said with innocence and kept eating.

"That's okay. Thank you for inviting Beth anyway. Is everyone ready for dessert? Laiklyn brought a chocolate cake, and we have pumpkin or pecan pie. Tia, would you mind helping Irma and me? If everyone would like to go back to the living room, we can have dessert by the fire. Boys, will you please clear the table?"

"Boys clear the table?" Laiklyn asked before anyone left the table. "Grandma says that's for girls to do."

"Well, in the olden days that was true. When Sean and Tyler grew up, they helped me with cooking and clearing the table every day. Yep. They know how to cook and even iron. These days it is not just for girls to do all the housework. Since it takes both parents to earn an income, they should both share the work at home also. That is how I see it. I also do yard work like mowing the lawn, plant flowers, and pull weeds. What do you think about all this?"

"I think I agree with you, Auntie. Let's have some cake!" Laiklyn said with a big smile.

"Cake is coming up!" Jeannette told her.

Jeannette was right about Rebecca. She sat in judgment the entire afternoon. Jeannette kept a smile on her face, but it was getting harder as the day went on.

In the kitchen, Sean whispered to Jeannette, "I thought they wanted to mend fences? What is with these people? The only one that likes to talk is Laiklyn."

"I know, honey. It is tense. Let's get through the rest of the day, okay? Would you get my guitar out for me, please?"

While everyone was eating dessert, Jeannette decided to play some music to see if it would break the ice. It didn't.

"Auntie you play the guitar really good!" Laiklyn complimented.

"Thank you. Come here, and I will show you how to play a chord."

"You got your guitar out to show off? To make sure we knew you could play and that you have a big recording company?" Rebecca accused.

"No! Everything seems so tense I thought maybe some Christmas music would lighten things a bit. Guess I was wrong. Okay, I am going to ask you a question I have wanted to know the answer to since I was seven years old. I have intuition. Yes, intuition. I was BORN with it. Does that make me evil? Do you think I am evil, Mom? Warren convinced you of this, didn't he?"

"It is not from God! I don't know how you got it!" Rebecca shouted.

"Did Warren blame you for me having this gift?" Jeannette asked.

"Mom, I think we should go now," Rose said. "Jeannette, will you get our coats out please?"

Sean stepped forward and pointed a finger directly at Rebecca's face and said, "You, old woman, are horrible! I have stood back and watched you and Warren treat my mother disgracefully! You have pushed her out of your family since she was a child! I will not sit by and let you be mean to her in our home! I am glad I never got to know you! You are not the grandmother I wanted to know! One more thing, Tyler or I do not have my mom's gift of intuition, but I am proud of her because she does. If she didn't have the gift, Mark's restaurant would have burned down three days ago! By the way, Mark is her husband and my stepfather. He embraces her God-given intuition! Now, I want all of you to leave! You are not welcome here! Never come back!" Sean shouted with Tyler standing by his side.

"You are going to let him talk to me like that?" Rebecca asked Jeannette.

"Mom, he spoke the truth. He stood up for me. All those years I was growing up, never once did you stand up for me. You allowed dad to whip me or whatever he wanted to do for punishment, and you turned your back on me. He lied to me countless times, and you didn't say a word. You knew he was lying to me. Because of him, I was pegged as a liar and troublemaker by the teachers. I didn't see anyone stand up for you today. Could it be that they agree with Sean? That you have turned into a horrible old woman?" Jeannette said without emotion.

Rebecca slapped Jeannette hard across the face, and Sean caught her hand in mid-air before she could do it again. Jeannette did not make a move toward Rebecca. Jeannette was afraid if she hit her back, there would be no stopping her. Instead, she put her hand to her cheek, and tears welled in her eyes. The tears were partially from the sting, and the rest was from hurt feelings, again.

"I want to respond with a slap to your face, Rebecca. But I will not stoop to your level. Besides, I might not stop with one slap. If I read this room correctly, nobody would stop me," Jeannette said quietly.

"Get out!" Sean yelled.

"Gladly. Evil lives here," Rebecca said and grabbed her coat.

"Evil does not live here, evil is walking out of the door!" Sean yelled.

Tyler brought their coats from the closet and passed them out. He didn't say a word, only glared at Rebecca.

"Goodbye, Auntie. I liked eating with you," Laiklyn said and hugged Jeannette and kissed her red cheek.

"Thanks for coming munchkin and thank you for the kiss," Jeannette said.

Irma stood at the door and handed the dishes they brought back to them and the leftover chocolate cake to Laiklyn. She glared at each one as they retrieved their dish.

As Rebecca walked by Irma, Irma grabbed her arm and spun her around. She said, "You are despicable! You call yourself a Christian. God is going to judge you, harshly!"

Rebecca raised her hand as if she were going to strike Irma.

Tyler grabbed her arm and said, "Never again will you raise your hand to any one of my family! My mom is one hundred times a better person than you! I swear if you try to hit one more person, you will be picking yourself up off the floor! Get out!" Tyler shouted inches from Rebecca's face at the top of his lungs then took her by the shoulders and spun her around to face the door.

Jeannette watched them in the driveway from her living room window. She held a cold, wet rag on her cheek. They couldn't see her. She watched her family exchanging gifts in her driveway. Sean made a move toward the door, but Jeannette stopped him.

"Son, it's over. Thank you for having my back. I am done with them. It will take me a little time, but I will get over this. They are not going to hurt me again."

Sean bent down and hugged his mom with compassion. Tyler, Zach, Tia, and Irma joined in and made it a group hug. Jeremy gave grandma a big wet kiss on her cheek and patted her face.

Jeannette pulled back, and with tears streaming, she said, "Thank you. I am so proud of all of you. If you don't mind, I am going to wash my face and call Mark. Would you all please help Irma with the dishes?"

Irma made her way into the huddle, grabbed Jeannette, and held her tight. No words were needed; they were felt.

Jeannette felt better after talking to Mark. He was upset he could not be there for her. After her phone call, she joined the family in the living room for hot cocoa and wet kisses from Jeremy. Since her biological family left, the atmosphere in her home had lightened. She felt a heaviness while they were there.

"Mom, your guitar is still in here, why don't you play some Christmas songs for us?" Tyler suggested. He knew music would calm his mom and soothe her soul.

She began to play, and Jeremy joined in. He clapped, and he tried to sing along. Everyone laughed, which made him laugh more. Jeannette had to stop playing; she was laughing so hard.

"This young man is going to say goodnight. It is past his bedtime," Tia said. "Give Grandma kisses."

"Goodnight, sweet boy. I love you," Jeannette said and threw him kisses. Jeremy waved at her.

"It's been quite an eye-opener of a day, today," Zach said. "Are you sure you didn't get switched at birth, Mom? Those people are nothing like you. I am impressed with how you turned out."

"Thank you, Zach. Let's not talk about them anymore, okay? Let's eat some pie!" Jeannette suggested. "Is Irma still here? There you are. Are you headed home? The kids are all flying to Chicago in three days, so take some leftovers home for you and your hubby. Oh, I wanted to give you this card before I left for Chicago. Merry Christmas. Open it."

"Oh, Missy, it is a beautiful card," Irma said. She opened the card and saw five one-hundred-dollar bills and an extra paycheck.

"Irma, you are always ready to help whenever I call, and I appreciate you so much. We all do, and we want you to have a wonderful Christmas. Go wild. Do something you have wanted to do for a long time. Take a vacation. This is a gift for fun. We love you. Merry Christmas!" Jeannette's generous gift shocked Irma.

"I don't have a gift for you!" Irma said through tears. "I don't know how to thank you. This is too much."

"It is not too much. You are my gift, and you are very welcome. Tyler and Zach, would you mind driving Irma home? I am afraid she won't be able to see the road. One of you drive her car the other follow in my car. The keys are by the door."

"Come on, Irma. I'll drive your car," Zach said.

The door shut, and there was silence. Sean sat beside Jeannette, put his arm around her, and said, "A penny for your thoughts."

"Naw. I can't take your money. My thoughts aren't worth a red cent right now. Sean? Thanks for being a good son."

"I am a good son because that's how you raised me — not the way those people raised you. It took every ounce of strength in me not to slap Rebecca back after she hit you. I don't understand how you held yourself back from slapping the crap out of her. Your cheek is still red. Mom, you are so much better than they are, and they don't see it."

"It's okay. That slap was nothing compared to what I went through as a child. I knew if I started hitting Rebecca, I might not stop! Someday my family will realize I am a good person, but it will probably be too late. When Rose reached out, I hoped it was going to be better than it turned out. I had to try one last time. I think I will turn in early and watch a little TV before I go to sleep. Before I do, I almost forgot to give you the plane tickets. Here you are. I'll let you hand them out. I will be at the airport in the morning before you guys get up. So, I will say goodbye now, and I will see you for Christmas. Kiss Tia and Jeremy for me. Tell Tyler and Zach; I love them. I love you, too."

"Goodnight, Mom. Oh, I forgot to ask about *My City*. When is it opening?"

"Tomorrow. Mark will be working on the last things until late tonight. I hope he goes home to get some sleep before he opens. Mark has to go in early for a staff meeting. He is putting some new protocols in place, so something like this will not happen again."

"Get some sleep, Mom," Sean said. "You look tired."

14

Jeannette was happy to be back in Chicago. She had David take her straight to *My City*. She wanted to hold Mark. He was waiting for her at the head-waiters area.

"Oh, my love. You feel so good in my arms," Mark said in her ear. "Are you okay?"

"Yes, I think so. I had to try one last time. It was awful! When Rebecca slapped me across the face, I had to hold on to Sean. He wanted to slap her back. Then he threw everyone out! It was horrible, and yet, I was thankful he stood up for me," Jeannette cried into Mark's shoulder.

"It is all over. You never have to go through it again."

"Rose stressed no presents, but I saw them in the driveway exchanging gifts amongst themselves. They left me out, again."

"Sh-h-h, honey. You are back in Chicago again. They are not coming here. Dry your eyes and let me see your smile. There it is. Come with me and see how nice the repairs look. It's brand new again. One of the new systems I had installed is a security entrance. Every employee has a number they are assigned. They have to punch in that code to unlock the door. Then if something like this happens again, I can check to see who the last one to enter the room was," Mark explained with pride.

"That is a great system. Did you find out who the culprit was?" Jeannette asked.

"Yes. No one wanted to confess at first. I asked who smokes. Some hands went up. I excused the non-smokers. I told the group of smokers if someone didn't confess to smoking in the storeroom I was going to fire all of them. All eyes went to one person. I stared him down. He admitted to it, and then he tried giving me a stupid excuse about not wanting to go outside, it was too cold. I fired him on the spot. He was a dishwasher. I have already replaced him."

"You have done an excellent job with all of this. I am impressed, and a little turned on," Jeannette giggled at the look on Mark's face. It was priceless.

"I would love to do something about it, but we opened fifteen minutes ago. But if you come with me to my office, I will kiss you," Mark told Jeannette.

"I will race you to your office," Jeannette said and laughed at Mark's raised eyebrows. "Not really, I will walk quickly."

"You are in a rare mood today," Mark said. He took her into his office, and passionately kissed her. "Welcome home, my love."

"I would have rather stayed in Chicago and helped with the repairs. But after seeing them, you did fine by yourself. I really am impressed."

There was a knock at the door. Mark said, "Come in."

"I am sorry to interrupt, but there is someone here asking for you at table 25," A waitress informed Mark.

"Okay, I will be right out. I would like it if you stayed for a while."

"I planned on it. I am going to say hi to your chef," Jeannette said. In the kitchen, the pace had picked up considerably from thirty minutes ago. "Hi, Chef. Do you need a hand?"

"The aprons are over there. Dive in!" Chef said.

An hour went by, and Mark made it back to his office, but Jeannette was not there. He knew where to find her. In the kitchen. Mark stood across the countertop from her with a big smile.

"Chef, who is the recruit? Shall we keep her?" Mark asked.

"If you try to take her, this meat cleaver might have something to say about it! She is doing great, and I need her right now."

"Jeannette, do you mind helping Chef for a while? We have a packed house. There are people lined up to come in. Okay, I am going to leave you with Chef. I love you, Honey," Mark said and left.

"Bye!" Jeannette shouted.

She thought while dishing orders, "I needed to work with my hands to keep me occupied and busy. I'll bet Mark is going to be open on Christmas Eve to make up for being closed for four days. His manager can close that night. We will have a good Christmas now that the ugly is out of the way."

Three hours later, things started to slow down, giving the wait-staff time to prepare for the dinner rush. Mark walked into the kitchen and found Jeannette helping the dishwasher put dishes away.

"Sweetheart, what are you doing now? It is time for you to go home. I called David, and he will be here in fifteen minutes. Take your apron off and come with me," Mark instructed.

223

"Bye! Mark is kidnapping me, Chef. I will come back again sometime," Jeannette shouted over her shoulder.

Without looking up, Chef gave her a quick wave.

Mark took Jeannette to his office. Inside he said, "I need my hands on you. I have missed you so much." He crushed his mouth over hers.

"You make my knees weak! I wish we were home right now. I would show you how much I missed you. Hey, I just had a thought. Are you going to be open on Christmas Eve?"

"We are going to be open for lunch only and close at 3:00. I see a look in your eye that means trouble. What are you thinking?" Mark asked with caution.

"What would you think about having dinner for your staff and the staff at *Windy City* on Christmas Eve? I know it would be a big job and it is only a few days away. *Windy City* would foot the bill. It will be a good tax write-off. We can serve them for a change. They do everything for us all year long. I think Clay is going to be in town. I can give him a call to see if he wants to play for a while and make it a real party — that way the band can enjoy it also. Sean, Tia, Tyler, and Zach, I am sure, would help serve. Jeremy will entertain. Better yet, we could make it buffet style, and they can serve themselves. I can cook. What do you think?"

"That is going to be a lot of work, Jeannette."

"I know, but our staff does so much for us all year long, we can give a little back," Jeannette tried to convince Mark.

"I will make a deal with you. If Clay will come and play and if enough of my staff wants to have dinner, then I will say yes."

Jeannette squealed. "I am calling Clay right now." Mark could not hear what she was saying, but he could see the smile on her face. "He and The Band said yes! They will be in town on the 23rd. I had to promise him they could eat dinner. It is turning out to be a party! Now I have to call the kids and tell them I have volunteered them to help with a big dinner. It is going to be so much fun! Clay is going to blow the roof off this place!"

"I love seeing you this happy. You are like a little kid," Mark said, shaking his head. "I will start by asking the staff if they are interested. You know if they have a significant other, they will come too."

"Yep. So, we need to get a headcount, so I will know how many prime ribs to order," Jeannette started in planning mode. "I know it will cost quite a bit, but I have not used much of my expense account for the last several months, so I have built up quite a bit. I think prime rib, baked potatoes, salad, rolls, and green beans will make a good meal and relatively simple. You and the boys can carve the meat. We can have you guys set up in three places, so there won't be a line waiting to get their food. And . . ."

"Okay, okay take it down a notch. We need to talk to Chef about using his kitchen, and we need to see if both your staff and mine want to do this. This is at the last minute, and they might have plans," Mark warned her.

"I am calling Bridgett. Hi, it's Jeannette. Yes, I got back a few hours ago. I have been at *My City* helping out. I had a great idea, but I want you to talk to the staff or send each one an email, whatever, and ask them if they would like to have a Christmas dinner at *My City* on Christmas Eve. Mark and I will be serving and cooking. Clay and The Band are coming and will be playing. I need a headcount. Of course, if they have a significant other, they can bring them. It is our way of saying thank you for all your hard work this year. We are going to blow the roof off this place! I will need to know ASAP how many will be here. If you could get that started right away, that would be great. I will be in the office tomorrow. Thanks, Bridgett."

Mark talked to Chef while Jeannette was on the phone. To Mark's surprise, Chef gave the okay. But he said if it were going to be anyone other than Jeannette cooking, he would not agree. Mark's employees were interested also.

"Jeannette, are you sure you want to do this? Chef has agreed, and the staff wants the dinner. How about *Windy City* staff?" Mark asked.

"I am confident my staff will be all for it, especially since Clay and The Band will be here. It looks like there is going to be a party at *My City* on Christmas Eve! I will invite David and Raelene also. You can invite Skylar, Shannon and Ken, too!" Jeannette said, adding to her list.

"You are going to be exhausted," Mark warned.

"We all lay around on Christmas Day anyway. It is going to be so much fun. You will see." Jeannette told him. Her phone rang. "Hi, Bridgett. Everyone? Hooray! It's a party. Okay, tell them to plan on 6:30. Thanks, Bridgett. Bye. Mark! Every person on my staff will be here. I told them 6:30. Was that, okay?"

"Yes," Mark answered shaking his head. "You amaze me with the ideas that pop into your brain. Sweetheart, you better go home and start resting up for Christmas Eve. I love you."

"I love you, too. Oh! David is probably waiting for me outside. Bye, honey. See you at home!" Jeannette disappeared out the door.

At home, Jeannette began making lists and laid out a plan. She called her accountant and informed him about using her expense account to pay for the dinner.

Her accountant said, "That's a great idea. It will help your bottom line, too. I was going to give you a call about spending some money between now and January first. You have not used enough of your expense account. Frugal is good, but you have to spend money also for the tax breaks. I am glad to hear your happy voice. Let me know how much the bill is. I will make sure there is plenty of money in the account to cover it. Have fun!"

"It is Christmas Eve!" Jeannette said to Jeremy. He was sitting in his highchair, watching grandma make breakfast. "Tonight, is going to be so much fun! Isn't that right Jeremy?" Her excitement was contagious. Jeremy was laughing and clapping his hands.

Sean came into the kitchen and saw Jeremy and grandma having fun and laughing.

"What is all the racket going on in here?" He said with a big smile. Seeing daddy had Jeremy banging even louder on his tray with a spoon. "You two are having too much fun. Are you trying to wake everyone up?"

"Why not? We are excited about having a Christmas party tonight. See? Jeremy knows." Jeannette said, and Jeremy banged harder, kicking his feet and laughing.

"Okay, that's enough of that," Sean said and picked Jeremy up. "Let's let mommy sleep a little longer. You are looking forward to tonight, aren't you, mom?"

"Yes! You know how I love Christmas. The idea popped into my head, and it snowballed. Clay and Amy are in town. Clay and The Band will be playing tonight. It all fell together. Clay is playing for a New Year's Eve event here in Chicago, so he came to town early. I think they are looking forward to tonight. Who knows, I might get up and play with them if I don't forget my guitar. I need to put it on my list."

"I expect you to play with them tonight! Jeremy needs to see grandma jamming with Clay and The Band."

"Sean, I need to go into *Windy City* for an hour or two. I am sorry to leave you with this mess my partner in crime made. I will be back before lunch. I love you, boys." Jeannette kissed each one and swept out the door.

Mark had left before Jeannette, and he was already at *My City*. He expected the prime ribs to be delivered by 9:00 a.m. He also ordered pumpkin pies and apple pies for dessert. The bakery is sending those over at 10:00. Mark sat at his desk and began to think, *"My life has changed so much since I met Jeannette. I would never have volunteered my restaurant for something like this dinner tonight. I think I was getting a little stiff like my parents were for so many years, just not as bad as they were. Jeannette made me see what I had been missing all these years. If anyone can pull off this dinner tonight, it is Jeannette."* Mark jumped when he heard a knock on his office door.

"Yes? Come in."

"Did you order a bunch of pies? We have the bakery here wanting to drop them off," one of the kitchen staff asked.

"Yes, I did. I will be right there. We need to put the pies in the walk-in. They are for tonight's dinner," Mark told him. "Are you coming to dinner tonight?"

"Are you kidding? I wouldn't miss it! Free dinner, Clay and The Band, and you are serving us dinner. It's going to be fun!" The young man told Mark.

Mark chuckled as he walked with the young man to inspect the pies.

"These look good." Mark signed the invoice to accept the delivery. "Come on. I will help you get all of these in the walk-in."

"You are going to help me?" The young man asked with a surprised look on his face.

"Why wouldn't I?"

"Well, you are the boss, and I have never seen you do this before."

"I might not have done this lately, but I have experience with every job here. Way back in my early years, I started as a dishwasher in a little restaurant. I wanted to know this business inside and out because someday I planned to open a restaurant. I worked hard, and here I am today. That is probably more information than you wanted to know," Mark said with a smile. "My wife must be rubbing off on me."

"More information than I expected but interesting. I never thought of you to be a dishwasher. It is hard for me to imagine that. You are the boss."

"Hum. I might have to change some things and take a page out of Jeannette's book."

The young man looked puzzled. "Excuse me?"

"Sorry. I was thinking out loud. How do you see me as a boss? Are you afraid of me?" Mark asked, wanting an honest answer. "This is not a trick question, and I will not fire you for the reply. I want you to answer honestly."

"Well, I am not sure afraid is the word I would use. Respectfully nervous is more like it. You are not the type of person I would feel free to approach to carry on a conversation. I am not on the same level as you," the young man attempted to explain.

"Level?" Mark asked.

"Yes. You are way up here, and I am way down here. That's how I feel when I am around you."

"Oh. Thank you for telling me. Okay, it looks like we have managed to fit all the pies in here. Good job. By the way, what do you think of my wife? Do you see her as the boss's wife? Or is she someone you can approach and talk to and not be respectfully nervous with?" Mark asked. "This is not a trick question either. Answer me honestly."

"I know she is the boss's wife but at the same time I can easily talk to her without judgement or feeling I am on a lower level than she is. She is real and sincere. She's cool. Hey, man, thanks for the help," the young man said and gave Mark a wave as he went back to work.

"You are welcome!" Mark said with a raised voice. He said to himself, *"That is an eye-opener. Respectfully nervous. Hum."*

Last-minute Christmas shoppers were out in force with a look of panic on their faces. Only a few hours left to find that perfect gift.

Business slowed down by 2:00 at *My City*. When the last patrons left, Mark locked the door. Jeannette was in the kitchen prepping the prime ribs. Chef was sitting on a stool, watching her. Sean, Tyler, and Zach were wrapping potatoes in foil, getting them ready for the oven. Mark was arranging three carving stations. One for him, Sean and Tyler. Zach will be the runner, refilling everything. Tia and Jeremy will be in the kitchen with Jeannette.

Mark entered the kitchen and saw Jeannette had everything under control. He smiled, watching Chef on the stool, talking to Jeannette and laughing at Jeremy. The boys were teasing each other while they prepared the potatoes. Tia had the salad in the bowls and was ready to be served. As for Jeremy, Tia had him corralled in the highchair for now. He was enjoying the show. Mark felt warm inside. "This is family," he whispered.

"Hey, Mister! Yes, Mark, I am talking to you. Grab an apron and put the potatoes on the pans!" Jeannette told him.

"Yes, Ma'am! I am on it!"

"Oh, no! Mark, I forgot about dessert! What am I going to do? The pies!" Jeannette yelled, putting her hands on her face. She forgot she had seasoning from the prime rib on her hands. Now it was all over her face. Everyone burst out laughing.

"Honey! It's okay. I remembered them. They are in the walk-in — pumpkin and apple pies. You are a mess! Why don't you go wash up?" Mark suggested while laughing.

"It's a good thing I brought my makeup with me and a change of clothes. Okay. I will be right back." Jeannette laughed along with everyone.

At 5:30, Mark yelled, "One hour to go! Are we ready, team?"

"Yes, we are!" Zach yelled back.

"Okay. Everyone has changed clothes except me. Mark, could I use your office? There's more room in there," Jeannette asked. "Hey, you guys Clay and The Band should be here any minute. They will knock on the back door. Let them in."

"My office is always open to you, Baby. You guys keep an eye on those prime ribs. Your mother will have your hide if they burn," Mark warned, as he walked Jeannette out of the kitchen and scooped her up in his arms as soon as his office door shut.

"Simmer down, tiger. That's for later. I love you, but you will have to wait until this is over," Jeannette told him and gave him a passionate kiss.

People started arriving at 6:00. Clay and The Band were set up on the stage and ready to play. The boys were seating people as they arrived. Clay and Amy were in the kitchen, talking to Jeannette as she prepared for dinner.

"Sweetheart, the tables are full. I believe everyone is here. Clay, if you don't mind, we will have you play after dinner. For now, we will let the stereo play," Mark instructed.

"Sweetheart, before we go out in the dining room and start, how about we have a toast with the good stuff that I happened to bring along, with our team? Okay, everyone has a glass. You too Chef. Raise your glasses to this wonderful Christmas Eve. We are truly blessed to have our two staffs, friends, and family we love gathered together. May we all be filled with joy, thankfulness, and love in our hearts. Salute!" Jeannette shouted.

"Okay, Honey, come with me so we can welcome everyone." Mark and Jeannette walked onto the stage and took the microphone, holding hands. "Good evening *My City* and *Windy City*. We are so glad you came to dinner this evening. All of you work hard all year long for us, so we wanted to show you our appreciation by serving all of you dinner," Mark said as applause broke out.

Jeannette took the microphone, "I want to thank my staff for a beautiful and profitable year. You all worked very hard, and I am so thankful for my family. I should explain to all of you from *My City*, I call my team at *Windy City,* my family. We work together, help each other, and we care about each other. I love them all. And thank you to *My City* staff for always making me feel welcome. *Windy City* staff members, see Bridgett before you leave tonight."

Mark and Jeannette together, holding hands, said, "Let the party begin! Let's eat!"

The feeding frenzy began. There was laughter, talking, sounds of silverware on plates, and sounds of a happy holiday season throughout dinner. Mark did not stop smiling the whole time he was carving. He had a better time than he expected. When everyone had their plates full, Jeannette, Mark, Sean, Tyler, Tia, and Jeremy sat down with Clay and Amy to eat. The Band sat at a table on one side of them and at a table on the other side of them, Shannon, Ken and Skylar joined Chef for dinner.

Jeannette excused herself long enough to get the bottle of the good stuff she brought to propose a toast at their table, The Band's table and with Chef's table. She handed it to Mark to pour each one a shot. She took her glass and stepped to the microphone.

"Ladies and gentlemen. I want to propose a toast in a minute. But first, my sincere thanks goes out to every one of you for being in my life. I feel blessed, and I am sure Mark feels the same. Did you get enough to eat?" Applause broke out signaling yes. "I hope you found the dessert table. I hear a lot of moaning, and I am going to take that as a compliment. Raise your glass with me. May you all have a glorious, joyful, and blessed holiday season with many more to come. Salute!" They shouted together,

"Salute!" Jeremy tried to say it, but all he got out was a yell with his arms in the air.

Jeannette continued to announce, "We are going to clear the plates away, and then we will have some entertainment." She and her kitchen crew began clearing dishes but stopped. They looked around the room, and everyone was clearing their table and taking the dirty dishes to the kitchen.

"Mark, I didn't expect them to clean up the dishes. Why are they doing that?"

"Because they want to help you. It is their way of saying thank you to us for dinner. Sweetheart don't cry. They love you."

"This is the best Christmas present ever," Jeannette sobbed.

Clay and The Band took the stage. Clay addressed the crowd.

"Are you ready to get this party started? Here we go!"

The applause and cheering were deafening. After two songs Clay asked Jeannette to join them. She jumped up and grabbed her guitar. It is the first time Sean and Tyler got to see their mother play with Clay and The Band. They were cheering just as loud as everyone. Maybe louder. Clay, The Band, and Jeannette had so much fun on stage they played for an hour straight. It wasn't like work. It was fun. Clay and Jeannette, of course, got into a war of guitars. It went on for several minutes, back and forth, until Jeannette blew him away.

"Ladies and Gentlemen, it has been our honor being with you tonight," Clay said. "It is time to call it a night." The crowd started chanting, 'one more song!' "How can we say no to that? Let's slow things down. Hey, Pretty Lady, let's do the first song of yours." The song ended, and the applause began, again.

Jeannette took the microphone, "Goodnight and Merry Christmas! Be safe on your way home."

Instead of leaving, the crowd all filed into the kitchen to help clean. When the kitchen was back to normal, the *Windy City* staff pulled Jeannette aside.

Bridgett began, "Jeannette, we wanted to give you a little something for always being there when we need you." She handed Jeannette an envelope." We all chipped in. "*My City* stopped to watch.

She opened the envelope. There were tickets for the next six plays at the theatre Mark took her to when her arm was in a sling. She could not stop the tears. With Jeannette in the middle, they made one huge group hug. Jeannette whispered, "Thank you, family. I love you."

The party was over.

15

Five months later, Jeannette's family's lives were still non-stop and always on the go. It was Jeremy's first birthday, Tyler and Zach are scheduled to graduate in a month, and Mark is planning to open a new restaurant in Clark City. Jeannette is working on the new recording company she named *Old West Windy City* that is being built with a large parking lot that Mark's new restaurant and *Old West Windy City* will share. Thanks to the notoriety at the wedding, Skylar was inundated with new clients. She had to hire two more seamstresses to meet the demand.

Tyler designed Sean, Tia and Jeremy's new home before he started on the restaurant and recording company. The little family took Jeannette and Mark up on their offer for a one-acre plot. The house was finally finished after months of dealing with contractors. Moving in with a one-year-old running everywhere was, to say the least, hectic.

The estate was going to be full of adults plus a one-year-old. It is just the way Jeannette likes it.

She had arranged for Shannon, Ken and Skylar to come to Oregon to celebrate Jeremy's first birthday then stay to attend Tyler and Zach's graduation in Corvallis. Of course, they were staying at the estate. The day after graduation they would catch a plane in Corvallis to fly home to Chicago.

At Jeremy's birthday party everyone wore a party hat. Shannon shocked them all when she put one on making Jeremy laugh at her. It was just family and Zach in attendance. The little guy had a personal cake he dug into with both hands then attempted to put fistfuls of the sweet treat in his mouth. He had cake and frosting everywhere on him and the floor.

It was a new experience for Shannon. She kept trying to clean his hands. That was a battle she was not going to win. Ken finally told her to let him play. There was probably one-hundred pictures taken of the little cutie.

After the party died down, Jeremy was bathed and taken home for bedtime, Tyler asked Jeannette and Mark if he could have some time alone with them.

In the office, Tyler began, "What do you think of Tracy? Tia's bridesmaid. Did you like her?"

"I didn't get to visit with her very much. We were on the go the whole time she was here. What I observed, I thought she was nice. But I wasn't sure about her. I didn't get a real bead on her. How about you, Mark?" Jeannette asked.

"I feel the same way. Sean told me a little bit about her. He said he and Tia introduced her to you. Why are you asking us this, son?" Mark asked him with a slight frown.

"We have been dating since the wedding. I broke it off with the other girl. Zach doesn't mind Tracy so much. The reason I wanted to ask you about her is, I need to marry her," Tyler announced.

"What do you mean you NEED to marry her?" Jeannette knew the answer, but he was going to have to say it.

"Well, she...Uh. . . She's pregnant," Tyler said with nervous fear. The silence was deafening. "Mom, Mark, are you going to say anything?"

Very calmly Jeannette said, "Do you love her?"

"I think I do," Tyler answered.

"How does she feel about you?" Mark asked.

"She has told me she loves me," Tyler said with a shrug.

"Do you think Tracy would get pregnant on purpose to trap you into marrying her?" Jeannette asked point-blank.

"Mom! She's not that kind of girl!"

"When she went to brunch with us and found out who I was, I saw her attitude change. She was overly impressed with our house, too. My advice is not to ask her to marry you just yet. Please, honey, I am not saying she is a bad person, or that she is lying. Let me ask you this. Do you think about her every minute, have no appetite, can't sleep because you are thinking about her? Talk countless times on the phone every day? Do you think you have a relationship like Sean and Tia or Mark and me?"

Tyler sat with his head down in deep thought. He raised his head and said, "No."

"Did you use protection every time?" Mark asked.

"As far as I can remember, yes," Tyler answered.

"Are you positive she is pregnant?" Jeannette asked.

"She told me she was. I didn't think about her not telling the truth. She said since she was pregnant, we didn't need condoms anymore," Tyler confessed.

"Please tell me you didn't fall for that?" Mark said with urgency.

"We haven't had sex since she said that. I was getting ready to come here, and she needed to study for some tests. Besides that, I was pretty freaked out!" Tyler responded.

"Thank God! Listen. You MUST use a condom IF you have sex with her again. Do not let her talk you into not using protection! It is possible, since she said that, she may not be pregnant and is trying to get that way. After graduation, you will go your separate ways, so she has to act fast if she is not pregnant. Son, women will say and do a lot of things to get what or who they want. I am not trying to make you cynical toward women. All women are not like your mother. I want you to think before you act. If you have sex with her again, make sure you use protection!" Mark instructed sternly.

"Honey, did she tell her parents yet?" Jeannette asked.

"I don't know for sure, but I don't think so."

"Okay. We need to get to the truth. Let me think about it. In the meantime, do not say anything about this to anyone until we know for sure, okay?" Jeannette instructed. Tyler nodded and left the room. She looked at Mark and said, "How about you and I take a walk, maybe in the direction of Sean and Tia's house? I will give them a call and see if we can stop by for just a minute."

Before Jeannette and Mark left the house to journey across several acres to visit with Sean and Tia, Shannon and Ken excused themselves to turn in. They were exhausted from the days' activities.

"Hi. I hope it wasn't too late to stop by. That is why I called first. I know you were just at our house, but we wanted to ask you about your friend Tracy. How well do you know her? The reason I ask, Tyler has been seeing her for a while, and we only met her the one time. So, what do you think of her?" Jeannette questioned.

"I have known her for a couple of years," Tia began. "She is nice. Although, Tracy has made a few comments about people that made me uncomfortable. For instance, if she thought someone was poor, she looked down her nose at them and made snide comments. Tracy's smart and comes from a professional family but had to get student loans to pay for school. If I remember right, she was not happy about it. She expected her parents to pay for college. I did not pry. It was not any of my business."

Sean added, "They are a cute couple, but I have not seen that spark that two people get when they are a good match. I think Tracy keeps the relationship going. You know how Tyler is. He is laid back and will go along with whatever she wants. I am not sure if she is good for my little brother. Sorry, Tia."

"Do not be sorry, honey. You tell it as you see it. I take no offense. That's one of the reasons I love you. Your honesty," Tia said.

"Well, thank you for your opinions. My bed is calling me. That sweet boy wears me out! I love you kids. Bye," Jeannette and Mark said and exited the house.

As they strolled home, hand in hand, they talked about a strategy to get the truth about the pregnancy. Jeannette and Mark will not have Tracy investigated like Jeannette was. That was not a pleasant experience. They needed HER, to be honest. By the time they arrived home, a plan had hatched to take place at graduation. Nothing mean or underhanded. Just a kind of truthful confrontation.

Tyler went back to school to take two more finals. Then he would be done. All that would be left is graduation. All week Tracy did her best to seduce Tyler. He always made some excuse. Packing his things was a good excuse he used a lot because it was true. It upset her when she failed. Tyler watched her stomp out of his apartment like a spoiled child.

The family arrived Friday afternoon in Corvallis for graduation on Saturday. Mark made reservations at a nice restaurant not far from campus for dinner. Tyler did not invite Tracy. He didn't even tell her about it. During dinner, Tyler received a text from her asking where he was. He told her he was having dinner with his family. She asked where. He did not respond.

Tyler had everything in his apartment packed and ready to leave as soon as the graduation ceremony was over. The moving trailer Jeannette rented was loaded and hitched to his car, so Friday night he spent the night at the hotel with his family. Mark requested a cot for their room. It was Tyler's bed for the night. Tyler knew Tracy would be calling and texting all night, so he turned off his phone.

They had breakfast in the hotel restaurant early the next morning and then accompanied Tyler to the campus. Tracy immediately spotted them when they arrived.

"Tyler! I tried calling you all night! Where were you? I would have had dinner with you, but I did not know where you were!" Tracy scolded.

"My phone died, and I forgot to plug it in. Oh, well. We both made it here," Tyler said with no care.

"Tyler we need to talk about our situation," Tracy said in hushed tones.

"Hello, Tracy! Good to see you! Today is a big day. It signifies you are an adult and ready to make your way in the world. It is the beginning of the biggest adventure of your life. What you do now carries a lot of weight in the direction where your life is going from here. Are your parents coming? I want to meet them." Jeannette commented.

Tracy's face got a little pale. She answered, "Yes. They are already here. I think they went for a walk around the campus one last time. I will tell them you want to meet them. Tyler, we need to take our place. I am sure I will see you after the ceremony, Jeannette."

Mark and Jeannette watched them walk away, all the while Tracy was chewing out Tyler for leaving her out last night. Tyler did not say a word, just walked.

"They do NOT love each other. Tracy is forcing this relationship, and we are not going to let our son be dragged down by her! Tyler deserves a better woman in his life!" Mark promised. "She is ruining his graduation day. When he looks back on this day years from now, it should make him smile, not remember a bad day because of Tracy."

Their family took up an entire row of chairs. Skylar sat next to Jeannette so she could cheer with her when Tyler walked by. Sean played with Jeremy to keep him occupied and hoping he would sleep through the ceremony.

Pomp and Circumstance began to play. The graduates filed in. Zach came in first with a smile from ear to ear. Jeannette and the family erupted into cheers. Then Tyler came into view, and once again the cheering squad clapped and yelled. Skylar put her fingers in her mouth to whistle as loud as she could. Tyler grinned. Tracy walked alongside Tyler. The look on her face told Jeannette she was not happy. Tyler kept smiling, not letting Tracy affect his mood.

After the ceremony, Tyler found his family. Jeannette and Mark, along with the rest of the brood, met him with hugs and kisses of congratulations for his accomplishments. Zach joined them after being with his parents for pictures. The family took so many pictures of Tyler and Zach that their cheeks hurt from smiling. Every photo taken was absent of Tracy. It was not an easy task, but Jeannette managed to work around her.

Jeannette noticed Tracy looking across the lawn and acting a little fidgety. *"That must be her parents coming this way,"* she thought and tapped Mark to get his attention.

Mark and Jeannette quickly approached Tracy's parents. Mark said, "Hello. Are you Tracy's parents? My name is Mark, and this is my wife, Jeannette. We are Tyler's parents."

Denise and Duane looked confused. Duane said, "It is nice to meet you. My name is Duane, and my wife is Denise. You said Tyler is your son? I apologize for not recognizing who that is. I assume he must be a friend of Tracy's. She has not mentioned him."

"Really? From what I understand they are pretty good friends and have something in common that will make us more than good friends," Jeannette said.

"That's nice. Since Tracy's fiancé has been at college in Boston, we are glad to hear she has made some friends. She was lost when he left," Denise explained.

Tracy spotted her parents talking to Mark and Jeannette. She scurried to the group before Jeannette and Mark told her parents something she had to explain. Worried, she asked, "Mom, Dad, what are you doing?"

"They are not doing anything, Tracy. They are talking to us. You remember, Tyler's parents? We thought it is important to visit with Denise and Duane since you and Tyler have gotten so, shall we say, close," Jeannette said cheerily.

"Of course, I remember who you are!" Tracy snapped.

"Tracy! Where are your manners? Why are you talking to these people like that?" Denise scolded.

Jeannette waived for Tyler to join them. "Since you have not heard Tracy speak of Tyler, let me introduce him. This is our son, Tyler," Jeannette introduced. "Tyler, how long have you been seeing Tracy?"

"About eight or nine months, I think. Maybe more," Tyler answered.

"You must be mistaken, Tyler. Tracy is engaged. They are getting married in the fall. I am confused. I don't understand what is going on," Denise said.

"Engaged? Are you kidding me? Tracy told me she is pregnant, and I am the father!" Tyler shouted.

"What?" Duane gasped. "Pregnant? Is that true? You told us you were saving yourself for John! Explain yourself, Tracy!" Her father was furious. Heads were turning at the group because of how loud Duane was shouting.

"Daddy, he is lying. I am engaged. I have been true to John," Tracy said, sounding like she was innocent of any wrongdoing while trying to manipulate her father.

"I AM LYING?" Tyler screeched. "We had sex almost every night and YOU initiated it! I just went along for the ride. I used protection every time, but then you tell me you are pregnant! I was ready to do what was right and marry you for the sake of my child!" He paused for a minute, then said, "Now I get it. You were determined to marry me for my family's money, weren't you? Was money all you wanted from me? You saw easy street if you married into my family?"

"Money? Tracy, this is crazy!" Denise declared loudly.

It was clear Tracy was not going to give up any information, so Jeannette nudged Tyler to explain.

"I am sure you have heard of *Windy City Publishing and Recording Company* out of Chicago? They have produced hundreds of albums and made Clay, and The Band famous with number one hits my mother wrote for him. Jeannette, my mother, owns that company! My stepfather, Mark, owns *My City Restaurant,* which is an upscale restaurant and club in downtown Chicago. Tracy thought she could force me into marrying her if she were pregnant, enabling her to live a life of the rich! Am I right, Tracy?" Tyler fumed.

Duane glared at Tracy with fire in his eyes and fists clenched. He ordered, "Tracy! Tell me the truth! Did you say these things? Were you trying to trap him? I am warning you. Do not lie to me!"

"Yes!" Tracy hissed. "You made me get loans to pay for school! You were supposed to pay for it! I shouldn't have to! He doesn't have any loans! He is rich! Now I am stuck with paying those loans! It is not fair! If I were married to him, he would pay for them for me, and I would not have to work! I didn't go to college to get a degree! I went to find a rich husband! I am not going to be poor for the rest of my life!"

"What about John?" Denise shouted.

"He will NEVER have any money. He is going to be a public defender! I would have to work, and we would still not have any money! I am NOT going to live like that! I almost got Tyler to marry me! YOU messed it up! I could have been rich!" Tracy roared.

Jeannette spoke up and said very calmly, "First of all, Tracy, Tyler is not the one with the money. I am. Mark is. Although you have been seeing Tyler for most of this school year, you know nothing about Tyler or our family. Tyler is not a spoiled rich kid. You didn't know we were rich until Tia and Sean's wedding. Tyler worked his way through college. We did not hand him money, and he did not ask for anything unnecessary. He learned at a young age that integrity and responsibility were very important character traits to possess. Money was earned, not given. Tyler EARNED his education. I am very proud of the man he has become. I am so very thankful my son did not get stuck with a liar like you. He deserves much better. Goodbye and good luck, Tracy. You are going to need it," Jeannette told her.

Mark took Jeannette's hand, squeezed it, and smiled from ear to ear. He was proud of his wife. Tyler, along with his family, walked away with smiles. They could hear Tracy in the distance yelling at her father and stomping her foot like the spoiled child she is.

"Jeannette, I am so sorry I introduced them. I had no idea what kind of person she was. Tyler, please forgive me?" Tia pleaded.

"Tia don't beat yourself up. Somebody would have introduced us. There was a reason Tracy came into my life. She taught me a lesson. Not everyone is who they say they are. I look back, and I should have seen it. I turned a blind eye to her actions and comments. I should have paid more attention. Instead, I was having a good time and ignored all the warning signs. Tia, this mess is NOT your fault. I take responsibility for it. It will not happen to me again. Lesson learned. To think I almost married that girl! Scary," Tyler shuddered. "Thanks to Mark and Mom, I will not be strapped to a psycho! There is no blame on your shoulders. I still love you, Tia. By the way, Mom, you and Mark did a great job of getting her to admit she had lied. It was genius to watch you work." Tyler said.

"That's my boy! My baby boy! He has learned so much," Jeannette sniffed.

"Aw, mom. You aren't going to cry again, are you? Geez," Tyler moaned.

"I am a proud mother, and I will cry if I want. Come here so I can hug you," she told him. Jeannette sobbed with pride into his shoulder.

"Oh, good grief! Is she crying again?" Zach yelled.

"Zach! Congratulations, again! It's about time you came back! You wandered off and missed all the excitement. I am as proud of you as if you were my real son!" Jeannette gushed.

"Oh, man! Are you EVER going to stop crying when we do something amazing?" Zach asked with a smile.

"No! It is my pride that rolls down my cheeks. Remember it for future reference," Jeannette explained.

Mark gave Zach a hard hug. He had come to love Zach as his own, too.

"Oh, not you too! You have been around Jeannette too long! You have picked up her bad habits," Zach protested and smiled at the same time. Mark shed a few tears for being part of a family that cared so much for each other.

"My mom and dad gave me $100.00 for graduation!" Zach waved his $100 bill in Tyler's face then stopped in his tracks. "Wait a minute. What excitement did I miss? I heard some yelling but didn't know in what direction to look. Was that you guys?" Zach asked.

"You should have seen the look on Tracy's face when mom and Mark got Tracy to admit she was lying about being pregnant with my baby. It was priceless!" Tyler reported laughing.

"We wanted to get you worked up so you would realize Tracy's real plan. We just gave you a nudge," Jeannette explained.

"Pregnant? What? Tracy? What?" Zach had no clue what happened.

"Don't worry about it. Tracy wasn't pregnant. Life can go back to normal. I will tell you the story later," Tyler promised.

Jeremy trotted to Zach and Tyler to hug them as everyone else had. He said the best he could, "Pisure," pointing to Tyler's chest.

"Do you want Grandma to take our picture?" Tyler asked, holding Jeremy. He nodded in agreement.

Jeannette already had her phone out and was obliging the little man's request. Tyler, Zach, and Jeremy were the focus of another photoshoot. Jeremy was a real ham when it came to getting his picture taken. He smiled and made faces. It was always a surprise what he would do next.

They had a family dinner that night, at an older restaurant which did not mind if they got a little louder than usual. It was Shannon, Ken, and Skylar's last night in Oregon. Tyler told the group the story about Tracy during dinner. The table was quiet, listening intently. Shannon and Ken were shocked.

Skylar, Ken, and Shannon had gone for a walk around the campus while all the drama played out. Zach punched Tyler in the arm for not telling him.

Everyone had stories to tell around the table about college adventures. Jeannette enjoyed listening to all the tall tales since she did not have any of her own. Sean noticed Jeannette had not said a word, and he knew why.

"Oh, Mom, I'm sorry," Sean said.

"What on earth for?" Jeannette asked.

"We are all telling stories about college, but you never had the opportunity to attend college."

"Oh, sweetheart. Don't be sorry. I'm not. I chose to stay with my boys. Nobody forced me. It was the best decision of my life. If I had to, I would do it all over again. I am not sorry for staying home with you two. I am proud of how my boys turned out because I did. Together we have created this wonderful family that keeps growing. I love my life and everyone at this table. So don't feel sorry for me," Jeannette explained.

"A toast to Mom. Thank you, Mom, for everything you have done for Tyler and me. I love you. Salute!" Sean declared.

The adults raised their glasses, and so did Jeremy, the best he could. He tried to say salute, but all that came out was "sssssoooooot" and spit. It made everyone at the table laugh. Jeremy laughed and clapped his hands.

Family night in Corvallis was wonderful.

The next morning it was time for Shannon, Ken, and Skylar to say their goodbyes to Jeremy, the graduates, Sean, and Tia. It was time for Mark and Jeannette to drive them to the airport. It was so hard for them to leave their new family behind.

"Tyler, since you and Zach will be home before we are, I wanted to warn you about two things in the driveway. I think you will be pleased. Congratulations!" Jeannette said with excitement.

"Really? Did I get a car? Did you get Zach and me a car? Thank you! Thank you! Thank you!" Tyler and Zach yelled at the same time and threw their arms around Jeannette and Mark.

"I am going to beat you home, Tyler," Zach yelled as he ran to his car.

"I bet you twenty-dollars you don't," Tyler retaliated.

"Drive safely!" Mark shouted. The boys gave him a wave of acknowledgment.

In Jeannette's car, she turned in her seat and said to Ken, Shannon, and Skylar, "I hope you enjoyed your time in Oregon. We have truly enjoyed having you here."

"Someday, I am coming back! I love it here! I wish there were a market for my designs in Oregon. I would move to Oregon in a heartbeat," Skylar dreamed out loud. Her head flopped back on to the seat headrest.

Jeannette's business mind kicked in. She said under her breath, "If she advertised some of her creations in Portland and Seattle, I will bet they would sell. Those women are always looking for the latest designs and trends."

Shannon and Skylar started to sniff. Jeannette turned away from the girls and handed tissues over her shoulder.

"Thank you, Jeannette," Shannon said and wiped her nose. "I have watched you while we have been here. You are a good person, inside and out. I am so sorry, Jeannette, for investigating you. It was a huge mistake. We should have, like you said, observed and listened. If I could have seen this side to you, I would NEVER have doubted you."

Jeannette turned halfway in her seat to face Shannon.

"That is water under the bridge. I forgave you a long time ago. In my mind it is forgotten, now you need to forgive yourself. It will truly make you feel better. I speak from experience. It is easy. Just ask your heavenly father to help you forgive yourself. That's what I did. I felt a heaviness lift from me. It made me feel so much better. Carrying guilt and unforgiveness is like a black cloud hanging over your head. It clouds the mind with negative thoughts, which conjures more negative thoughts, and so on. It has a snowball effect on our actions as well as in our physical bodies. You might get sick with a serious disease, have aches and pains you have never experienced before, depression, or migraines, naming a few things. Until you clean up the negativity, the positive cannot get through," Jeannette said. "You look confused. Did I not make sense?"

"Just the opposite! I was thinking back. I know exactly when I became negative. I am not going to go into the story right now, but I will be taking care of this negativity in short order! I do not like being the person I have become. Mark, Skylar, I am so sorry for not being a good mother when you were young. Despite me, you both turned out to be wonderful adults with a lot of talent. I have another chance with my great-grandchildren. Ken, I want to move to Oregon!" Shannon declared and burst into tears.

"You what? I have been thinking the same thing! I was not sure how I was going to breach the subject!" Ken exclaimed. "Mark? Is that a problem for you? Would you have a problem if we lived in Clark City?"

Mark's head snapped to look at Jeannette. He was tongue-tied.

"What about your friends and your clubs? You have lived in Illinois all your life. Do you really think you want to uproot and move over two-thousand miles away?"

"YES!" Shannon and Ken said in unison.

Jeannette gently put her hand on Mark's arm. She did not take her eyes off him when she replied, "I think it is a fantastic idea. We would love to have you here, and I know Jeremy would enjoy seeing you all the time. I think it is a great idea. Honey, what about you?"

He paused for a moment before he answered, "Mom and Dad, I love you. I like who you are now. If you ever revert back to who you were before you met Jeannette, I will pack your things myself and send you back to Chicago. That is a promise. Do we have a deal?"

"DEAL!" The couple shouted.

"What about me? I am going to be left in Chicago all by myself!" Skylar burst into tears. "This is my family, too, and I love all of you! Now I know what a family can be, I don't want to go back to the way it was!"

"Skylar, I have been thinking about this," Jeannette began to voice her idea.

"The building for *Old West Windy City* will have office space for five more businesses. Tyler and Zach are opening an architect design business in one of them. There are four more spaces available. It will be at least a year until the building is complete, maybe longer. That should give you time to find someone to manage your store in Chicago. You can set up a Skype account and talk with clients, if need be, even facetime with them. You would still be designing; only you will be doing it from Oregon. Your designs can be faxed or emailed. Your clients in the Chicago area could go into your store there for measurements. Oregonians could catch designer fever, too! With enough advertising in big cities such as Portland and Seattle, it would generate new clients, I am positive. I'll bet if you asked your brother, he might let you have a fashion show at his new restaurant. If it is slow in the beginning, remember your shop in Chicago will be generating income. I think it is a brilliant plan! So how about it, Skylar?" Jeannette suggested.

There was silence from the backseat until Skylar let out a loud yell, "Brilliant! Why didn't I think about that? I could even design western wear! Oregon is going to love me! Maybe I could put on a style show in Seattle? Now I cannot wait to get back to Chicago to prepare for moving! Hurry up, Mark! Drive faster!"

Mark laughed before saying, "Holy crap! The whole family will be here! What have we done? Jeannette, can you handle having all my family here?"

"They are my family now, too. It will be a good thing for all of our family to be together," she stated. "It will be wonderful for Jeremy to grow up knowing his grandparents, great-grandparents, great-aunt, and of course his uncles, Tyler and Zach. Our family will grow larger when Sean and Tia have more children. When Tyler marries, there will be even more children. Oh, my goodness! My head is spinning. That is a lot of people," Jeannette paused at the thought of how huge their family might become. She caught her breath and said, "Skylar, you and I will be best friends, as well as sisters, I know it. Your work is cut out for the three of you. If you need help, let me or Mark know. We will do what we can to help."

Shannon asked, "Would you start looking around for a house for us? Give us an idea of what the going price is? That will tell us how much we need to get out of our house. It is going on the market as soon as we get home!"

"I will start checking on prices right away. As time gets closer to moving, I have a great Real Estate agent I will call," Jeannette told her.

The goodbyes at the airport were not sad, but happy with the prospect of moving and embarking on a new adventure. Skylar's mind was already whirling with what needed to be done and arranged in priority order. She made lists just like Jeannette always does. Shannon and Ken did not stop talking about moving the entire flight home.

Lesson learned: Be careful with your tongue. Even though it does not possess any bones, it can be strong enough to cut someone to the quick, break a heart, and also destroy someone's life.

Lying has a ripple effect and there is no way of knowing how far out the ripple goes. Lying to get what you want will come back and bite you in the butt! If you can't speak the truth, keep your mouth shut.

16

Jeannette and Mark left for Chicago the next day. They were exhausted in a good way.

With only one year to get their established businesses running smoothly without them at the helm, was not a lot of time. Although it will take longer than a year to get the new ones built, Mark and Jeannette will need to be in Oregon overseeing the construction as much as possible.

Jeannette and Mark had to go before the City Council and present their proposal to build because the amount of land they needed for this endeavor was in Clark City but also in the county. The vote was unanimous. The city offered to sell them a large parcel of land just over the city limits line, in the urban growth boundary of Clark City where Jeannette wanted. They agreed to give the new businesses city services such as water, sewer and garbage even though they were not annexed into the city, yet. The county gave them tax break incentives to build, which sealed the deal, in Jeannette's opinion. The parcel was purchased, and they were on their way.

Tyler and Zach had the design for both the restaurant and *Old West Windy City* finished before graduation. Jeannette had her contractor working on permits for construction immediately after the purchase of the acreage.

Ten months later, the construction of Mark's restaurant was close to being finished. The paving of the parking lot was underway, landscaping was being put in, finishing touches on the inside were being completed, and a huge sign was being installed that read: *Our City Dining*. Another sign just below reads: *Family Dining or Dinner and Dancing, Live Music Every Night*. The final thing will be moving the kitchen equipment, tables and chairs, and food stock in.

Mark was designing the interior similar to the theme of *My City*. He had Tyler and Zach design the restaurant with two distinct halves with separate entries: the family dining side, with a comfortable, homey feeling and lots of windows. The dinner club needed a stage for live music, a dance floor and an unusual seating area.

There was a circular fireplace in the center of the family dining room with glass encasing the flames. Pictures hung on the walls of Clark City starting from the time of the founding of the city to the present. Fun facts about the town were etched in wood and hung alongside the pictures. The tables were round. Instead of tablecloths, the tables had a dark blue cloth runner that draped over the side slightly. Two half-circle bar areas were situated close to the kitchen for the older group that enjoyed having coffee in the morning and discussing the issues of the day. Together it made a complete circle with an opening that separated the half circles to allow the waitresses to move around and through freely from the kitchen.

The dinner and dancing side was set up in the fashion of *My City*. One half of the dinner area was at a slightly higher level. The other half encircled the dance floor. Being on the upper level made the dance floor and stage seem sunken, in the style of the 1930s and 1940s. The entrance was three steps up into the dining area that encompassed a lower level of seating. All of the tables were round with white tablecloths and a small lamp in the middle. The walls were light blue with photos of the Blue Mountains and of Oregon's deserts and forests. It was like no other place in the west that Mark could find. Because of its originality, Mark was hoping it to be a hit.

Old West Windy City was going to take longer to complete. It was more substantial in size and more complicated. In other words, it was a lot bigger than *Our City Dining*. The building was two floors in height, with an elevator. The entire main floor space will be filled with the recording company. It will consist of three sound rooms and sound booths, five offices, an employee break area, two conference rooms (one small one large), a storage room, and several restrooms. Jeannette's office will be the largest with a private restroom and decorated for comfort with a couch and several overstuffed chairs. In one of the corners by her desk, an area was reserved for toys. If her grandchildren should visit, it was vital for her to have something for them to play with. There also could be times that a client might bring their child with them because of an absent caregiver. The toys would give the child something to do while the adults talked business.

The second floor is made up of five very large office spaces. Two of them were already reserved. Tyler and Zach with building designs, and Skylar with her clothing designs. The other three vacant areas will be advertised for rent.

Jeannette was in constant contact with her contractor asking about timelines. She was anxious to stay in Oregon with maybe only one trip to Chicago each month. When that time comes, Jeannette decided to give up her apartment and stay in a hotel when she came to the city. It will save the company money. Mark will be traveling with her to check in on his restaurant and go over the books.

Skylar was ready to move as soon as Jeannette gave her the go-ahead. Shannon and Ken would be moving in two months to a house Jeannette picked out for them with her real estate agent, Shirley. She used her 'super-power' to choose the right home for them.

Starting on Monday, Mark will be staying in Oregon and setting up his restaurant, staff, and expecting to open in a month. Their lives were in upheaval.

It had been three weeks since Jeannette had seen Jeremy and needed to hug him and kiss those sweet cheeks while he wiggled and laughed. It was time for a family gathering.

Bridgett interrupted a conversation Jeannette was having with Sean on the phone.

"Jeannette line two is a woman by the name of Rose. Do you want me to put her through?"

"Yes. That is my sister. I will take it. Sean, I will call you back. Hello Rose. You never call me so there must be a problem. What is it? Who died?" Jeannette inquired.

"Mom passed away this morning from a stroke. Beth, Leroy and I set the funeral for Saturday. Can you make it?" Rose questioned.

"I already have plans to be in Oregon this weekend, so I will be there. What time and where will it be held?" Jeannette asked.

"Since she has lived in Stokes Landing since birth, we thought it was appropriate to have it there. The service will be at 11:00 a.m. at the church. Mom wanted to be cremated. Do you want us to wait so you can say goodbye?" Rose wanted to know.

"There will not be time for her to be cremated before the funeral if you wait for me. My flight will not land until Friday, late afternoon. I will say goodbye in thought and prayer. Thank you for letting me know. I will see you Saturday," Jeannette cited and hung up.

She called Mark to tell him about the phone call she had just received. The next two calls were to Sean and Tyler. All three gave her their condolences. It was sad to think Rebecca did not know her grandchildren or great-grandchild. Jeannette's boys were never a priority in Rebecca and Warren's life. Jeannette considered herself to be the "black sheep" of the family who went off to make her way in the world.

On Saturday, Mark accompanied Jeannette to the funeral. On the drive to Stokes Landing, Jeannette talked a lot about what it was like growing up in the tiny town.

"Mom wasn't a bad person or as grumpy as she was when I last saw her. Rebecca was married to a control freak, Warren, who told her what to do and when to do it. She was not a confrontational person, so when Dad was *'disciplining'* us, she turned her back and went into the kitchen. I have always thought Mom believed if she didn't see it, it didn't happen. Rebecca never stood up for any of us against him. Even when he lied to me and got me in trouble at school, she did not defend me. She knew it was lies he had told me because she was there when he said them. In some respects, there was no doubt she was afraid of him. One thing that still plagues me, is why did Warren find it necessary to constantly lie to me? He did not do that with my siblings. Humph. I will never know."

"This will be over soon, sweetheart, and then we will have our family dinner. I asked Irma to make prime rib," Mark commented as he pulled the car into the parking area of the church. "Who is the woman staring at us?"

"My sister Beth. She is the one who does not like me. The last time I saw her was at Warren's funeral. Sorry, dad's funeral.

I said some things I felt I needed to say about how she has treated me all these years. I left her with her mouth hanging open and furious with me. Hold on to your hat. It is going to get interesting," Jeannette promised.

"Who is the other woman that just stood by her?" Mark inquired.

"That is my other sister, Rose. She is a lot younger than the rest of us. She treats me, okay. The man that is talking to them is my brother Leroy. Well, no time like the present to meet them. Let's go," Jeannette suggested.

"Hello everyone, this is my husband, Mark. Mark, this is Rose, Beth, and Leroy," Jeannette informed her siblings.

"You got married again? Whoa! Is this number three?" Beth asked with a smirk.

"Yes, and the last. Now, do you have anything you want me to do?" Jeannette asked flatly.

"No. We have it all covered. We didn't think you wanted to help, so we made the arrangements with Pastor Dave. You could have come here earlier in the week if you wanted to help. Laiklyn was asking about you. You remember your niece, don't you?" Beth asked.

"Of course, I do. You don't remember, sorry, you can't remember someone you have not met. You do not know your nephews, Sean and Tyler or your great-nephew. Neither did Warren or Rebecca. My children were not a priority in their lives. Yes, I am a grandmother and loving it. My children did not have the experience of a grandparent like yours did and I am glad they did not experience Warren and Rebecca. I see you did not take my advice about finding happiness. Well, enough of this lovely conversation. I am going inside," Jeannette decided.

"Just a minute, Sweetheart," Mark said. "From what I have just witnessed, Sean and Tyler have not missed out on knowing his aunts and uncle. For your information, they have attended college, graduated with honors, and gotten degrees. One in business and the other is an architect. Jeannette did a remarkable job raising her boys. You sounded surprised Jeannette married again. When you have a heart as big as Jeannette's, love will find you. She is an amazing woman."

Mark went on to say, "She survived marriage to Jeff, which said a lot about her strength. I am sure you do not know the whole story, and I will not bore you with it. Robert did not leave her by choice, as you well know. She had no intention of marrying again until she met me, her third and final husband. You should be proud to be related to her. She has accomplished a lot. Can you say the same thing about yourselves or your children? I didn't think so."

Mark took Jeannette's hand to escort her into the church. It was his turn to leave her siblings with their mouths' open.

Laiklyn caught a glimpse of Jeannette as she strolled into the church holding a stranger's hand. She rushed to her and shouted, "Aunt Jeannette! I am so glad to see you! Why do I only get to see you at funerals?"

"It seems that way, doesn't it?" Jeannette remarked as a question. "Life and business keep me very busy. You will have to come visit me. Oh! I am sorry. I did not introduce you. This is Mark, my husband. Mark, this is my favorite niece, Laiklyn." Laiklyn hugged Mark without regard.

"It is nice to meet you, Laiklyn," Mark replied. "You are certainly not like your mother! Don't tell her, but you are much prettier than she is! You will have to have dinner at my new restaurant in Clark City when it opens."

"Oh, Uncle Mark! Thank you. Yes, I am the pretty one, according to Auntie. I will talk to mommy about your restaurant. We don't go out to eat very much. You can sit next to me in the church if you want," Laiklyn told him.

"Thank you I will," Mark promised.

Pastor Dave meandered over to greet Jeannette and Mark.

"Jeannette, isn't it? I remember you from Warren's funeral. I must say a funeral was much easier and faster to plan when you were present." He looked at Mark, wondering who this gentleman is.

"Pastor Dave, this is Mark, my husband. Mark, this is Pastor Dave," Jeannette introduced.

"It is nice to meet you, Pastor. How long has this been your home church?" Marked asked.

"Fifteen years in this nice community."

"Did you know the family well?" Mark questioned.

"As well as anybody, I guess. Warren and Rebecca were good supporters of the church. Rebecca attended and participated in every function and service we had. Warren was the opposite. God forgive me, I will not speak ill of the deceased." The Pastor stopped talking long enough to look to the ceiling, then continued. "Were you acquainted with Warren and Rebecca?"

"No, I was not, and I thank God for that. Rebecca probably attended everything she could to get away from Warren. But that's another subject for another time. I am from Chicago. I am opening a new restaurant in Clark City. Have dinner with us sometime," Mark invited.

"I am sure I will. Please excuse me. It is time to start the service. I see Laiklyn is motioning for you to sit by her," Pastor Dave pointed out.

Mark and Jeannette obliged Laiklyn and took a seat next to her. She moved to sit in-between the couple and held a hand of each.

In attendance were three times as many people who came to pay their respects for Rebecca than at Warren's funeral. It was a mystery for Jeannette to understand why her mother would stay with such a mean spirited, controlling man. She also became mean spirited in her old age — a lot like Warren. I guess living with him as many years as Rebecca did, Warren rubbed off on her.

In her head, she heard a small voice say to her, "She was unable to leave. That was not how Rebecca's parents raised her. They raised her in the old beliefs of the church 'do not spare the rod' and 'be submissive unto your husband.' It was the path she was destined to take. If she had not, would you be who you are? You broke the cycle of abuse. You learned your father's way was not the way of love and Rebecca was not the mother you wanted to be. Your path has been long and complicated but necessary. Because of Rebecca's path, you are the woman you are today. By her example, you knew what kind of woman you did not want to be. You broke free. You obey your gift from God, and God honors your obedience."

Tears ran down Jeannette's face. Laiklyn handed her a tissue.

Patting Jeannette's hand with comfort said, "It is okay Auntie. Grandma is in a better place. We do not have to worry about her anymore."

Jeannette smiled at Laiklyn for the kind words. She could not tell her the tears were not about the passing of Rebecca but from the words spoken in her mind.

Beth and Rose, in Jeannette's opinion, made the service too long. She will be biting her tongue, not to say anything negative about the ceremony.

At the end of the service, they decided not to attend the potluck, which disappointed Laiklyn. Jeannette did not speak to her siblings before leaving. She wanted to avoid any more negative conversations. Chances are she would not see them again, and she was okay with it.

During the drive home, Jeannette told Mark what she heard in her head. He was silent for a minute, thinking about what she confided to him.

He finally spoke, "I believe you heard a voice. You have a special gift, and this might be an extension of your intuition. It might have been God, an angel, your heart, I don't know. I do not doubt that little voice. I believe it tells you the truth, and I am thankful for it."

Jeannette reached across the console to hold his hand. She whispered, "Thank you for believing me. I appreciate it more than you will ever know."

For dinner, Irma and her husband were invited to join them. Of course, Zach was in attendance. There was food involved. The table had smiling faces feasting on prime rib and discussing the latest sporting event and the latest scuttlebutt in Clark City. Jeannette sat next to Jeremy to help him with mac & cheese Irma made just for him. Jeremy did not use utensils. Hands were much better tools to eat with. Spoons were for banging on the highchair tray.

Sean tapped his wine glass for attention.

"I have an announcement! Cheers to family dinners!" It was agreed by all. "I do have one more thing to say. It is my pleasure to tell you all, in six months we are adding another grandchild to our family!"

The group applauded his announcement. Jeannette squealed with joy, "Mark another grandbaby!"

It was Tyler's turn for an announcement. The tapping began once again.

Tyler shared, "I have found a wonderful woman that I like very much. I want you all to meet her tomorrow. She could be a permanent addition to our family, but first, I need everyone's approval. Zach has already given his. I have invited her to swim with us around two. Her name is Christine. She was born and raised in Clark City. She went to college in Idaho on a softball scholarship to study agriculture. Christine graduated at the top of her class a year ago and works for the county to help local farmers identify problems with their crops. She is thinking about looking into opening an office in the new building. She wants to broker crops and offer pesticide-free fertilizer as a service for the local farmers. The farmers would not have to worry about finding a market for their crops. If they hired her, Christine would market their crops and arrange to sell them in the U.S. or anywhere in the world. She believes the farmers need a boost in selling what they grow, by an honest person who knows them and can find the best price possible. She is the absolute opposite of Tracy, thank God. I believe I might have found the *one*."

Jeannette shouted, "It is about time! I have been waiting for more grandchildren!" There was a burst of laughter and clapping. Tyler's face turned red.

After meeting Christine and watching the two together, there was no doubt they belonged together.

"Christine is a lovely young woman, Tyler," Mark told him. Jeannette agreed and complimented Tyler. That evening Jeannette and Mark took Tyler to the office for a discussion.

Jeannette began, "Tyler, are you planning on asking Christine to marry you?"

"Yes."

"There is something I need to tell you," Jeannette began. "Before Robert died, he wanted you and your brother to be taken care of, so you would never have to struggle as I did. He set up a bank account for you to be used for a ring, your wedding, honeymoon, and set up a household."

Tyler was shocked. It took him a minute to regain his speech. "Really? He did that for us? Sean never said a word to me about it!"

"Yes, I know. I asked him not to say anything. I wanted you to be as surprised as he was. Now, we need to give Mr. Baker a call. He is in charge of Robert's estate. Your account is the last of his duties. Let me get Mr. Baker on the phone." Jeannette dialed. "Mr. Baker, this is Jeannette. It is time to tell Tyler about the account Robert set up. Yes, he is right here," Jeannette said with a smile and handed the phone to Tyler. She and Mark left the office while Tyler spoke to Mr. Baker.

Tyler walked out of the office in shock.

"Mom, do you know how much was in that account? There was $75,000.00! Mr. Baker just transferred it to my account. I can't believe it! Now I can buy her a ring. I am going to start designing a house for us right away."

"Okay, son but before you get ahead of yourself, don't you think you should buy a ring and ask Christine the big question?" Mark suggested.

Tyler's mind was on overload. As he paced, he said, "Oh, yeah, I guess I should. Mom, will you help me pick out a ring? What jewelry store do you suggest? When should I ask her? How should I ask her?" He started to sweat.

"Slow down, Tyler. Take a breath. Tomorrow, I will help you with the ring. It will be up to you when and how you will ask her," Jeannette said with a giggle.

"I wish Robert were here so I could thank him. I loved him. I hope he knew how I felt?" Tyler said and stopped pacing. "Please don't take offense to that, Mark. I love you, too. Robert was the only real father I knew before you."

"I didn't take offense. I wish I could have known Robert," Mark said. "I am here if you need any male advice, and I have a suggestion about where to propose. How about *Our City Dining*? Maybe I could talk to the owner about a special dinner for two the night before it opens?" Mark suggested with a chuckle. "It would give some of my wait-staff a little experience on how things work. Jeannette and I will eat in the family dining area so if you have a problem; we will be there. I will also have the band play for you. How does that sound?"

"That is perfect! How soon do you open?" Tyler asked.

Mark answered, "If I had my way, it would be tomorrow. But give me around ten days."

"It sounds like you have a plan," Jeannette said.

She rose to hug Tyler. Her baby is getting married. She cried into his shoulder while Tyler moaned. Mark looked at Tyler with a big smile and a chuckle. Tyler rolled his eyes.

Jeannette and Tyler set off the next morning to buy a ring. She took him to her favorite jewelry store in Clark City. It was on the same block Robert's office had been, which distracted them both for a minute. Their eyes met with a look of sadness.

Jeannette snapped back to reality and said, "Okay, enough sadness! We have come to start a new adventure with happiness. This is a good day! Let's find that perfect ring."

Shopping did not take long for Tyler to spot the perfect ring. It resembled an older style of ring. It was white gold with a square one carat diamond in the center of the engagement ring, and a small band of diamonds for the wedding band

"This says Christine all over it. She is old fashioned in a lot of ways, and this simple ring is just right. What do you think, mom?" Tyler asked.

Tears welled in her eyes when she said, "It is beautiful, honey." Jeannette turned away to let the tears fall.

Tyler made his purchase. With his bag in hand, he led his mom out of the store. "Thank you for coming with me. I am a nervous wreck! What if she says no? Oh, God!"

"Sweetheart I have seen how you look at each other. She will say yes. Remember your old mom is always right about these things," Jeannette said with a compassionate smile.

The big night came, and Tyler was sweating through his clothes. Mark could see how nervous he was, so he tried to help with a shot of top-shelf whiskey.

"Here," Mark said and handed Tyler the glass. "This will help. Son, this is the biggest decision in your life. Do you think you have made the right choice? Are you always thinking about her? Do you want to be with her 24/7? Are you interested in any other women?"

"Yes, she is the right one. She is always on my mind. When I am away from her, I feel like half of me is missing. I haven't looked at another woman since I met Christine," Tyler recanted.

"Then, son, I believe you have made the right choice. Everything will be fine," Mark said reassuring Tyler. "Oh! Look at the time. She should be here any minute."

Mark cued the band to begin then headed to the kitchen to check on dinner. Jeannette saw Christine walk in. She couldn't help herself. She peeked around the corner to watch.

The table had a lit fat candle surrounded by a fresh bouquet of flowers made of all colors of the rainbow and sat atop a white linen tablecloth. The band played soft music to help set the mood. Tyler went down on one knee and. . . .

"Jeannette, what are you doing?" Mark asked from behind her. She jumped and almost let out a scream, but Mark pulled her away from her perch before she disturbed the big question. "Honey, leave them alone. I know he is your baby, but Tyler has become a man, and he can handle this on his own."

"I know, I know. Oh, Mark, he is a man," Jeannette said and melted into Mark's shoulder.

Christine said yes, and the evening was perfect.

Another wedding. This time Jeannette hoped Christine had a mother who would help. Until they decided on a date, preparations for the *Old West Windy City* building to be completed was still the order of the day.

Lesson learned: Never be with someone who does not treat you well. Be with someone you can laugh with, understands you, treats you with respect, listens to you, knows the good and bad about you, and will make you a priority. That person is a keeper.

17

Our City Dining opened with a capacity crowd in the family dining area. The club side was half full. It was new, and word needed to get around about it being a dinner club. In a short time, with more advertising and word of mouth, Mark had faith his new creation would be flourishing.

Old West Windy City was a week away from opening. Already the music community was buzzing about the new studio. Tyler and Zach had already moved in on the second floor and was ready for business. Opening day could not come fast enough for Jeannette.

Skylar moved to Clark City two weeks ago. She was so excited about setting up her new shop, she spent long, late hours working on her new space, wanting everything perfect when she opened the doors. Skylar borrowed Jeannette's wedding coat for display on a mannequin as a sample of her designs. Pictures from the wedding were hung on the wall to show the entire ensemble. Skylar was anxiously looking forward to opening and would be ready to take the fashion world of Oregon and Washington by storm.

The evening before the complex was scheduled to open, Jeannette hosted a cocktail party at *Old West Windy City* for politicians of the city and county as well as pivotal business owners and real estate brokers from the area to unveil her new complex. The purpose of the gathering was meant to give them a tour and explain what Jeannette's business does and how everything works. She introduced the tech people, which gave demonstrations about recording.

The guests also toured the second floor where Tyler and Zach were in their office and ready to show them what they do, and some of their designs. They also bragged about their designing *Old West Windy City* and *Our City Dining*. Those designs were pictured on the wall.

Next door was Skylar with some of her clothing displayed, and several drawings of new designs that will be coming out soon. Skylar impressed the females as they toured. They were very interested in Skylar's new designs.

The real estate agents noted three more spaces were still for rent. One was on hold. The two left had several interested parties. Jeannette was not worried about finding a renter for the vacancies.

Jeannette was told by one of the politicians, constructing the restaurant and the recording complex will bring income and jobs to a city that needed it. More people will be working, making more disposable income, which will lead to more business for the stores. There will be an influx of business for the hotels and motels when the recording company is in full swing. Jeannette and Mark made a tremendous boost to the city economy.

The morning after the opening, Jeannette got a call Tia was on the way to the hospital to deliver a new member of the family. She bolted from the office, shouting instructions to her secretary. Mark was unable to meet her at the hospital. He had a huge banquet needing his attention.

She made it just in time to witness another birth. The new baby was a little girl they named June Marie. The name fit her. She was perfect in every way with ten fingers and ten toes. The moment she was born, June had daddy wrapped around her finger. Sean was such a good and loving father and husband. Jeannette was so very proud of him. She knew Tyler was going to be the same way when he and Christine started a family.

Jeannette teased, "This is just great. Our second day open and our business manager and attorney are taking a vacation," she chuckled. "Sean, take the next two or three days off to help Tia and June get settled. Tia, can you work from home for the next couple of months? Does that sound acceptable?" Tia agreed.

Jeannette kissed little June on the head before leaving and said, "Welcome to this crazy family, little one."

That evening the entire family was at the hospital by Sean and Tia's side getting to know June. Jeremy was very loving toward the little bundle of joy. After all, June is his little sister. He stood by whoever held her as if he was her protector. From time to time, Jeremy, ever so gently, kissed her on the head. It was evident big brother loved his new little sister.

Tyler and Christine set a date for the wedding. The date was in three months, September 15th. Christine thought it was plenty of time for planning a wedding. When they announced the date, it sent her mother into a frenzy of making lists and phone calls.

Two weeks after the wedding date was announced, Tyler visited Jeannette in her office.

"Do you have a minute, Mom?"

"Of course, I do. There is always time in my day for my boy," Jeannette acknowledged. The look on Tyler's face gave her a jolt. "Okay, son. I believe I know what is on your mind. Humor me and tell me anyway."

"Christine is pregnant," he blurted out.

She sat quietly, watching Tyler squirm. She questioned, "Why are you so nervous to tell me this wonderful news?"

"Wonderful? You are not upset because we are not married yet? Whew!" Tyler relaxed and slumped onto a chair.

"Tyler. You love her, and she loves you. I don't understand why you were nervous about telling me. A child is something to celebrate! Your wedding is in a few short months. I grew up in a different time when a woman was expected to be married before pregnancy. If she got pregnant, she was looked upon as a loose woman and scorned. After any and all weddings the older women in the community kept calendars and counted the months before a couple's first child was born. Those women were the busybodies and made sure they knew all the gossip to spread."

"Some unwed mothers were sent away to live with relatives until she delivered, and the child was put up for adoption. Other girls were *forced* into adoption to save face. Some chose abortion. These days the old ways are gone. People live together for years, have several children, and then get married. Sweetheart, I certainly do not look down my nose at you or Christine. Instead, I congratulate you!"

"Oh mom, what a relief. I don't know why I was so nervous. I have always been able to tell you anything. It seemed like such a major thing, and I wasn't sure how to tell you. I guess after the Tracy thing I was a little gun shy. I love you," Tyler told Jeannette.

"Do you want to move the wedding up? I can talk to Mark about using one of his banquet rooms. Wait a minute. Have you told Christine's parents yet?"

"We are telling them tonight. I wanted to tell you first. We just found out Christine is pregnant, so we have not talked about moving the wedding, yet. I am sure there will be a lot of discussion this evening at dinner. Christine's parents are old fashioned Christians. It might not go over very well," Tyler commented with rolled eyes. "This is totally against what they believe. Christine was a virgin. We love each other so much, it just happened. It was not planned."

"Would you like Mark and me to come to dinner with you for support when you tell them the news?" Jeannette asked.

"Oh, Mom, would you? I would appreciate that a lot! Let me talk to Christine first. I will call you. Do you think Mark would have an empty table in the club tonight for us?" Tyler nervously inquired.

"Don't go. Let's give Mark a call right now," Jeannette suggested. "Hello, sweetheart. Tyler just gave me some exciting news. Christine is pregnant! Yes! Isn't that great? I know! Another grandchild! They are going to tell her parents tonight. Tyler would like us to be there for moral support. Do you have an open table tonight in the club for the six of us? What time, son? He said 7:00. Wonderful! I love you. Bye. We are all set. Let me know right away if I need to cancel."

"Give me ten minutes. Thanks, Mom. I love you," Tyler said.

Christine sounded relieved when Tyler called knowing they would have extra support. Dinner was all set.

The table at *Our City Dining* was in a quiet spot, so it was easy to carry on a conversation amongst the six. Jeannette and Mark sat sipping a glass of wine before the arrival of the other four.

"Tyler was nervous to tell me he is going to be a father," Jeannette began. "My baby is going to have a baby. We will need to call your parents tomorrow. Although they will be moving here next week. Then again, we should let Tyler tell them."

"I think it would be nice for Tyler and Christine to tell them. How is *Old West* doing? Any new clients?" Mark asked, changing the subject.

"Business is good. We have new artists coming in all the time. Two offices on the second floor signed a lease today! I have been holding on to one for Christine, if she wants it," Jeannette explained.

"Hi, Mom. Mark. I see you are relaxing with your favorite wine," Tyler observed.

Jeannette rose from the table to hug Christine.

"Congratulations! I think it is wonderful! Another addition to our family!" Jeannette gushed with excitement.

"I feel the same way," Mark confided and hugged Christine. "You two will make wonderful parents."

Tyler ordered a glass of wine, and Christine ordered iced tea. Their conversation was centered on the anticipation of a new bundle of joy until Christine's parents were spotted walking toward them. The group hushed up their conversation.

Jeannette could see Christine's hands were shaking under the table and thought, "This poor girl is scared to death of her parents. This evening might get very interesting."

Christine introduced the couple, "Jeannette, Mark, these are my parents Davin, and Cyndi."

Jeannette spoke up, "Cyndi, it is nice to finally put a face to the voice on the phone! Please, sit. Would you like a glass of wine before dinner?"

"No, thank you," Davin said. "We do not drink alcohol. Iced tea would be nice."

"Jeannette, I wanted to talk more about the wedding with you," Cyndi began.

"I am all ears, but first I think the kids have something to say," Jeannette suggested.

Christine opened up by saying, "We have some news that might come as a surprise. We are thinking about changing the wedding date, but that is not the surprising part," she paused and looked at Tyler. He gave her a wink. She blurted out, "I am pregnant."

Cyndi gasped in shock as her mouth dropped open. Davin's face instantly turned red with anger.

"You couldn't wait a few months? I thought we raised you better than this!" Davin hissed. Do you expect us to be happy about this and congratulate you? You have shamed us in the eyes of the church!" Tyler reached for Christine's hand and squeezed it.

Cyndi added, "I am shocked! Did he force you? In a world where there are so many options of birth control, you still let this happen! You shouldn't have been involved in sex anyway! I can't believe this! Davin, what are we going to do?"

"Cyndi, Davin, don't you think this kind of thinking has been overturned by acceptance in the last twenty or more years? You are unapprovingly over the top with your reaction," Jeannette commented. "In my opinion, a child is a blessing and a reason to celebrate. Christine and Tyler love each other and conceived a child from their love. It was just a little earlier than expected. Your daughter was a virgin. She did not have sex with anyone besides Tyler. She saved herself for him. The man she is marrying. Quite frankly, I am looking forward to another grandchild," Jeannette smiled with happiness and shocked Christine's parents.

"Well, I never!" Cyndi spat out. "What are the people at church going to say?"

"If you ask me, to snub your nose at a pregnant girl is not the Christian way. You are judging her for having a lack of morals. The act of sex was created by God, and doesn't the bible say don't judge or you will be judged? What about you without sin cast the first stone? Have you never done anything to be unfairly judged? If you have not, you are putting yourself in the same category as Jesus: Perfect. Are you or Davin perfect?" Jeannette questioned.

Davin spoke up, "Of course we are not perfect! But our family is looked up to by the members of our faith. Now, this! It will shame us!"

"Then you need to find another church! If what I am about to say offends you, I ask your forgiveness in advance. The people in your church are hypocrites. I just explained that. If you think your daughter has sinned, then that is *her* issue with God. Not yours. Not the church. Not the people who attend your church. You are guilty of nothing. There is no shame in this. Your church of so-called Christians is judging this young couple in the ways of the Old Testament of the bible. How can anyone judge against another for participating in an act that God created? He said, *love one another,"* Jeannette argued.

"We need to go home and discuss what we are going to do about this!" Davin demanded.

"What you are going to do about this?" Tyler repeated with panic in his voice. He looked to Jeannette and Mark for immediate help.

"Davin, please stay and talk to us? No more talk about pregnancy. Just a nice visit," Mark suggested.

"I apologize if I have thrown gasoline on the fire," Jeannette said. "Wouldn't you like to stay and have a nice dinner with us? Please? We should get to know each other. We are going to be in-laws in a short time from now. You have my word, I will not speak one more word about this pregnancy tonight," Jeannette promised. "Please stay? The food here is exceptional. Of course, dinner is on us."

Cyndi looked at Davin with pleading eyes. Davin gave in, and they stayed for dinner.

With each course, Davin calmed a little more. By the time dessert was served, he was chuckling at something Mark said.

While enjoying coffee, Davin spoke up, "I hate to admit this, but I think Christine struck the jackpot marrying Tyler and having such good in-laws. I have been thinking about what you said while we enjoyed this nice dinner. Jeannette, thank you for keeping your word. I am going to break it for you. I have observed how much Tyler and Christine love each other. You were right. A new life was created out of love. If some of the church members look down on us, I know enough about each of them to shut their mouths and put them in their place. Cyndi, I think we should get them married right away and make sure this baby is born into a family who loves him or her. What do you say?"

For a moment, Cyndi was tongue-tied. She gathered herself and sat a little straighter in the chair.

"Let the church talk. We are good people, not perfect, but good people. Besides, I know how to throw a stone and I know who to aim it at!" Cyndi said with a giggle.

Christine jumped up and hugged both of her parents. "Thank you, Mom and Dad! I love you!"

Cyndi asked, "Okay, now we have to figure out how soon you want to have your wedding? Christine, have you thought of a date?"

"We were thinking in two weeks," Chris informed her mother.

"Two weeks?" Cyndi screeched and then quieted herself. She was drawing attention to their group. "How do you think we can put such an important and major thing together in two weeks? We have to find someplace to have it, a florist, a photographer, a cake, a caterer. My head is spinning!" Cyndi protested.

Mark had a suggestion, "I have an open banquet room. You are welcome to use it. You won't need a caterer. We serve food here. I have a great chef. I will bring in another chef to cook for the restaurant that day. As far as the cost goes, we would be happy to pay half. Of course, you get a discounted rate, anyway. We are family."

Jeannette added, "I know a good florist in town, who is reasonable, and I am willing to bet, they can handle it on short notice. The bakery makes wedding cakes with only a couple weeks' planning. That should not be a problem. I only see two obstacles. Getting the word out and a photographer."

"Wow, Jeannette, you and Mark have the know-how to get things done! Okay! We are having a wedding in two weeks! Christine, we will shop for your dress tomorrow. Tyler, you need to get a tux fitting. Now I am in planning mode!" Cyndi admitted with a slight giggle.

"Ahem," Davin cleared his throat. "I think it is time to go home. It has been an interesting evening, to say the least, but enjoyable. Cyndi are you ready?"

"Now I wish we could stay and discuss a lot more, but I am too tired and too full to do any more planning tonight! Yes, I am ready. I have to kiss my daughter first," Cyndi declared.

When the couple was out of sight, Tyler started the conversation, "Mom, I cannot thank you and Mark enough for being here! We should have told you they are big church people and not downplayed them as just Christians. It turns out you and Mark did quite well, as always. I have even more respect for you than I had. I did not think it was possible, but here we are!"

Christine reached across the table to pat Jeannette's hand and said, "Please accept my gratitude for what you have done for me this evening. My parents are very old-fashioned. Their reaction was better than I thought it would be. They were not screaming at the top of their lungs! I was shocked when my dad gave his permission for me to move up the wedding."

"No worries. I negotiate all the time in my line of work. If I can help one of my children, that is what I will do. I have already accepted you as my daughter. I love you. Whew, I was worried I got too overbearing. I was afraid I might have gotten too bold when your father was ready to leave. Thank God, they stayed. They are lovely people when you cut through their outer layer. Okay, all is well," Jeannette said with relief. "Now, you have a lot of work to do in the next two weeks! If you need help, just ask. Mark and I will do what we can. "Mark agreed.

"One more thing before you go. After the wedding, I am going to need a firm answer regarding the office space. I had to turn several businesses away that wanted it."

"Yes, ma'am. I will have a definitive answer for you after the wedding. Tyler will you please take me home?" Christine asked.

The young couple left with smiles on their faces and holding hands. Mom had come through again.

18

Over the next eight days, Christine and Cyndi were consumed with wedding details. Phone calls were made to Jeannette for advice daily. Hundreds of emails were sent out instead of invitations. The count two days before the wedding was one-hundred-twenty-five emails had sent back an R.S.V.P. confirming their attendance — a nice amount for a small wedding with only two weeks' notice.

Making things even busier, Shannon and Ken arrived to move into their new home. Their house was perfect. It was just what they wanted. Jeannette hired a local moving company to move all their belongings in, thank God. With Mark and Jeannette working at their new companies as well as helping with the wedding, there was not enough time in the day to help with the move. It only took one day for everything to be unpacked and put where it belonged by a team of strong young men — a very efficient way to move.

Tyler and Christine shared their news with Shannon and Ken the day they arrived in Oregon. Surprisingly, they were not upset. They were of the older generation that did not believe in pregnancy before marriage. The reaction was one of joy and congratulations, which astonished Jeannette, Mark, and Skylar.

The rehearsal dinner was at Jeannette and Mark's estate. It was more of a family meal. Only one person was not related, the maid-of-honor. Of course, Zach was there, but he is family. The family was growing by leaps and bounds. Jeannette loved all the commotion and laughter that went along with this brood of people. She longed throughout her life for a family like this. They all got along with each other and loved one another. Jeannette had made her dream come true.

After dinner, Shannon took Jeannette aside to say, "I never knew what it was like to belong to a big family, a happy family. My parents were what you might call *stiff* people. They did not show affection toward their children, and I didn't realize I was the same way. It was because of the role models of my parents, I'm sure. You and your family have shown Ken and me what it is like to belong to a REAL and loving family. The little ones bring us such joy. I love you, Jeannette, and I love every one of those nuts in the other room. I have only one regret, Mark did not find you years ago! Thank you from the bottom of my heart. You are one in a million." Shannon threw her arms around Jeannette and gave her a tight hug.

"You are the best mother-in-law in the world. I love you, too," Jeannette said with a cracking voice. She put her arm around Shannon as they joined the loud group who were laughing at Jeremy and passing June around for baby loves. Jeremy always kept a close eye on his little sister. If she made the slightest whimper, he was quickly by her side.

19

It was the morning of Tyler and Christine's wedding. The big event was set to begin at 5:00 p.m. The bride and groom had the wedding jitters. Sean, Zach, Davin, and Mark were with Tyler having a toast to his last hours of bachelorhood. They were ready to toast when they saw Jeremy climbing on a chair with a juice box in hand. He intended to toast with the men because he believed he was one of the guys. Jeremy raised his juice box in the air and yelled "salute" with all the men.

Tia, Shannon, Cyndi, Skylar, and Jeannette were with Christine helping her put her gown on. The maid-of-honor was applying final touches of makeup and last-minute changes with her hair. June sat in her baby chair and watched intently as women were chattering, spraying, and giggling. She was entertained and let out a laugh or a coo occasionally.

The banquet room looked impeccable. The perfume from stargazer lilies filled the room and wafted into the dining areas. Music from a stringed quartet softly played as the guests visited with one another and found a chair.

It was time. Mark flashed the lights, signaling it was time to sit down, the ceremony was about to get underway.

The quartet played a beautiful love song as the bridesmaid and maid-of-honor walked toward an arch of flowers where Tyler awaited. They were dressed in simple royal blue and white velvet, floor length gowns with sheer long sleeves. They carried a bouquet of blue roses and white lilies. The girls looked elegant.

The men wore black tuxes white shirts, a royal blue vest and a royal blue bowtie. On their lapel was pinned a single white lily. Tyler was starting to sweat through his shirt.

The volume of the music grew. It was Christine's cue to make her appearance.

At first glimpse of the bride, Tyler's mouth went dry, and his face lost its color. *"Christine is a gorgeous bride, and she is going to be my wife. What happened to my legs? I can't feel them! She is beautiful,"* Tyler thought. Sean saw his brother's legs wobble and reached behind him to grab his belt to keep him from falling.

Sean whispered in Tyler's ear, "Hold on little brother. It will all be over in a few minutes."

He was right. It was over in a few minutes. Although he remembered nothing. He had been in a daze. Tyler did what the minister told him to do and was successfully proclaimed to be a husband to Christine.

Dinner began after the cutting of the cake. The evening filled the guests with a sense of romance and joy. Jeannette glanced at Cyndi and Davin throughout the evening. Never once did she see them without a smile on their faces. Shannon and Ken were in a state of pure happiness.

The bride and groom were only going to have a four-day honeymoon at the Oregon coast. They both had to come back for work.

Because of the wedding, many more people who had never visited *Our City* were eager to come back. Mark received a lot of compliments about his restaurant from the guests. It boosted his pride and fed his ego, but he was still humbled so many appreciated his vision of making dining an event and not just ordering a meal.

Mark brought the chef out to take a bow for the excellent dinner of Prime Rib, Mark, and Jeannette's favorite.

Jeannette whispered in Mark's ear, "I still say Irma could give your chef a run for his money at cooking a Prime Rib." Mark gave a little chuckle.

The bride and groom left at 7:00. They had a three-hour drive to the Pacific Ocean shore. The last guest left at 10:30. Afterward Skylar lingered with Mark and Jeannette for a relaxing glass of wine. The ladies took off their heels and rested their feet on a chair next to each other.

Skylar broke the silence by saying, "It was a lovely wedding. I am impressed you girls pulled it off in two weeks! Whew! Tyler told me Christine was a big help. It's about time somebody helped you! I visited with Cyndi and Davin during the reception. I like them."

"Thank you for the compliment," Jeannette began. "Yes, it was a busy two weeks, but worth it. They look so happy together, and so much in love. I have to agree with you about Cyndi and Davin. They are nice people, since we broke through their hard shell, close to fanatics, with their church ideals. Don't get me wrong. The Bible is my go-to book. I read one scripture a day. It is not like that for them. They were so immersed in religion, to the point I think if the church had cast Christine out, they would have gone along with it!"

"Kudos to Christine for putting up with it all these years," Skylar remarked.

Mark had a smile sweep over his face, making the girls stare at him with wonder.

"Did I tell you what Jeremy did with the men? We were ready to make a toast to Tyler when Jeremy pulled up a chair to stand on next to Sean during our toast. He had a juice box that he raised and touched all our glasses. He was one of us. That little man was so cute. We treated him as one of the men and tried not to laugh."

"Did you get a picture? I would love to see that little stinker being one of the guys. I love my grandchildren!" Jeannette told them.

After the newlyweds returned from the coast, Christine decided to begin her dream of being an Agriculture Broker and rented the space from Jeannette. She opened for business two months after the wedding. She made a corner next to her desk for the baby she was expecting in five months. A fold-out screen separated it from the office. She was surprised to have customers almost immediately, but it shouldn't have surprised her. The farmers and Ranchers, all knew her, which made for a smooth transition. They trusted this home-town girl. She could not only help with problems with their crops but help with selling them for a reasonable price just as she planned.

Because the seed of business Jeannette and Mark started, the area began to boom. Tyler and Zach were designing more buildings and houses every day, making it necessary to hire a secretary.

Oregonians and Washingtonians had accepted Skylar and her designs with open arms. She was designing more out of her Oregon office than Chicago! A big seller was to western royalty courts for their appearances in parades, rodeos, county fairs, and special events. Her first fashion show is scheduled in the spring in Seattle, Washington. She hired a secretary and three seamstresses to sew the designs and was still turning a profit. Jeannette's idea of skyping with clients proved to be brilliant. Skylar did not have to travel to Chicago. She was able to talk to her banker and accountant and shop manager via skype, leaving her with much needed time at her drawing board. Plus, it cuts down on the expense of traveling.

Mark's restaurant and dinner club were filled every night. Oregonians loved the new idea in dining. It had caught on like wildfire after the wedding. Any tourist traveling remotely close to Clark City made a detour to visit *Our City Dining and Dinner Club*. The Chamber of Commerce added the restaurant on their web site as a MUST dining experience. Mark hired an exceptional staff and took a page out of Jeannette's handbook on how to treat employees. He had a happy and satisfied team.

Old West Windy City had taken off just as Jeannette thought it would. She had Rap artists, Rock and Roll artists, Country Western artists, jazz, and all other types of music coming in, hoping to get a recording contract. Others just wanted to make a recording for themselves. She had been correct in tapping the talent in the west. It helped to have the parent company *Windy City Publishing and Recording.* That made it easier to become established. Every artist and non-artist alike had heard of it. With Jeannette at the helm, the company had a lot of respect and a lot of business.

Windy City was operating smoothly with Greg in charge of the business end in Chicago. Jeannette no longer made monthly trips to Chicago. She took the advice she had given Skylar and did a lot of skyping. But it did not stop her from being in Chicago in person. Jeannette had stretched it to every other month and stayed for three days, meeting with Greg, her accountant, the attorney, and the bank. Greg was a perfect choice. Of course, he always had her listen to tapes to see if they needed any tweaking while she was there. Sometimes he sent her a disc for her opinion, but his idea was usually correct, not needing Jeannette's advice, but there were times she used her exceptional ear for music to make the song a hit.

20

The months flew by and the time for Christine to deliver had come as quickly as a snap of two fingers. Tyler was a nervous wreck expecting Christine to go into labor any minute. He had her bag in the car, the car seat was installed and ready to be filled with a cooing bundle of joy. The only thing left was waiting for Christine to go into labor. Like Sean and Tia, they did not know what gender they were having. It will be a surprise. Not to Jeannette, she already knew, but honored their wishes and kept it to herself, well...Mark and herself.

Christine was overdue by two weeks. The doctor told her if she had not gone into labor by Friday, he was going to induce. Christine and Tyler did everything they could think of to get labor started. He took her for rides down bumpy roads, they walked several blocks each evening, she drank cod liver oil, but nothing worked.

Early Friday morning, Christine was induced to give birth. The labor pains started almost immediately. Tyler walked her up and down the hall at the hospital. Every hour the nurse checked to see if she had dilated. After six hours, the contractions had gotten very intense, but still no dilation. Her doctor was growing concerned and told her no more walking. He made her stay in bed with a monitor strapped around her belly to listen to the baby's heartbeat. If the baby went into distress, he would have to rush her to the operating room and perform a caesarian section.

By this time the entire family and Christine's parents were by her side. Tyler held her hand, Cyndi rubbed her back, and

Jeannette massaged her feet. The monitor started doing something odd and caught Jeannette's attention. She slipped out of the room to get the nurse so as not to alarm anyone. After Jeannette told her about the readings on the monitor, she immediately paged the doctor to come to room 226 stat! Jeannette quietly went back into the room and put her arm around Tyler. A minute behind her, the doctor and nurse came rushing in.

The doctor told them, "The baby is in distress. Christine, we are taking you to the O.R. Everything is going to be alright. You need to relax as much as possible. Tyler, as soon as the baby is born, one of the nurses will let you know. We have to go now!"

Tyler quickly bent down and kissed Christine on the top of her head and whispered, "Mom said you are going to be fine, and so is the baby. Do what the doctor says and try to relax. I love you."

Christine was whisked off and quickly disappeared down the hall. Tyler turned into Jeannette's shoulder and cried.

Jeremy stood at Uncle Tyler's side and tugged on his pant leg. Looking up, he said, "Unkie sad?" He hugged Tyler's leg.

Sean picked up Jeremy. He told him, "Unkie is a little sad right now, but he will be alright. Auntie Christine had to go into another room with the doctor. When she comes out, you will have a new cousin. A baby. Then Unkie will be happy." Jeremy shook his head with understanding. He leaned over and patted Tyler on the cheek.

Sean's heart hurt for his brother. He grabbed Tyler and locked himself around him, hoping to give him comfort.

A nurse took Tyler down the hall to a door with a window where he could see down a hall that led to the O.R. She told him it was where the nurse would come from, and he would be the first one to see her through the window of the door where he stood. Of course, the formidable family followed and waited with him. He stood staring through the window, his hands placed on either side of the pane of glass without moving or saying a word. Jeannette held her arm around her youngest son so he could feel the support and love from her and the family.

Nervousness had spread throughout the group. Whispered chatter was taking place behind Tyler. None was of any importance. They needed to fill the silence.

The doctor was right when he said it would not take long for Tyler to know the outcome. A nurse came around a corner and mouthed the words, "It's a boy!"

Tyler shouted, "It's a boy! It's a boy!"

The nurse opened the door to let them know everything went very well, and Christine was going to be fine.

"You have a good-sized baby boy. He weighed eight pounds three ounces! That is a big baby for such a petite woman. He has all his fingers and toes and is crying at the top of his lungs! That is a good thing. You can go back to her room if you'd like. We will be bringing her back, along with your son, in about an hour, maybe less. Congratulations, Daddy!"

"Oh, thank God!" Tyler said and slumped to the floor. "I have never been so scared in my life," He looked up to see a sea of smiling faces. "I have a son!" He exclaimed.

Mark helped him to his feet and locked him in a familiar hug.

He told Tyler, "I love you, son. Your mom and I thought you might need these." Mark handed him a box of cigars that read, "It's a boy."

Tyler looked at his mother with surprise, then said, "You knew. Of course, you did. Thank you for not spoiling it. Thanks, Mark, for the cigars. Everybody have a cigar! I am a dad!"

Jeremy started clapping. He said, "Unkie, happy!" Then he reached out his little hand for a cigar as all the men had.

Sean smiled at how cute Jeremy was but had to tell him he was too little.

He was in Sean's arms and was about to be disappointed when Grandpa Mark said, "Little man, I have a special cigar just for you. It is a blue candy one. See?" Jeremy grinned and gently took the cigar and placed it in his mouth, just like the men. Now he felt like one of the guys. Grandma Jeannette snapped a picture for the baby book.

They filled Christine's room, waiting for her return. The tension was broken now the little guy had made his appearance, so the conversations returned to louder, happy ones.

They were interrupted by a nurse saying, "Beep! Beep! New mommy coming through!" She wheeled Christine into the room. Following them was a nurse holding a little bundle wrapped in a blue blanket.

She asked, "Which one of you is daddy?"

Tyler said with a crack in his voice, "Me. I am the father."

"Say hello to your son," the nurse said and put him in Tyler's arms.

At first, Tyler stared at him, then kissed him on the forehead. Jeremy wiggled in Sean's arms until he got close enough to see his new cousin. He touched the new little person on the cheek with his hand, then scrunched up his mouth, wanting to kiss him. Tyler held him closer so Jeremy could kiss him. Jeannette was snapping pictures without notice. It was her routine when a grandchild was born to take lots of pictures and start a baby book.

After the sweet baby was held and kissed by the family members, it was time to give the new family some privacy, but first Mark asked, "What are you going to name him?"

Christine offered the answer, "Zach's middle name is Michael, and so that is his first name. His middle name is after my father, Davin."

"I like it," Mark said. "Michael Davin. A good strong name for a big boy. We will see you tomorrow. We love you."

Davin and Cyndi stayed a little longer. Davin did not want anyone to know the birth of his grandchild brought tears that were threatening to spill down his face.

"I am truly blessed. My daughter has married a wonderful young man, she has made me a grandfather, and the best thing is she named her son after me," Davin acknowledged. He let the tears flow. After he regained his voice, he said, "And to think I was upset because Christine was pregnant with this little miracle. Thank you, Tyler, and Christine, for standing up against our old beliefs and helping me see what was important."

Tyler hugged both Cyndi and Davin. "It wasn't just Christine and me. You should thank my mother and Mark, too."

The new family was left to enjoy their new addition.

The next day Jeannette and Mark visited the hospital to make the same offer to Tyler and Christine as they had with Sean and Tia. A one-acre parcel would be theirs, with a house built on the property. What funds they have for the house will be used until it is depleted then Jeannette will take over and finish paying for their home.

Mark encouraged them, "Take your time to decide. I know you want a house; you need a house now that you have little Michael. Talk it over and let us know what you decide. We do not want you to feel pressured...B"

Tyler interrupted, "We don't have to think about it. We were hoping you would make this offer! Christine and I talked about this, and we agreed. Right, Christine?" He asked.

"Yes! It is a wonderful and very generous offer! How can I thank you? Oh, Tyler a new house!" Christine gushed.

"Guess who is designing it?" Jeannette said with a giggle. "Tyler, I would suggest you get busy with the design right away. I will contact the contractor this afternoon. Can you have the plans ready in two weeks so I can make an appointment for him to look them over and give us a price? Mark and I will be there, and I will work on getting the price lower than what his quote is."

"Don't worry about the designs. I already have some of the designs on paper. Yes, it will be ready in two weeks. I have no doubt you will get the price down, mom. I have seen you in action. The nurse said we could go home as soon as the discharge papers are ready, about an hour from now," Tyler stated.

"As soon as Mark and I get our baby fix, and kiss his sweet head, we will leave you to pack up," Jeannette told the couple.

Jeannette and Mark left the hospital arm in arm.

"I am so thankful for my gift of music. It has brought joy to my heart, and the ability to afford to help with my children's happiness," Jeannette told Mark as they drove home.

Tyler had the plans ready and was waiting for the contractor. They met at Tyler and Zach's office. Jeannette worked her magic and got the price down by ten-thousand dollars. It was always a negotiating game with Jeannette and the contractor. They both enjoyed the battle of bantering. In the end, the contractor would rub his face with his hands in frustration and agreed to Jeannette's price. It always finished with smiling faces and a handshake. They respected each other and their tactics just as Clay and Jeannette mirrored the same tactics with one another and ended the same, with a smile and a handshake with one bonus; A glass of the good stuff to seal the deal.

Eight months later, the family of three had finally moved in and was enjoying the space of their new home. Tyler felt good living between Sean and Tyler's parents. All within walking distance. Shannon and Ken lived a mile down the road, Skylar lived two miles away, and Davin and Cyndi lived the furthest at just over three miles. They were all close, but not so close they felt smothered.

21

Several years went by.

The restaurant, the recording company, architect design, clothing design, and agriculture brokerage were all turning a profit, and a respectable profit it was.

Zach finally found that special woman whom Jeannette had to give her approval of before he asked her to marry him. Her name is Kim and she is a native of Clark City. They married a year ago and were expecting their first child in six months. Jeannette and Mark helped them with a significant down payment on a house. However, they did not get the same deal as Tyler and Sean. Kim and Zach found a piece of property a mile away to build their home.

Tyler and Christine were expecting another child in five months. The doctor told them Christine will have to have another cesarean section. They already had the date picked out when she will deliver. It will remain a secret, again what the sex of the baby is.

Christine delivered another boy, Seth Alan, weighing in at 8 pounds 6 ounces.

Tia gave birth to another son eight months ago, making them a family of five. They named him Nolan Thomas. That was it for them. They informed everyone — no more babies at the last family dinner. Three was enough.

Sean, Tyler, and Zach's children were all close in age and were always together. The family told them they were all cousins, and Zach and Kim were their aunt and uncle. That is how they will grow up, like family.

Jeannette and Mark and their vision of business had put Clark City on the map. Their businesses never slowed down, attracting more tourists and customers all the time. New companies and stores sprang up all over town. Mark and Jeannette took a chance, spent several million dollars, and woke a slumped town back to life. Although that was never their intention, it was the icing on the cake. It started with an idea Jeannette had about moving home and tapping into the talent hidden in Oregon. It had a snowball effect in one way or another and trickled down to every person in the city and county.

Clay and The Band were still at the top of the charts and in the limelight. Clay kept buying songs from Jeannette when she had time to write. Her price had gone up substantially, which always made Clay cringe, but she was well worth the price. Without her, they would probably be a group struggling, trying to make a hit, and hoping to be famous. Together, their music had made Jeannette and Clay very rich. But for Jeannette, the money was an extra blessing. For her, it was all about the music. Thank God, she dared to sell Clay that first song.

The county Clark City was situated in had the county fair every year in Clark City. The Fair Board asked Jeannette if she could get Clay and The Band to play one night on the main stage. She made the call and Clay jumped at it. He was finally going to get to spend time in Oregon where Jeannette and Mark lived. Best of all, he was looking forward to seeing Jeannette and meeting the new family members. Of course, she planned a big family dinner including Clay, Amy, The Band, and all the in-laws and great-grandparents. She also invited Clay and Amy to stay at the estate while they were in Clark City. They gladly accepted. Jeannette made reservations at a new hotel that just opened to house The Band.

During the county fair, there was also a pro-rodeo that ran the full week. It took place at the center of the fairgrounds. Cowboys and cowgirls from all over the country, and some from Canada, came to participate. Clark City had one of the best arenas for the rodeo on the rodeo circuit, so it was no surprise how many cowboys and cowgirls it drew to compete.

Jeannette managed to secure box seats straight across the arena from the bull riding chutes, which are considered prime seats. They planned on attending two nights, Thursday, and Saturday. Friday night, they were on stage. She was excited to show off her town and what they had to offer to her old friends.

On Sunday afternoon before all the festivities of the fair began, Jeannette and Mark met Clay, Amy, and The Band at the airport with two vans she had rented, along with drivers, to transport instruments, equipment, and The Band for the week. Clay and Amy rode with their host and hostess.

That evening was the family dinner. Jeannette made arrangements for one of the vans to pick up The Band and deliver them to Jeannette and Mark's estate. Each person was greeted at the door by the couple while Clay and Amy watched as people kept filing in. They did not think there was an end to how many people were now in Jeannette and Mark's family. They were overwhelmed at how big the family had grown.

"Tell me these are NOT all family?" Clay asked with a gaping mouth.

"Every last one of them! I take that back. Zach and his wife, Kim, are considered family, but not related. He and Tyler have been best friends since high school. They even went to college together, and they have an architect design company that is doing very well. I will show you their office tomorrow when I give you a tour at *Old West Windy City*," Jeannette informed him.

"It seems like yesterday you were a timid young woman, with two young boys and a gift for music. You have come a long way, Pretty Lady," Clay recalled. "I hear your name mentioned in conversations all over the country. You have made a very respectable name for yourself in the music world. Of course, I always tell them you are my friend."

Jeannette's face turned red, as usual. That was the one thing she could never overcome.

"Clay, if you are trying to suck up to me to get the price of my songs at a cheaper price, think again, buddy," Jeannette teased, and Clay grinned. Amy shook her head at the two.

"Sweetheart, you are the youngest looking grandma I have ever seen. Oregon agrees with you," Amy complimented. "Mark, you look wonderful, too. Did you ever believe in your wildest dreams you would one day be a grandpa to this huge family? It is amazing how quickly life can change with an introduction. I will take the credit for that!" Amy beamed.

Mark took Amy's hand, kissed it, and said, "I am in your debt for a lifetime. Thank you, a million times! Excuse me for one minute."

Mark went into another room and brought back a bottle of the good stuff.

"Clay and Amy, this is for your part in getting Jeannette and I together," Mark said as he presented the bottle to Clay.

"I'll take that. Thank you very much! It was my idea. Clay was unsure if we should introduce the two of you. I pressed the issue until he agreed. So, this bottle goes to me!" Amy declared.

"Okay, okay," Clay said. "It was your idea, but I am going to help you drink this!"

"After dinner, we might have to sample the contents," Amy said with a wink.

Jeannette looked around to make sure the family was all present and accounted for before disappearing into the kitchen.

"Irma, it is time to put all the food out. I will help you. We can enlist Tia and Christine, too."

The food was spread out on a separate table, banquet style, for serving. It was a help-yourself kind of dinner. If anyone went away hungry, it was no fault of Jeannette's.

After all the food was arranged, Mark tapped his glass with a spoon to get everyone's attention for a toast.

"Before we start filling up our plates, I would like to say thank you to family and friends. May you all be blessed with love, happiness, and a lifetime of joy! Salute!"

In turn, the group yelled, "Salute!"

After everyone had left, several hours later, with full stomachs and tired children, Jeannette, Mark, Clay, and Amy sat around the fire pit, enjoying a glass of wine.

Clay broke the relaxing silence by saying, "Pretty Lady, you have a fantastic family. They all seem to like each other, too. That's rare. You have come a long way, and no one deserves to be happy more than you. How about you and I play a little fireside music?"

"I will have to get my guitar. Give me a minute," Jeannette told him.

"No, you don't. It is right here," Mark said and handed it to her.

"You know me too well, Honey. What shall we play? Something soothing for full stomachs," Jeannette said with a chuckle. "You start. I'll jump in."

They played a song from years ago. It was one of the songs they performed the first time she played with Clay and The Band at a wedding reception. She was married to Jeff at the time. That was the night Jeff crushed her dreams. She bounced back several years later with a vengeance and made new dreams come true.

"You did not forget this old song! It really is an old one," Clay said.

"No, I didn't forget. It was the first time I performed with you and The Band that we played this song. Dang, that takes me back. The boys were little guys. I loved that night and playing with you. I was in seventh heaven. I wanted so badly to go on performing with you, but it wasn't meant to be," Jeannette reminisced.

Mark looked confused and asked, "Why didn't you join his band? He invited you, and you turned him down? Why?"

"Well, Jeff would not allow me to. Before you get all excited, let me explain. At first, Jeff plainly said, 'no.' when I begged him, he gave me a choice. He told me if I joined the band, I would never see my boys again. Jeff would take them from me. I knew he would make good on that threat. He didn't want them, he used them to control me. My boys always came first. There was no choice to make, and he knew it. I stayed home. I have NEVER regretted my decision. There were times, during my younger years, I cried, thinking I would never have another opportunity to make music, but I reminded myself being a mom was more important. If you think about it, everything I went through led me to *Windy City*. None of this would be a reality, and I would not have a good friend that I love playing guitars with, so it all worked the way it was supposed to," Jeannette recalled.

"Sweetheart, you never told me that story," Mark interjected with sadness.

"It's alright. It is over and in the past. It was just a hard time I went through and came out on top. I made the right choice. My boys have now grown into men, and I am very proud of them.I take all the credit for that!" She boasted and got a good laugh from the others."

"Let's play some more, Clay. Here's one I used to play for my boys when they were having a hard time falling asleep."

Jeannette began to play a sweet lullaby that seemed to float through the night air. Clay caught on quickly and played harmony. Mark got a text from Sean and one from Tyler. They heard the music from their houses. They told Mark to thank Mom and Clay for the lullaby. It was a perfect ending to a perfect night. The song not only had a calming effect on young children but the adults, too.

Amy broke out the good stuff, and they toasted to old friends. Then the yawning began, and it was time for the adults to go to bed.

The next morning the four went to breakfast at *Our City Dining*. Mark wanted to show off his creation. The Band joined them for a tour, and of course, breakfast. They were impressed with what he had done. It was beautiful, with a warm and welcoming feeling.

"I was noticing the stage in the dinner club. If you need any new music one evening, we would be happy to help you out," Clay suggested. "Right, Band?" They all gave a nod of their head; their mouths were full.

"I am glad you offered. I was thinking about asking you. How about Wednesday night, on one condition? If you get my wife on stage to play with you. It has been so long since I've seen her on stage, I know she misses it," Mark asked, almost pleading.

"Deal! I am going to enjoy this!" Clay agreed, rubbing his hands together.

"Alright you two, I am sitting right here! Of course, I will play! Wednesday night was the only time I didn't have anything planned for you. I want to make sure you have a good Oregon experience. Who knows, maybe you will retire here?" Jeannette suggested.

"Whoa, Pretty Lady! I'm not that old, yet!" Clay roared.

After breakfast Mark joined them for a tour of *Old West Windy City*. Jeannette impressed them with the design of how things were efficient, modern, and much more extensive than *Windy City*. Jeannette explained she was also doing some upgrading in Chicago with the sound system.

The tour carried on to the second floor. Amy was particularly interested in Skylar's creations. She stayed longer with Skylar while the group moved on.

"Jeannette, I think you just cost me a lot of money," Clay told her.

"What are you talking about?"

"Skylar and her designs! Amy is still there, and I am sure she is having Skylar design her something. Not just one thing either, it will be several," Clay forecasted and rolled his eyes.

He was right. Amy caught up with them in the sound room an hour later. She was all smiles and admitted to having Skylar design her three outfits, making Clay's eyes roll, again and made Jeannette chuckle.

"Clay," Jeannette started, "I have a surprise for you. A new song. Why don't you all bring your instruments tomorrow afternoon and set up in this sound room? I will play it for you first. If you like it, how about we get it on tape while you are here?"

"It's a date. I have a feeling this is going to cost me money also! Oregon is expensive!" Clay declared, shaking his head and making Jeannette laugh.

The sound booth and room were ready for Clay and The Band when they arrived. The Band set up their gear and was prepared to listen as Jeannette played her song for them. It wasn't a fast song, and it wasn't slow, just a nice in-between.

"Yep! It is going to cost me! Another good one, Pretty Lady. It could make the charts. Let's try it out tomorrow night at the dinner club," Clay suggested.

"I'm game, but can the band keep up?" Jeannette asked teasingly. There was a lot of moaning and complaining about her comment.

The drummer spoke up, "Try us! We can keep up with anything you dish out!" He teasingly retorted.

"Okay, you heard the song. Let's see what you've got!" Jeannette challenged and gave the nod to the sound booth to record.

"Well, drummer-man, you proved it. Nice job. Justin, in the sound booth, has it cued up and ready to play it for you. Shall we give it a listen?" Jeannette asked.

In the design of this sound area, Jeannette had the booth made larger to accommodate larger groups. They were all able to fit inside the room comfortably. The tape finished, Clay looked at Jeannette, and both were smiling.

"It is another good one, Pretty Lady!" Clay confirmed.

"I like it, but I think it would sound better with this at the bridge," Jeannette said, grabbing her guitar. "Instead of what we just recorded. Let's do it one more time with this one tweak."

"You heard her, boys. We need to tweak it," Clay admitted.

When the second recording was finished and listened to, Clay said, "You were right. That one change made the song. You amaze me. How do you do that?"

"I don't know. I can hear it in my mind, and I have to get it out. That's it," Jeannette revealed. "Do you think it is a keeper? Shall we put it on a single?"

"Yes. Give me the contract to sign, and I will get out my checkbook," Clay groaned.

"I have it typed and ready for you. You know you are going to make a lot more money than what you are paying me. So quit whining! Tell him, Amy!" Jeannette demanded.

All Amy could do was laugh at the two. It was always entertaining to watch them work a deal. Jeannette would tell him just how it was going to be, and he would act like it was killing him. When the contract was signed, and business concluded, they laughed, and everyone had a drink of the good stuff she kept hidden with several glasses at the ready. Mark had snuck away from the restaurant so he could join them in sealing the deal with a costly glass of whiskey.

Jeannette loaned her car to Clay and Amy so they could drive around to see what the town had to offer. They saw horse trailers galore coming into town for the fair and rodeo. Many had already arrived. Clay pushed the buttons to roll down the windows to hear all the sounds of a county fair. It was attractive to both Clay and Amy. Chickens crowing and clucking, cows mooing, horses whinnying, pigs squealing, and he heard other sounds he could not identify, but enjoyed hearing.

Clay and Amy met Jeannette and Mark back at the estate. The Band was invited to swim and have a burger on the grill. Sean and Tyler heard the splashing and laughter. Together they walked over to see what was going on. Jeannette saw them and motioned for them to join in.

There were grandchildren, along with adults of all ages around the pool, laughing and talking. Clay, Amy, Mark, and Jeannette chose not to get in the pool with all the activity. Instead, they watched from a comfortable chair, under a huge umbrella with a cold beer. Of course, the littlest ones stayed close to grandma.

On one of her trips into the kitchen, Jeannette grabbed her guitar. She asked the little ones if they would like to sing the frog song. On the plush grass, they jumped up and down and clapped their hands. Grandma began playing, and the grandchildren jumped around the best they could trying to be frogs. The children were so cute, the adults could not help but laugh.

"How about the Choo-Choo song?" They began trying to make toot-toot sounds like a train. It was hilarious. They were on all fours trying to be an engine chugging along adding a toot-toot as they chugged down a make-believe track. When the song ended, they jumped to their feet and wanted another one.

Grandma told them, "After dinner, I will sing you a lullaby, but right now we need to put the hamburgers and hot dogs on the grill. Do you want to help me cook?" The little ones took off running to the patio. "Amy, would you like to join this wild group and me? It should be entertaining."

Amy laughed and said, "I would love to."

Clay and Mark observed all the hubbub taking place on the patio. Clay said, "Those were cute little songs Jeannette sang to the kids. Where did she pick those up? Or did she write them?"

Mark answered, "She wrote them for her boys when they were little. They loved them. They had the same reaction you just witnessed. She promised to sing them a lullaby after dinner. It will be the one you heard the other night. That song always settles them down for mom and dad. By the time she finishes the song, they will be yawning and ready for bed. I'm sure it is the reason she promised to play it."

"Jeannette is a wonderful grandma. I can only imagine what it was like having her as a mother," Clay imagined.

Tyler and Sean joined Mark and Clay under the umbrella.

Tyler answered Clay, "We have the best mom in the world. You see her cooking with the kids? She let us cook with her every day. We had aprons and wooden spoons that made us feel like we were helping. She played and sang to us, just as you heard a few minutes ago. She was with us 24/7 until we started school."

Sean added, "Our father didn't treat her very well, and we knew it, but there was nothing we could do. We knew she was unhappy. Sometimes we heard what he said or yelled at her. She never let her sadness show around us. She put a smile on her face and kept on doing what she needed to. Sometimes we heard her cry when we got older. She told us a few years ago Jeff crushed her dreams and used us to do it. We are glad she got away from him. We have never had a relationship of any kind with him and never will."

"Your mother is an exceptional woman," Clay began. "It is amazing she is not bitter and grumpy but look at her. Jeannette is having as much fun as the children are! She has earned happiness and love. Remember that Mark! Do not hurt our girl!"

Mark held up his hands and said, "I won't, I promise! I love her too much."

"Come and get it! Burgers and dogs are ready! Let's eat!" Jeannette yelled.

Grandma helped each one of the little ones with preparing their food and settled them at their own children's sized table. The adults had dinner family-style, passing food around to serve themselves as the dishes went by.

"Hey, Clay!" The drummer yelled across the table. "We should come to Clark City more often. It's like a vacation!"

"For the most part, yes, it is, but Oregon is costing me a pretty penny," he gave Jeannette a wink. "Just remember tomorrow evening we are playing at the club and Friday night at the Fair," Clay reminded.

"We also have two days at the rodeo! Those cowgirls are pretty! Have you noticed those jeans they wear? It is a wonderful sight when they walk away," the bass player commented, and all the men agreed. The women rolled their eyes.

After dinner, Jeannette played and sang a lullaby as promised. Just as predicted, the children were yawning and ready for bedtime. Their parents said goodbye and disappeared into the dark of the evening.

Wednesday rolled around before they knew it. Mark stood at the microphone in the club, to make an announcement.

"Ladies and gentlemen, I know you enjoy the sounds of the orchestra here at *Our City Dining*, but tonight we have some special guests that have graciously offered their services for your listening pleasure. With the fair in town, I see a lot of new faces, but the faces you will see in just a minute are very well known. It is my pleasure to introduce, Clay and The Band!" The club erupted into applause as they walked on stage.

Without saying a word, they started playing. Jeannette joined them on stage. Mid-way through the first song, Clay began a guitar challenge with Jeannette. There was no doubt, Jeannette won, as she always had. They finished the song, and the crowd clapped, cheered, and whistled.

Clay stepped to the microphone and said, "Thank you! If you do not know the little lady that just showed me how a guitar is played, her name is Jeannette, owner of *Old West Windy City Recording Company* right across the parking lot, and my longtime friend. Give it up one more time for Jeannette. She writes a lot of the songs on our albums. We have a brand new one no one has heard, yet. We recorded it yesterday as a single. It should be out in about four weeks. Is that right, Jeannette?" She nodded. "We want to use this audience as our test audience to see what you think. It's called *A Little Bit of Lovin.*"

The dining patrons loved it. Clay gave Jeannette recognition for being the author once again. Her face turned red like it always had. It was the one thing she had not overcome. It just proved she was still humble.

An hour later, it was time for the orchestra to take over. The crowd cheered Clay, The Band, and Jeannette off.

Mark took the microphone and said, "That lovely lady with the guitar is my wife! Isn't she great? I think so, too! Clay and The Band will be playing at the fair Friday night on the main stage. Now, enjoy the big band sounds of our orchestra."

The rodeo was exciting for the group from Chicago. It was a new experience watching the cowboys and cowgirls compete. The Band made 25 cent wagers amongst themselves on who was going to get bucked off, if the calf would outrun the horse in the calf roping competition, or if the bull or the cowboy would win in bull riding. It was the type of sporting event that was a normal thing to witness in Oregon, but something altogether new to The Band. The Oregonians showed them how to whoop it up.

Friday night Jeannette performed with Clay on the main stage and enjoyed every second of it. At the end of their concert, they got a standing ovation. The fans convinced them to play one more song.

"Since you asked so nicely, we will play one more. This song is a brand new one. It will be out in about four weeks as a single. Here we go!"

They got the same reaction from the audience as they had at the dinner club. They loved it.

After the concert, Clay turned to Jeannette and said, "This just might be another hit!"

Jeannette responded with, "Each hit I write for you the price of my songs goes up!" She cracked herself up, but Clay gave her the usual cringe and made her laugh even harder.

Saturday was the last day for the group to be in Clark City and the last day of the rodeo. It was the finals, so only the best was participating, which made it all the more exciting. The bets between the members of the band continued through the evening. Each stake was still a quarter. The bass player ended up winning the most quarters.

Sunday morning, they all ate breakfast at *Our City Dining*. They were tired but relaxed at the same time. Jeannette had been great at keeping them entertained and fed, not to mention recording a possible hit while they were in Clark City.

It was hard saying goodbye at the airport. Jeannette hugged every person before they left. Amy and Clay got special bear hugs.

"Your home is gorgeous, and your family is...Well, big and wonderful. A million thanks for including us in your family and letting us stay with you," Amy proclaimed. "We enjoyed your grandchildren so much. Can we come back again?"

"You don't have to ask! You are welcome ANYTIME. Just give me a heads up when you are coming, and our house is your house. I will miss you. Take care of the big guy. Send me pictures of Skylar's designs when you get them," Jeannette instructed.

Mark and Jeannette enjoyed a relaxing afternoon by the pool. After all the activities of the past week, Jeannette and Mark needed a day of relaxation.

A year had passed. The last song Jeannette wrote for Clay put him at the top of the charts, again. Tyler was the father of two, Zach had one son, Sean and Tia had three children, Skylar's business was booming, Mark's restaurant was busy every day of the week, and Jeannette's new recording company was more active than ever.

22

Mark got a call from a frantic Ken, "Shannon, had a stroke! She is in the hospital." Mark and Jeannette rushed to her side.

The doctor came into Shannon's room to give a diagnosis and report to Mark, Skylar, Ken, and Jeannette.

"It was a massive stroke. Four blood clots showed on the M.R.I. One of which is in her brain. She is in a coma. We have done everything we could to help her. I am not sure she will wake up. We have to wait and see. That's all we can do for now."

All of the young adults came to say goodbye and kiss her forehead in case Shannon passed.

Shannon did not wake up. She lasted eight more hours. Ken, Mark, Skylar, and Jeannette stayed by her side until she was gone.

Mark cried on his father's shoulder.

"I loved her, Dad. She was a good great-grandmother. I am so glad we have spent the last several years together. She was a different person."

Skylar and Jeannette joined the two and made it a group hug.

Skylar said through sobs, "I loved her, too. Her heart opened, and that hard shell she had, broke wide open when she moved to Oregon. It amazed me every time I watched her playing with the great grandkids. She was good with them. I am sorry I didn't give her any."

Jeannette added, "I loved her, too. We got off to a rocky start, but it all turned out well. I am going to miss her. The little ones will not understand where she went. They loved playing with her. They laughed when she tried getting up from the floor. They thought she did it for their entertainment. She would get frustrated, and that made them laugh all the harder. I like to think we made her last years, happy ones."

Ken finally spoke, "She was the happiest I had ever seen, after we moved to Oregon. She loved each of you, and she adored those great grandbabies. She and I had grown close once again. Thank you, Jeannette, for melting her heart and mine." They all broke into sobs again.

The memorial service was at the cemetery. Shannon made friends with more people than Mark had realized. That made the turnout more substantial than expected. It blessed his heart to see how many people cared about his mother.

All the family members gathered at Jeannette and Mark's house. Irma made finger food to eat, and people kept dropping by with more food and expressing their condolences.

Three months had gone by since Shannon passed away. Ken was in a deep depression and could not find his way out. He spent every evening with Mark and Jeannette. They tried to convince him to talk to a counselor, have a checkup, or go to the senior center to be around other people his age. He always listened and shook his head in agreement but did not take their advice. He felt lost without Shannon.

Within six months Ken passed away in his sleep. The doctor said there was nothing physically wrong with him. The only answer he had was, Ken might have passed from a broken heart after losing Shannon. He gave up the will to live.

"I can't believe they are gone. Several years ago, I don't know if I would have mourned their passing. They finally became the parents I always wanted them to be. Now they are gone," Skylar said and broke down and cried. "I loved them both."

Jeannette put her arms around Skylar to comfort her.

"Sweetheart, I wish you had been able to spend more time with them since they changed. They have always loved you and Mark, but they didn't know how to physically show it. Your mom once told me that her parents never showed affection to her or her siblings. She figured it was why she didn't show her feelings toward you and your brother. Remember, the love for you and Mark was always there; she or your dad just didn't know how to express it," Jeannette explained.

Skylar began to laugh. "They learned that first Christmas eve at your apartment. I can still see the look on their faces when the kids gave them those hugs. That was priceless!"

Jeannette joined her in laughing. "You are right. I thought Shannon might run screaming from my apartment, thinking she had been accosted or something. From that moment on, she was a changed woman. Ken was easier going. For whatever reason, I think it was easier for him to accept. They had so much fun playing with the little ones. They almost became kids again themselves."

"My mom did not want to be called a grandmother, although she kept after me to get married and have children. I don't think she thought that through." That got a giggle from Jeannette and made Skylar laugh. It was contagious. They both could not stop laughing.

Mark was concerned the two women had lost their minds. The stress had finally caught up to them, and they snapped.

"What is so funny? Is this how you show respect for our parents?" Mark questioned.

"Lighten up, Mark!" Skylar told him. "We were remembering that first Christmas at Jeannette's apartment. The look on their faces when the kids hugged them."

Mark smiled and chuckled a little. He remembered. "I will admit, it was hilarious. Their hearts melted that night."

"Oh, sweetheart. Remembering the good times and the love you shared with them after they moved to Oregon brings healing. Talking about them helps you heal. These are things no one can take away from you. They live deep down inside. They loved you very much. I watched them when we had family functions. Love was written all over their faces. They were proud to be your parents," Jeannette told Mark.

Mark took Jeannette's hand and kissed it. "I love you."

A few months later, Skylar met a man at Mark's dinner club. He was there having dinner with friends when he spotted Skylar from across the room. He excused himself from the table and walked to Skylar.

"Hello. My name is Ayden. I noticed you from across the room. Would you like to dance?" He held his hand out, and Skylar slipped her hand in his. She felt a spark. That spark lit a fire.

Ayden and Skylar danced for the rest of the evening. The friends Ayden was sitting with finally left. Jeannette and Mark gave up on Skylar coming back to the table, so they left the restaurant with smiles on their faces. They saw love in bloom.

The music had stopped, but neither Skylar nor Ayden noticed until a young man with a broom came by them and said, "Get a room. The band is done playing, and we closed fifteen minutes ago." He went on sweeping and shook his head.

"I guess it is time we left," Ayden said.

"I guess it is. I don't remember an evening I enjoyed more. Thank you," Skylar said.

"May I see you home, Skylar? I want to make sure you get home safely," Ayden said.

"I have my car in the parking lot, so there is no need for you to go out of your way. If you would like to meet me at my house for a glass of wine, I wouldn't mind the company," Skylar suggested.

"If it is not too late, I would love to. I will follow you in my car."

"Okay. But let me be clear about one thing. I am not asking you to come over to have sex. That is off the table for now. I am enjoying the conversation and would like to get to know you better," Skylar told him.

"Yes, Ma'am! No sex. Only wine and conversation," Ayden repeated his instructions.

They talked through the night until the sun came up.

"Ayden, did you know it is light outside? You have been here all night. I am not tired. Are you?"

"Not at all. Why don't I go home and take a shower and meet you at *Our City* and I will buy you breakfast?" Ayden asked.

"That sounds great. I will meet you there in forty-five minutes," Skylar said.

They fell in love that night. From then on, they were a couple and always together. Skylar had finally found her perfect man.

`A year later Ayden and Skylar were married. They made a sweet couple. He had one child from a previous marriage, a boy who was grown and married with a daughter named Nicole. Skylar was a mom and a grandma, finally, and the family grew by four.

Five more years went by. Jeannette was seriously thinking about retiring. She knew her company would be in good hands with Sean and Tia at the helm. She had been grooming Sean to take over for years. He had an ear and talent for music, but no one was as good as Jeannette. After six months of contemplating, she handed over the reins to Sean. She felt like she was giving away a child.

She told Sean, "I don't think I am ready to do this. Maybe I should stick around another six months or so?"

"Mom. Don't do this. I know it is hard for you. This company is your baby. You deserve to have some fun and travel like you have dreamed of. Mark has cut back on the time he spends at the restaurant, so there is no reason you two cannot have some time away from work. That is all I have ever seen you do, work. You both have plenty of money so you can afford to go anywhere in the world you want. Take some time to play. It is your time. I've got this."

She knew her oldest son was right. There was no doubt he would do a good job. Jeannette was just having a hard time letting go. Sean and Tia walked her to the car, arm in arm. She pulled out of her parking space, stopped, and stared at the building for several minutes before driving away. She was amazed at what she had built.

23

The first thing she did when she got home was search online for a place to vacation. She found the perfect excursion. When Mark got home, she sprung it on him.

"Mark! I found the perfect trip we can take! A cruise to New Zealand! What do you think?"

"Honey, I will go anywhere in the world with you. When do we leave?" Mark agreed.

For three weeks they cruised, ate, went sightseeing, visited ancient runes and generally had a wonderful time. They didn't have a schedule to keep, they didn't need to fly to Chicago, Jeannette did not have a meeting she needed to attend, and Mark didn't have a group at the restaurant that required the owner to be there. They wondered why they had not taken the time before now to do this.

Over the next several years, they visited every country they desired to see, always bringing mementos home to their grandchildren. They even talked Clay and Amy into taking a couple of cruises with them. One was an Alaskan cruise.

On the Alaska cruise Jeannette and Clay were recognized by the crew and were asked to play. The emcee stood on stage with 2 guitars in either hand. Jeannette's face turned red as usual, and Clay smiled. They walked to the stage and began playing one of their favorite songs. It was the first one Jeannette sold to him. The audience applauded and whistled. Clay looked at Jeannette and started a guitar challenge. She gladly accepted and blew Clay away. They walked off stage bantering about who won.

"I don't know why you keep challenging me. You know you are going to lose," Jeannette boasted.

"Hey now Pretty Lady. I think this time was a tie," Clay corrected her.

The conversation went on with each claiming victory until they reached their table. Finally, Clay conceded again.

"Pretty Lady, I swear one day I will beat you," Clay promised.

"Keep the dream alive," Jeannette said with a very large smile on her face.

Another cruise they enjoyed was around the Hawaiian Islands. After that cruise it was time for the aging couple to stay closer to home.

Jeannette and Mark filled their days helping with being a taxi service for the grandchildren. There was always someplace they needed to be after school. From time to time, the children had a break from sports, dance, music lessons, and anything else they wanted to try and just relaxed with grandma and grandpa. Their homes were within walking distance, so as they got older, they stayed at their own home after school, but they always saw their grandparents daily. They stayed a very close-knit family.

Sean had taken over the role of Jeannette at the head of BOTH *Windy City and Old West Windy City*. He flew to Chicago once a month as Jeannette had. After a while he skyped with clients, accountants, the banks, and any other place that was too far away. Greg wanted to be home as much as possible for his children, like his mother did. Greg and Sean got along like brothers. The companies never faltered. Tia was a force to be reckoned with and kept the legal works of the company in check. If a question arose, she was unsure about, she called Mr. Walker. He was still the attorney for the Chicago branch and was happy to advise her.

All five of the grandchildren had musical abilities. They all wanted grandma to teach them how to play the guitar. She had a guitar for each of them she kept at her house. Each day Jeannette taught them a little more, in secret. When they were all able to play, they surprised their parents and family members at a family dinner, with a concert.

One evening after the large family finished dinner, Jeannette gathered the grandchildren and told them to go into the living room. Their guitars were waiting for them.

"Ladies and gentlemen, we have some very special entertainment for you this evening. Please follow me into the living room," Jeannette announced.

Sean said with surprise, "What is this?"

"My students and I have been working very hard on a few songs for your listening pleasure," Jeannette explained and counted down her small band of guitars.

The new guitarists got a standing ovation.

"How long has this been going on, and why didn't you tell us?" Tia asked.

Jeremy stood and said, "We wanted to surprise you. Grandma has been teaching us for a while. So, are you surprised?"

"Shocked," Sean said. "You have your grandma's talent, and I am so proud of every one of you."

Sean, Tia, Tyler, and Christine were utterly taken aback at the talent and ability the five cousins possessed. Grandma beamed with pride at her protégés. Bringing their concert of three songs to a close, they played the frog song, then the train song and ended with *The Old Grey Mare*. The lullaby was not perfected, yet.

Skylar hoped Nicole, Skylar's granddaughter, possessed some musical talent. Nicole must have heard Skylar's voice in her head because Nicole looked at her and shook her head no.

Jeannette's legacy sat before her. She felt blessed and thankful to have been able to give her time, songs, and love to the precious gifts of grandchildren. To some, this might seem like a small thing. To Jeannette, it was monumental. When these beautiful young people grew to have children of their own, she hoped they would look back on this time with grandma as precious moments in their lives.

A month later, Jeannette was puttering around with a new song. Suddenly she dropped her guitar. Mark heard the guitar hit the floor and rushed to Jeannette. He helped her to bed and called the doctor. Amazingly, the doctor made a house call for her.

After examining Jeannette, the doctor and Mark stepped into the other room.

"She did not have a heart attack or a stroke. She's tired. Her body is worn out. She has had a hectic and adventurous life. Her age and life, in general, have caught up with her. There is nothing I can do. I suggest you hire a nurse to be with her at all times and keep her comfortable. I have a list of nurses for you. They are all good and trustworthy. She is not in pain. A nurse would watch over her, take her vitals, report to me daily of any changes in her health, and if she experiences any pain, I will prescribe something for her. Mark, this type of care, to be blunt, is the end-of-life care. As her time grows closer, her memory could start to fade, and she will seemingly go to sleep, possibly not wake up. There is no telling how much time she has left. It is up to Jeannette. She has led such a fascinating and busy life. Personally, I don't know how she did it. Spend time with her and notify your family. Encourage them to visit as much as possible before she is gone. I will be in touch. Call if you need me," the doctor reported and left the house.

Mark felt his heart break in two. The woman who had made him so happy was dying. He followed the doctor's instructions. He called a nurse and hired her over the phone. She was knocking on his door within an hour.

He showed the nurse where Jeannette was and introduced them, "Sweetheart, I want to introduce you to JaNessa. She is a nurse. JaNessa, this is Jeannette."

"You can call me Nessa. That is what all my friends call me."

Jeannette had a worried look on her face when she asked, "Am I sick?"

Mark answered, "No, no, honey. This nurse is here to make sure you do not get sick. The doctor said you were tired and needed rest. JaNessa will stay with you, keep you company, and make sure you follow doctor's orders."

"I am tired. Okay, Nessa, I will do what you tell me to do with no argument. I have guitar lessons to give my grandchildren this afternoon. I have so much to do. Maybe I will take a short nap?"

"That's a good idea. Anything you have to do can wait until later. You need to rest for now. I will be right here if you need anything at all, and Mark is just outside the door," Nessa promised.

That afternoon, as usual, five smiling faces came through the door, where Mark met them and explained what was happening with grandma. Each one broke down in tears and hugged Mark.

"Okay, let's dry the tears before you see grandma. We need to smile when we visit her. It will keep her spirits up. Be your normal sweet selves," Mark instructed.

They did as Grandpa Mark told them. The younger ones sat on the bed next to Jeannette and told her all about their day and what classmate got in trouble and who threw up. The older ones joined in about their day. It sounded like a typical day at grandma and grandpa's.

After Sean Tia, Tyler, Christine, Zach, and Skylar left work; they went straight to Jeannette's side. They talked and laughed about their earlier days.

Jeannette was quiet. After a few minutes, she said, "I know why you are all here. I am coming to the end of my life. I am fine with it. I am at peace with it. No tears, please. I want to tell you the lessons I have learned in my life so, hopefully, you will take them to heart and not make the mistakes I have made. I need to tell you before I am gone. Please, learn from them?"

Tia turned on the recorder on her phone, not wanting to miss a word.

1. "Never let go of hope. You do not know what is right around the corner.
2. Love with all your heart.
3. Remember, there are millions of people and millions of stories. You have one, your story. It is unique, just like you are. Make it a good one, a story that makes you proud. Before you do or say anything, ask yourself, would I be ashamed of this action or words I want to say? How would I feel if it was done or said to me? You will never go wrong if you take a second to ask yourself those questions and answer honestly. You can possibly change a bad situation into a good one.
4. Forgive the people in your life that have wronged you. If you carry around hatred or refuse to forgive, it will fester like a cancer. It can turn you bitter. It is not an easy thing to do sometimes but give it your best shot. You do not have to be friends with them, just forgive. Besides, it takes too much energy to carry hatred around. The energy spent on hatred can be used for something more positive and useful.
5. People say, "*The sky is the limit.*" I do not believe that. It is your beliefs that stop you at the sky level. Strive for the universe!
6. Decide to be happy. It is a choice. I know it sounds strange, but it is true. When you get up in the morning, tell yourself it is going to be a happy day. Believe it. See what happens.
7. Do not get involved with someone that dictates what you do or say. That person is controlling, and they will hurt you, change you, mentally abuse you, and turn you into someone afraid of your own shadow. Mental abuse is as bad as the act of physical violence. It is worse! Broken bones heal, bruises go away, but a broken mind or spirit sometimes never heals. I speak from experience about both mental and physical abuse. Never give someone control over you!

8. Be a survivor! Never give up! I was asked several times in my life how can I hold my head up after everything I have experienced? I told them because I chose to be a survivor and NOT a victim. Children, someday your parents will tell you about my life. I hope you will learn from it and be proud to say I was your grandmother.
9. Remember, if you love someone, it is through the bad times and the good. Not just when it is convenient.
10. Trust is a difficult or impossible thing to regain if lost.
11. Do not change yourself to please another person. Be who you are, and the right people will always be around you and support you. They love you just the way you are.
12. Take care of your body. Stay healthy. Your body is a temple God gave you. What we do to our bodies when we are young, we will pay for in older years. Do not physically abuse your body. Live a clean life, and it will be a long one.
13. Keep the negative thoughts out of your mind. What you think about will come about. Be positive so positive things will be attracted to you.
14. Know when you have had enough! It is not quitting. It is moving on to something better.
15. Do not keep making the same mistakes. Ask yourself what lesson did you learn? Then the lesson will not have to be learned again. The second time is a choice. Learn it the first time around!
16. Take responsibility for your actions. It is called integrity. You will earn respect and it will keep your soul healthy.
17. To know what a person is really like, observe their actions, and listen to what they say. If you see or hear things from that person that troubles you, chances are, that person should not be in your life.
18. Each of you has God-given gifts. Try things that interest you and discover what your specific talent or gift is.

19. Girls, this is for you. Women are strong. We can be warriors! We are not born that way; we make ourselves strong. We face our trials and tribulations head-on and find solutions. We do not hide our head in the sand and hope it goes away. Each time we face a situation and come out a victor, our strength grows. Hold your head up and move forward. You can weather any storm if you face it and deal with it.
20. Whatever you give will return to you. Make sure it is love, truth, and trust.
21. Everyone has bad things happen in their lives. Sometimes it puts us on the path to the best ideas.
22. Make good memories, like shake chic. (Jeannette smiled.)
23. Good things can take time. Be patient. Keep a positive attitude, and good things will happen.
24. Love who you are. If you don't, then make a change!
25. Do not let life beat you up. Remember, you can endure whatever comes your way. Stand strong. God does not give your more than you can take. You can overcome problems. Learn from each situation. Leave the bad behind and move on.
26. NEVER assume! Learn the facts.
27. Do not focus or think about what is trying to defeat you. It gives it power. The thoughts grow, and you defeat yourself.
28. Love is not based on sex. Love should be based on trust, honesty, and respect for the other person. Sex is just icing on the cake.
29. Respect yourself! Do not be lured into sex because of peer pressure or someone says they love you. That line is used a lot by boys who only want sex. They will say,"*If you love me, you will let me.*" Wrong! You should say,"*If you love me, you will wait.*" Anyone can say they love you to manipulate you into doing what they want. Do not get

sucked into their game of '*love them and leave them.*' You will know the difference if you stop and think. Listen to that little voice in your head when it speaks to you. If you are not sure, then you are not ready.

30. If your first attempt at trying something fails, do not give up. You are learning what *not* to do. Eventually, you will learn *what* to do.
31. It is okay not to be the strong one all the time. Sometimes you need to find a quiet place and let your tears flow. It cleanses the soul.
32. Remember always to take a step forward. Once in a while, look back and you will see how far you have come! But do not live in the past.
33. Sometimes you need to let go and be wise enough to wait for what you deserve.
34. If you find yourself in a bad relationship, be thankful. It teaches you and prepares you for the right one. Just don't stay in that bad relationship. Get out.
35. If you find faults in others, you are blind to your own.
36. There are no bones in your tongue, but it can break a heart and is strong enough to break someone's spirit for the rest of their life. Think before you speak and be careful with your words.
37. Set goals, not resolutions. Not far-fetched goals, but goals that are *possible* to achieve. I do it every year. I write them down and check them off as I achieve them. It gives you a sense of accomplishment.
38. If you are afraid, pretend to be brave, and it will happen.
39. Do not be a prisoner of things that are IMPOSSIBLE for you to change such as another person. It will not work out. Let them go!
40. If you believe you can do something, you are half-way to making it a reality.

41. Start your day with a grateful heart for what you have.
42. When you feel like you are at the end of your rope, tie a knot, and hang on a little longer. Things will change.
43. It is essential to make yourself a priority from time to time. It is necessary not to forget you are **valuable! You have worth**!
44. Be someone who inspires others.
45. Do not be impressed by how much money someone has, what titles they hold, or degrees they possess. What should impress you is their kindness, integrity, generosity, and humility.

46. You can overcome whatever life throws at you!

47. Life is always changing and adjusting. Go with it.

48. Everything in your life comes from the choices you make. If you chose wrong, the blame does not reside with your parents, your job, the economy, your age, or a disagreement. YOU and ONLY you are responsible for every choice and decision you have made. Own it.

49. Always give thanks and be grateful for what you have. It could be taken away tomorrow.

50. Finally, the last thing that comes to mind is: when there is an ending, God will give you a new beginning."

Jeannette had to take a break for a glass of water. All this talking was taking its toll on her, but she continued.

"I hope you remember everything I have taught you and the things you learned by my example," Jeannette began. "Sean, Tyler, and Zach, you are wonderful fathers. I love you so much, and I am so proud of the men you have become. You chose the right women to be your wife and the mother of your children."

"Ladies, I love you as my own. Make shake chick once in a while and make a mess. It will make wonderful memories of happy times. You are good mothers."

"Skylar, you are an amazing woman who I love very much. We have truly become sisters. Comfort Mark when I am gone. Give him hugs and a lot of love. I know he will need it."

"Mark, my beloved. You have made me so very happy. I love you with all my heart. You will always have a piece of my heart with you when I am gone. I don't want you to be alone. Do not deny yourself, love. I want you to be happy. My spirit will always be around you. Remember our happy times. Thank you for sharing this crazy life of mine and always being by my side. We have created a huge family that will love each other no matter what. When I am gone, lean on them for help and comfort. Keep love in our home. Without you, my life would not have been as happy as you made it. I love you so much, Sweetheart."

A woman pushed her way through the sea of people to get to Jeannette. She frowned, trying to see who it was.

"Hello, Jeannette. It is Beth. I heard on the radio you were not doing well. I wanted to tell you that I love you. I finally took your advice and found my *happy*. When I forgave, I felt the heaviness leave, just like you said. There is one person I need to ask for their forgiveness. That person is you. Will you forgive me for all the years I was mean to you? I wanted to be like the woman you became," Beth said with tears welling up in her eyes. "I was so jealous of you. I wanted to be strong like you. My jealousy got in the way of loving you. You are my sister, and I am so proud of you."

"Of course, I forgive you! You are my sister, and I love you, too," Jeannette said. She was having a hard time catching her breath. "There is so much I want to say, but I am running out of energy and breath. Give me a minute."

"Would everyone please step out for just a moment? I want to check Jeanette's vitals." Nessa told the family, "She is weak. Maybe you should give her some time to rest?"

"We are not leaving her side! She never left us, and we love her too much to leave her now!" Mark sternly informed Nessa.

They all went back in to be with Jeannette.

Nessa whispered in Mark's ear, "I don't think she has much time left. If you have anything else you want to say to her, now is the time."

"Sweetheart, my life was blessed when God sent you to me. I was only existing, not living until I met you. I don't want you to leave me," Mark broke down for a moment then continued, "If you have to go, then I will let you. I will be alright, and so will the rest of the family. We will stick together like you have taught us and love one another. God knows better than I do what his plan is. He must need another angel that plays the guitar." Mark broke down again. Some of his tears landed on Jeannette's hand that he was holding. "I love you to the moon and back."

Jeannette gave him a little smile. She caught a glimpse of movement and turned her head to see what it was.

"Honey! Look who is here! It's Irene, from our special place in Chicago! She came to say goodbye, too. Irene, you came all this way for me?" Jeannette asked, pointing to empty air.

Mark knew what was happening. Irene had come to take her. She was an angel.

Irene spoke only to Jeannette, "I did not come to say goodbye. I came to say hello. Come with me. Your family will be okay. I will watch over them. Take my hand, and I will show you how beautiful heaven is."

Jeannette's arm fell on the bed. She took her last breath and followed Irene to heaven.

Jeannette forged herself into a strong and confident woman with her will to survive along with her love for others.

At the beginning of her life, she was made to believe she was evil and worthless. They were wrong. Because of *Memory Holds the Key,* she discovered lessons she learned along the way for a reason. Her experiences with *What Now* were necessary and helped her recognize happiness later in life. *Full Steam Ahead* taught her to keep moving forward. She transformed a broken, unhappy life into a happy life full of love.

She had worth. She was the most valuable person in her family's lives'. No one taught them more than Jeannette.

EVERY PERSON HAS WORTH. EVERYONE IS VALUABLE.

www.ingramcontent.com/pod-product-compliance
Lightning Source LLC
LaVergne TN
LVHW021757060526
838201LV00058B/3133